A Week at the Beach

Virginia Jewel

Also by this author

Christmas in Hell

Across the Pond

Nuptials for Sale

Second Chance

Coming soon...

There's a New Sheriff in Town

Thank you to all my favorite chick lit authors!
You've inspired me beyond belief.

1.

"I cannot believe that we had to fly commercial! That house better be fantastic. If I had to fly commercial, then that house better be the epitome of luxury!" Chrissy's whining voice rang in my ears for the millionth time since leaving home.

I rolled my eyes in response and pretended to be engrossed in the rows of rental cottages speeding past us as we drove. I had no doubt that the house waiting for us would be luxurious, but Chrissy and I had different opinions on luxury. Having spent the better part of my life living in a three-bedroom apartment with my parents and two little sisters, to me luxury would be having a private bathroom. Chrissy's standards were a little higher.

Chrissy and I met our first year at Columbia University and we have been best friends ever since. The year before we met, Chrissy's mother had finally snagged the ridiculously wealthy, and much older, husband she had spent her adult life looking for. With that marriage, came the life of luxury. Don't get me wrong, being friends with Chrissy definitely had its benefits. Spring breaks in Cabo, summer trips to Europe, and frequent visits to numerous day spas, were just some of the perks of being Chrissy's best friend. I certainly didn't use Chrissy for the perks, but the truth was that being Chrissy's friend meant you needed those perks. Friendship with Chrissy was a full-time job, the kind of full-time job that requires you to be on-call at all hours of the day and night.

Take the previous night, for example. Chrissy's frantic three a.m. phone call woke me up and ended with me packing for this unplanned beach trip. Normally, our summer beach trips were spent in the Hamptons, but Chrissy's recent indiscretions found her on the bad side of the Hamptons' elite. To put it bluntly, Chrissy had sex with someone's husband. Actually, Chrissy had been carrying on a full-fledged affair with someone's husband. She was well on her way to getting a Park Ave apartment, and being a kept woman, when the wife got wind of the arrangement and put her foot down. After all, Chrissy was only five years younger than the wife was.

So, in desperate need of a vacation, and banished from the Hamptons, Chrissy begged her stepdad for the keys to the Outer Banks beach house. It doesn't actually belong to Chrissy's stepdad, it belongs to his family, but he agreed to let us stay in it for a week. Much to Chrissy's dismay, he wasn't able to get us the corporate jet also. That's how we ended up flying commercial. First Class in commercial, but commercial no doubt.

"Are you even listening to me, Cami?" Chrissy pinched me on the arm.

"Ow!" I leaned away from her and pulled my arm away. "Yes, I was listening! You were complaining about the same thing that you've been complaining about since we left the city. I'm sure the house is going to be amazing. Ned's family has vacation homes all over the world. Have you ever been to one that wasn't amazing?"

Chrissy gave me an indifferent nod, "The one is London isn't that great. It only has five bedrooms and no pool."

"Wow, really?" my mouth flew open in disgust. Heavy with sarcasm, I continued, "That's awful. I don't know how you managed to get through that difficult time."

Chrissy shook her head at me. With a heavy sigh, she scooted closer to me in the backseat and grabbed my arm. "I know I'm being a pain, Cami. Thank you for coming with me. I don't know what I would do without you." She rested her head on my shoulder and snuggled closer to me.

"You're always a pain, Chrissy."

Twenty minutes later, the driver dropped us off in front of the beach house.

"Wow!" I said as I took in the oceanfront mansion in front of me.

Chrissy smiled, "This is going to be an amazing week!" She took off for the stairs, leaving me behind to carry our bags into the house. Thankfully, she hadn't packed much. She planned to spend most of the week in bikinis, so there really wasn't much to pack.

I struggled up the steps and dropped the bags on the floor as soon as I got through the open front door. The inside of the house did not disappoint. Italian marble tiles, ridiculously expensive furniture, and lavish décor greeted me. I looked down at the busted flip-flops I was wearing just to remind myself that I did not belong in that world.

"Get your bathing suit on! Let's hit the beach!" Chrissy sped past me, scooped up her bag, and bounded up the stairs! "I've already chosen my room! Come on!"

I followed her up the stairs, past the second level, and all the way up to the third floor of the house. As I walked up towards the bedrooms, I glanced at the open spaces on the second story. I could see a billiards table, an entire wall of games, and the biggest television I've ever seen outside of an electronics store.

"These rooms are amazing, Cami. The ones on this end of the house have an ocean view so I figured we would take these." She pointed at the two doors on the end of the hall. Don't be mad, but mine has a private bathroom."

Chrissy disappeared behind her door and I opened mine. A huge smile formed as I took in the king size bed sitting in the room. As an adult who had been reduced to sleeping in a twin bed, nothing could have made me happier than the sight of that big squishy bed. I collapsed onto it, spread my arms out, and stretched.

"This is my kind of vacation!" I sighed and snuggled into the comforter.

A loud knock on my door pulled me out of my relaxed state. "Come on! Let's go down to the beach!"

"Give me a minute," I shouted back at her.

In less than five minutes, Chrissy and I were out on the hot sand. The beach wasn't that crowded, but as usual, as soon as Chrissy revealed her super sexy bikini, and bikini body, a crowd of men started to gather. Not wanting to get in the way, I headed towards the water to let the crowd thin out. Chrissy was in her element and loving every second of attention she was getting from the men.

Another thirty minutes later, Chrissy waded into the water with a big grin on her face.

"What's his name?" I asked when she was next to me.

"Who?"

"The guy in the blue shorts who was working hard to get your attention," I nodded in the direction blue-shorts-guy had walked off in.

She smiled at me. "David. He's taking me out tonight!"

The fact that Chrissy was going to leave me alone in the giant house was not the least bit surprising to me. In fact, it might be a good thing to get some alone time. When you rent a room in a house occupied by two sixty year old women, and three others, alone time is something you are in desperate need of!

I gave Chrissy a warning look, but smiled anyway. "Be safe. Call my cell if you need me to come rescue you, and please do not let him get behind the wheel after drinking!"

Chrissy cut her eyes at me, "Okay, mom!"

I looked back and said seriously, "I'm not your mom. Your mother would have asked how much money he makes, what kind of car does he drive, and whether or not he has a portfolio!"

Chrissy giggled and dove down under the water.

We played in the water and on the beach until just before sunset. Chrissy needed plenty of time to get ready for her date. I didn't mind, I'd put sunscreen on before heading out earlier, but I could feel a burn on my face and shoulders. A cool shower and cold drink sounded good to me.

By the time Chrissy finished getting ready for her date, I had already showered and changed into my comfy pajamas, consisting of my old Columbia t-shirt and a pair of baggy sweats. I'd also fixed my dinner. We'd made a stop at the grocery store on the way from the airport, so I was treating myself to a peanut butter and jelly sandwich.

"I can't believe you are eating that!" Chrissy gave my dinner a disgusted look. "You eat like a five year old!"

"I eat like someone on a budget, Chrissy. I'm a teacher. I can't afford Kobe beef and foie gras!" I walked past her and tossed my dirty paper towel in the trash.

Chrissy ignored my insult and flipped her hair off her shoulder, "What are you going to do tonight?"

"I am going to curl up in bed and read."

Chrissy's eyebrow rose, "You're on vacation, Cami, live a little."

"I am living a little. I'm not reading anything academic, just chick lit!" I smiled a big cheesy smile and left her standing in the kitchen.

"I meant for you to go out and find yourself a man."

I shook my head at her, "And do what with him? Should I spend an entire evening stroking his ego, on the off chance that he might actually do something to please me, only to end up disappointed? No thank you!"

Chrissy smiled, "If you spent the evening stroking something other than his ego, you might not end up disappointed."

"A penis can't solve everything, Chrissy."

"Maybe not, but it certainly doesn't hurt to let a few try!" She smiled brightly and grabbed her purse. "Don't wait up!"

"I never do!" I shouted at her as she walked out towards the front door.

It was true. Even though I always told her to be safe, and even told her to call me if needed, I never bothered to wait up for her. What would be the point? She wasn't likely to get home until morning anyway. Once, in college, she left for a date on Friday night and didn't make it back to the house until the following Tuesday. Apparently, that date went well.

I curled up in bed and got lost in my book. At some point, after I'd fallen asleep, a loud noise from somewhere downstairs woke me. Figuring it was just Chrissy returning from her date, possibly even with her date, I just turned my light off and pulled the blanket up around me.

2.

I woke up the next morning with a big grin. Sleeping in a king size bed was like sleeping in an ocean of softness compared to my twin bed at home. The sun was shining in the window, and I could hear the sea gulls screeching over the beach. I rolled around on the bed for a few more minutes before I finally got up and got dressed. It was still early, and since Chrissy probably wasn't awake anyway, I thought I'd eat a quick breakfast then go for a run on the beach.

Once I was dressed, I headed towards the bathroom but was surprised at the sound of running water. I thought Chrissy had said that her bedroom had a private bathroom, but maybe I was mistaken. I shrugged it off. It wasn't like there weren't at least five other bathrooms in the house!

Downstairs in the kitchen, I hummed happily while waiting for my bread to toast. I reached into the refrigerator for the butter, and when I stood up, I found myself face to face with a stranger.

"Good morning! I didn't know this place came with a cook," the tan blonde man standing across the kitchen from me said with a smile.

I studied his face for a second, searching my memory for what Chrissy's blue shorts man looked like. For some reason, I remembered him having darker hair.

"Hey, Nick! You won't believe this!" another male voice rang out from somewhere upstairs.

"What?" the blonde in the kitchen replied. He slid into one of the chairs at the table.

"I guess I was too tired to notice this last night, but I certainly didn't miss it this morning." The voice got louder until another tan, but brunette, man stood in the kitchen. He continued his story without even noticing me. "Clearly the cleaning crew that we employ is scamming us! Not only was the bed in my room not made, but the last person that was here left an entire suitcase, including a pair of dirty panties on the floor!"

The blonde at the table laughed.

"Don't get me wrong, they were nice panties. I wouldn't mind meeting the legs they used to wrap around, but I don't like it when I wake up with unidentified panties on the floor when I had no part in putting them there!" The second man laughed as he sat down.

"Where's Chrissy?" I asked when the men stopped laughing.

"Who?" they replied in unison.

"Chrissy? I'm assuming that one of you is the guy from the beach yesterday. The one she went out with last night?" I clarified and set the butter down on the counter.

"Who is that?" the brunette asked the blonde in confusion.

"The cook, I think," the blonde answered with a shrug.

"I am not the cook!" I answered. I was starting to get a little annoyed with this game.

"Well I certainly hope you aren't the maid, because if you are then you are doing a piss-poor job of cleaning this place!" the brunette snorted.

"Okay, this has gone on long enough! Obviously, you both followed Chrissy here last night and one of you slept with her. Which one of you was wearing the blue shorts yesterday?" I asked and put my hands on my hips.

The guys looked at each other.

"When the hell did you pick up a girl last night?" the brunette asked the blonde.

"Me?" the blonde pointed at himself in disbelief. "I didn't pick anyone up last night!"

"Then who the hell is Chrissy?" the brunette asked.

"I don't know a Chrissy!" the blonde responded.

"Here's an even bigger question," the brunette added. "Who the hell is this?"

Both men turned to look at me.

"I'm Cami," I answered, but they both continued to stare at me in confusion. "I'm Chrissy's friend."

The blonde shook his head, "Who is this Chrissy chick you keep talking about?"

"Wait!" the brunette put his hands up to shut his friend up. He turned to me. "If you aren't the maid, or the cook, then who are you? And why are you in this house?"

"Why are you in this house?" I shot back at him.

He stood up. "I asked you first."

I stared him down before answering in a confident tone. "I'm here for the week on vacation with Chrissy."

"This is a privately owned house, it isn't for rent."

"We didn't rent it."

The brunette and I stood facing each other in a standoff while the blonde's head pinged back and forth between us like he was watching a tennis match.

"How did you get the keys?" the brunette asked.

"Chrissy got them from her stepdad."

"I thought you said you called and checked to see if the house was being used this week," the blonde finally spoke up.

"I did. My dad said the house was open. Who is Chrissy's stepdad?" The brunette was still staring me down but the look had changed from anger to suspicion.

"Ned Davis."

The brunette shook his head and sighed, "Uncle Ned." He pulled his cell phone out of his pocket and pressed a number. "I'm calling my dad. We're going to get this whole thing cleared up."

I stood in my spot in the kitchen, listening to the brunette man talk to his dad on the phone. My eyes roamed over him. Both men looked to be in their mid to late twenties, very fit, and very tan. The brunette's nails looked manicured, but I couldn't be sure. I glanced over at the blonde, but turned away quickly.

Apparently, I wasn't the only one checking people out.

As I turned away, I caught the beginnings of a smile on the blonde's face.

"Well, dad talked to Uncle Ned and it seems like you girls are legit, although, I've yet to see this Chrissy girl that you keep talking about." He put his phone back in his pocket. "How long before you girls can be out?"

"What?" I asked in disbelief.

"Uncle Ned didn't follow the procedure. He was supposed to check the calendar and then mark it if he wanted it. Since he didn't do that, and I did, you girls will have to leave." The brunette shrugged nonchalantly.

"Like hell we will! It's not our fault Ned didn't follow the rules. We were here first, and we're not going anywhere!" I put my hands on my hips and looked him square in the eyes. There was no way I was going to let him bully us into leaving.

"I'm sorry Tammy, but those are the rules. You and the phantom Chrissy will just have to leave."

I took a step closer to him. "My name is Cami, not Tammy! I don't care what the rules are. We aren't the ones who broke them, and we were here first. That suitcase you found in your room was Chrissy's, and so were the panties. As far as I'm concerned, you two can find somewhere else to go for the week because we're not leaving."

"Listen here, Cami," the brunette stepped up to me and spoke angrily at me. "I don't care if you two girls have been staying here for the past month! In this family, we have rules about how to schedule time in the vacation homes and for the use of the private jet. The fact that Uncle Ned didn't follow them and let the daughter of his latest gold-digging whore of a wife have the keys is not my problem. Get your shit and get out!"

"Whoa! Wait!" the blonde stood up and got between us. He didn't touch me, but he put his arm out to stop me.

I had already lunged forward at his rude friend. His arm stopped me and kept me from being able to reach the brunette.

"This house has like ten bedrooms or something. There's no reason why we can't all stay here, right?" He looked from his friend to me.

I took a deep breath and stared at the brunette. As angry as I was for the rude way he had handled the situation, there really wasn't any meat to my argument against breaking the rule. As long as he kept his mouth shut, I could handle sharing the house with him.

The blonde looked at me expectantly.

I nodded in agreement.

The blonde turned to his friend.

The brunette looked me up and down. "I guess she can stay."

"Thank you," I said sarcastically.

The blonde dropped his arms and nodded at us.

The room was silent as we went back to our original positions. Both men sat back down at the table and I moved back to the counter and buttered my toast.

The sound of the back door opening made us all look up. Chrissy walked loudly into the room, couture heels in her hand, and her hair a mess.

She smiled when she saw me, but then flinched when she saw the two men sitting at the table.

"Jesus, Cami! I told you to go out and get yourself a man, not a set of men. Was there a buy one get one free special I missed?" Chrissy giggled and smiled at the men.

"I think we just met Chrissy," the blonde leaned across the table and said to his friend.

It only took a few minutes to fill Chrissy in on what she'd missed. Surprisingly, Darren, the brunette man, didn't put up a fight when Chrissy insisted on staying in the master bedroom that she'd left her things in. He agreed to move to the larger bedroom at the other end of the hall.

"So, you're Ned's nephew?" Chrissy asked Darren as she pinched off a piece of my toast.

"Yes," he smiled at her. "And you are the daughter of Ned's latest wife?"

Chrissy nodded, "Why weren't you at the wedding?"

Darren smiled at her, "I was at his first three, so you'll forgive me for not traveling across the country for this one."

Chrissy giggled.

I rolled my eyes and looked down at my breakfast.

"Who is that?" Chrissy asked.

I looked up and watched as Chrissy pointed at the blonde still sitting at the table.

Darren followed her gaze, "This is my friend Nick."

The blonde gave us all a quick wave.

"And you brought him here?" Chrissy asked.

I could tell from the smile on her face that she was up to something. I actually knew Chrissy well enough to know exactly what she was thinking and what she was probably going to say next. I tried to suppress the smile that was forming on my lips. I glanced from Darren to Nick, hoping to catch both of their reactions.

"We work together in LA and we were both in need of a vacation, so I got the jet and the keys to this place."

Chrissy smiled sweetly at them. "So, are you two together?"

A small giggle escaped, but I shoved a piece of toast in my mouth to mute it. Chrissy knew that they were straight. Even though they both obviously took good care of themselves, it was also obvious that they were both straight.

"We're not gay, if that's what you are implying," Nick, the blonde, quipped from the table.

A quick look up told me that he was smiling. He knew what Chrissy was up to. He glanced over at me before looking back at Chrissy.

"I was just asking," Chrissy said in her carefree cute girl voice. "Well, I'm going to go jump in the shower then head to the beach. Anyone care to join me?"

"I'm going for a run, so I'm out." I said, as I crumpled the paper towel my toast had rested on. "I'll see you down there later, maybe."

I didn't wait around to see if either of the men would join her. Knowing Chrissy, she'd have them both panting over her before the sun set over the North Carolina horizon. A smile played across my face as I set off down the steps and onto the beach.

I ran for a half-hour then walked in the sand for another forty-five minutes. By the time I made it back to the house, it was empty. After changing into my bathing suit, I headed back down to the sand. I couldn't find Chrissy so I just plopped down in an available patch of sand. With my flip-flops off, I buried my feet in the sand and watched the water. There were more children out than there had been the day before, and I watched as a group of them attempted to build a sandcastle. It was a little lopsided, but in the end, wasn't too shabby of a castle. When they finished, they quickly abandoned it and headed out into the water.

As I watched them running into the ocean, I caught a glimpse of someone sitting on a surfboard further out in the water. A wave built and he paddled to catch it. I watched as he quickly pulled himself into a standing position and rode the wave closer to the shore. He made it look so easy, and I marveled at how graceful it seemed. He dove off his board then reappeared above the water. He ran a hand through his hair before he pulled himself back onto the board.

It wasn't until he was seated on the board again that I realized who he was. It was Nick, the blonde from our house. I'd suspected he had a great body, but now it was confirmed. Even from this distance, I could tell that he was ripped. It took me a few more seconds to pull my eyes away from him. He wasn't Chrissy's usual type, but he'd probably do for a fling. She was on vacation, after all.

With a chuckle, I lay back onto my towel and closed my eyes. The sound of the water and the other sunbathers chatting almost lulled me to sleep, but a painful itch on my ankle pulled me out of my almost-sleep state. My feet weren't buried in the sand anymore, but it felt like something had bit me. I scratched and checked, but didn't see anything. I lay back down, but the itching started again. So, I headed out to the water in the hope that whatever was biting me couldn't swim.

"I thought that was you."

I turned to see Nick floating on his board a few feet away from me.

"How was your run?" he asked with a smile.

"It was good," I answered timidly. After admiring his body from afar, I was feeling a little shy as I bobbed along in my bathing suit. I wasn't out of shape, but I certainly wasn't as fit as he was.

"Do you run every morning?" he asked and paddled closer to me.

"I try to, but I'm not as disciplined as I should be."

He tilted his head to the side in question. "What do you mean?"

"I have to work to keep my shape. I can't just call up mommy and have her make me an appointment to get my trouble areas taken care of. Being out here on the beach makes me realize how much more running I should be doing."

Nick smiled, "I didn't notice anything wrong with your body."

I blushed and looked down at the water.

"I meant that you look healthy, to me," he added quickly. "You don't see a lot of healthy looking women living in LA."

I smiled and nodded. I still wasn't sure if he'd just given me a backhanded compliment or not.

"Do you surf?"

He was obviously trying to change the subject.

I shook my head, "No. I'm pretty sure that surfing is one of those things that looks a lot easier than it actually is."

He laughed, "It takes some practice to get good at it, but it's not impossible."

"Well, you are very good at it." I smiled, "I was watching you earlier."

He smiled again, "I know. I saw you watching me."

"You could see me from all the way out here in the water?"

He smiled then admitted sheepishly, "Actually, I saw you walking out from the house so I followed you until you sat down in the sand."

"That makes more sense."

We looked at each other for a few seconds as we both bobbed with the wave. He was still lying on his board and I was floating next to him.

I looked out at the horizon and saw other surfers catching some big waves. "Looks like you're missing some action out there."

He turned his head towards the waves then back to me. "Yeah, I should probably get back out there."

"Maybe I'll see you around later." I waved and swam off towards the shore. Before getting out of the water, I made sure to adjust my bathing suit. I wasn't sure if he was still watching me, but just in case I wanted to make sure my ass wasn't hanging out.

Back on my towel, I collapsed down and tried to brush the sand off my feet. Sand was the one thing about the beach that made the whole experience awful. No matter how hard I tried, I couldn't get all the sand off me. My ankles were still a little itchy, but not nearly as much as they had been before my swim.

I spent the rest of the morning on the beach. As the temperature on the beach rose, so did the number of people playing in the sand and on the water. By lunchtime, it was too crowded and I was feeling a little claustrophobic. Besides, my ankles were itching like crazy!

Back at the house, I brushed the sand off my feet before entering through the back door. The house was quiet and I carried my stuff up to my room. After a long shower, I carried my wet bathing suit out onto the deck by the pool. Next, I made myself another peanut butter and jelly sandwich then headed out onto the porch to sit on the swing and enjoy the slight breeze that was blowing past the house.

The whole experience would have been a lot better if it wasn't for the rash that was slowly inching its way up my legs. The itch that had started at my ankles seemed to be spreading and the pain was past the point of distraction. I was about to head in to see if there was a first aid kit, when the French doors opened and Nick sauntered out onto the porch. He must have just gotten out of the shower because he was still wet, but now he was wearing jeans. Still no shirt, though.

"Can I possibly bum some food off you? We didn't bring any food and I am starving." He smiled sweetly at me.

"Help yourself!" I smiled back at him.

He was back in two minutes with a sandwich of his own. He sat against the porch railing across from me.

"Did you have fun at the beach?" he asked between bites.

I pulled my leg up and scratched as I answered, "I did, until it got really crowded."

He nodded and took another bite of the sandwich.

"How were the waves?" I was trying hard to be subtle about my scratching, but it was driving me crazy. Both legs were itching and it was taking every ounce of self-control I had to keep myself from scratching like a flea-ridden mongrel.

"They started to die out a little, and the water was getting crowded." He shrugged and shoved the last bite of food into his mouth. When he finally swallowed, he asked, "Are you okay?"

"Me? I'm fine. Why?"

He looked down at my feet then back up to me. With a smile, he said, "Because you're scratching the hell out of your legs." He pointed at my ankles.

I sighed and scratched even harder. "I think I'm having an allergic reaction, or maybe I got bit by something. It's awful!"

"Let me see."

He leaned closer and grabbed my leg, pulling me, and the swing, towards him. His hand gripped my foot, turning it over in his hands, while the other hand ran up my calf and around my ankle. He dropped that foot and reached for the other one, inspecting it in the same way.

"Do you have any nail polish?" he asked as he inspected my foot.

"I hardly think that a pedicure is going to cure me." I tried to pull my foot back.

He held it firmly in his hand and smiled at me. "You have chiggers."

"Ew! Gross! What are they?"

He laughed, "They are little mites that get onto your skin and make you itch. They won't really hurt you, just annoy you and make you want to scratch your skin off. Nail polish?"

"I think I have some upstairs, why?"

"If you put nail polish on them it will suffocate them and they'll die quicker. Go get it." He ordered me and dropped my foot from his hand.

Eager to get rid of the itching, I ran up the stairs to my toiletries kit and searched for nail polish. Unfortunately, I had forgotten my clear polish and the lightest color I had was a shade of turquoise. I grabbed it and went back to the porch. Nick was still sitting there, watching as people walked past the house.

"So, do I just put it on the bumps?" I sat back down on the swing and shook the bottle of polish.

He sat up and reached for the bottle, "Here, give it to me."

I handed it over and watched him as he picked my foot up again. He rested it against his chest and started to twist open the bottle.

Suddenly feeling self-conscious about my feet, I pulled my foot off his chest. "I don't want to get you dirty."

He grabbed my foot and put it back on his chest, "Relax, your feet are clean." He opened the bottle and began carefully painting my ankle and shin turquoise. "This is a very nice shade of blue you've chosen. Would you like me to do your toes when I'm done?" He asked without looking up.

I blushed and laughed. "I couldn't find any clear polish."

He looked up and smiled, "I like it. It matches your eyes."

"Does that charm work on the girls in LA?" I asked with a sarcastic smile.

He laughed, "I do alright." He pulled my foot off his chest and brought the other one up to take its place.

"How did I get these chigger things, anyway?" I asked as I watched him paint my other ankle.

"Did you run on the edge of the beach, where the bushes are?"

"Yes."

"That would be the culprit." He kept his head down as we talked, concentrating hard on his painting.

"Perhaps that's a sign that I shouldn't be running while I'm on vacation." I smiled at the idea of taking the week off from working out.

He looked up and smiled. "I think so. I'd be happy to suggest some other form of exercise, if you'd like." He lowered his eyes back to his painting.

I blushed.

He looked up and grinned wickedly. "I meant that I'd be happy to teach you how to surf tomorrow. You get quite a workout doing that."

"Oh," I blushed again.

He lowered his head again and went back to work. "Unless, of course, there was something else you had in mind."

"No, there was nothing else on my mind." I lied. Of course, there was something else on my mind! How could there not be? His hands were caressing my leg gently, and my foot was resting against his bare chest. What else would I be thinking about?

"Better?" he asked.

"Much. Thank you," I smiled at him.

"Since I'm down here, do you want me to go ahead and do your toes?" He grinned at me again.

"No, thank you." I pulled my foot off his chest.

"Your loss! I'm pretty good at it."

I shook my head at him and he laughed.

"Where's your friend?" he asked as he closed the bottle of polish.

"I don't know. I haven't seen her since I left for my run this morning." I shrugged and looked past him at the people walking down the street.

"So, why did you come to the beach with her if you two weren't going to hang out the whole time?"

"I don't mind spending time alone, and Chrissy likes going out and meeting new people. We'll catch up with each other for a few hours every day." I was used to Chrissy's behavior, so the idea of being left alone as I vacationed with her wasn't unusual to me. Sometimes we only saw each other for a few minutes each day.

He laughed quietly, "You and Chrissy don't seem to be all that compatible as friends."

I shrugged, "Just because we aren't exactly the same doesn't mean that we can't get along. We complement each other, I guess."

"I suspect that the complement is mostly one-sided." He shifted against the porch railing.

"What does that mean?" I asked in a defensive tone. "Chrissy and I help each other a lot. I keep her grounded."

"And she keeps you up in the air?" He grinned.

I looked sternly at him, "If by that you mean she keeps me waiting around for her to dictate what we do, you're wrong." I stood up from the swing. "I'm not Chrissy's servant. I'm her friend. "

I took a step towards the door, but his hand reached out and grabbed my ankle.

"Cami, wait! I'm sorry. I didn't mean to imply that you were Chrissy's servant. I was just trying to make conversation." He gripped my ankle tighter, "Stay, please."

I sat back down on the swing and he let go of my foot.

"I know that Chrissy and I are very different, but she's always been a great friend to me, and the least I can do is return the favor."

He nodded silently in response.

I watched a family walking past the house, struggling to carry all their beach gear and keep their kids in tow.

"Where did you two meet?" Nick finally asked after a few minutes of silence.

"Columbia."

He raised an eyebrow at me and I laughed.

"The university, not the country," I clarified.

He smiled, "You both went there?"

"Yep, we met our first year, when we were assigned to the same residence hall."

"You've been friends ever since?"

"Yes."

"So, was that before or after Chrissy's mom married Darren's uncle?" Nick asked.

I wasn't looking at him, but I could tell that he was watching me.

"They married the year before Chrissy left for Columbia, so it was after." I wanted to change the subject. He was asking too many questions. I turned and smiled at him, "How do you know Darren?"

"We work together." He looked down and started to play with his hands.

"How long have you worked with him?"

"A couple of years."

"Do you always vacation with him?" I asked with a suspicious look.

He laughed, "No, but we both needed to get out of town for a few days and I'd rather go somewhere I can surf than anywhere else."

Another suspicious look flashed across my face. "Why did you two need to get out of town?"

He shrugged and looked away from me, "Just work stress, that's all."

"There you are!" Chrissy's loud voice boomed from the street down below the house. "I've been looking everywhere for you!"

I stood up and leaned over the railing to see her. "I looked for you on the beach, but you were nowhere to be found."

She grinned at me. "I met some guys and they took me out on their boat. Come down and go to the beach with me! I want to talk to you."

"I need to change back into my suit. I'll be down in a minute." I answered and headed for the door.

Nick pulled himself up, moved to the swing, and called out to me. "Have fun!"

I stopped and turned around, "Did you want to come with us?"

He smiled, "I might come down later. Thanks for letting me have some food."

"Thank you for painting my wounds."

He laughed, "Anytime."

I ran up the stairs and put on my other bathing suit, a new t-shirt, and a pair of shorts. I'd left my flip-flops by the back door, so I slipped them on as I headed out towards the beach. Chrissy was waiting for me by the gate.

"What is on your legs?" she asked when I got closer to her.

"I had chigger bites, so Nick told me to put fingernail polish on them."

"What are chiggers?" she asked with a disgusted look.

"Nick said they're little mites that bite you and make you itch." My ankles had stopped itching until Chrissy started to talk about them. Now I was fighting the urge to scratch again.

Chrissy looked at me for a minute then asked, "Who is Nick?"

"The blonde guy staying at the house with us," I closed my eyes and shook my head as I explained.

"Oh!" she nodded in recognition. She grinned widely at me, "He's cute, don't you think?"

I shrugged nonchalantly.

"You don't think he's cute?" Chrissy asked in her probing voice.

"He's attractive," I shrugged again, in a very noncommittal way.

Chrissy wasn't buying my nonchalance for one second. She grinned mischievously at me. "You like him, don't you?"

"Don't be ridiculous. I barely know him." I shook my head and walked past her towards the beach.

Chrissy caught up with me. "Well, if you don't think he's cute and you don't like him, do you mind if I have a go at him?"

I stopped walking and looked sternly at her.

She broke into a smile. "That's what I thought."

I rolled my eyes and started walking towards the beach again.

Chrissy laughed and caught up to me. "Don't worry. I won't even look at him. He's all yours."

"He's not mine, Chrissy! Besides, we're only here for a week, why would I want to get involved with someone." I dismissed her then added before she could say anything, "Plus, he lives in LA and I live in New York."

"Oh come on, Cami!" Chrissy sighed loudly. "I don't want you to marry him and have his babies! Just have a little fun with him."

"I'm not that kind of girl!"

Chrissy shrugged, "Perhaps you should give it a try."

3.

We sat on the beach for almost an hour before anyone interrupted us. We were watching a group of teenagers playing volleyball on the beach when a male voice called out to us.

"You do know you could go to jail for even looking at those boys, right?"

Chrissy and I both turned around to see Darren and Nick standing behind us. Both men were shirtless and wearing their swimming trunks. Both were also carrying surfboards.

Chrissy was the first to respond. "They want us to look. That's why they're out here for us to see them."

Darren's eyes sparkled as he quipped back at her, "Don't worry. We'd only let you spend one night in jail before we bailed you out."

"Only one night? You are so kind." I said sarcastically and smiled at Darren.

He, in turn, flashed a sarcastic smile at me.

Chrissy jabbed me in the side and gave me a warning look. Clearly, she wanted me to be nice to Darren. However, for the life of me, I couldn't figure out why.

"So, Darren," I turned back to him and forced out a genuine smile. "Are you a surfer too?" I nodded towards the surfboard he was leaning against as we talked.

He laughed and shook his head. "This?" he pointed at the surfboard. "No, I don't surf. I would have picked the habit up years ago, though, if I had realized how much of a chick magnet these things were. We practically had to fight the women off during the walk over here."

I smiled as I caught Nick raising an eyebrow at Darren's last statement.

"I'm sure that those looks had absolutely nothing to do with the designer flip-flops, swim trunks, and sunglasses you're wearing." Chrissy said as she surveyed his look from head to toe.

Darren smiled and said to Chrissy, "I doubt that the women on this beach would know a designer outfit if it fell out of the sky into their laps with the tags still on it."

Chrissy giggled and flashed him her most flirtatious smile.

Hoping to prevent any more flirting, I turned to Darren and asked, "If you don't surf, what's with the board?

Don't tell me you carried it all the way down to the beach just as a prop to pick up chicks?"

Darren took his eyes off Chrissy and smiled at me. "Nick said you asked him to teach you how to surf. Being the great friend that I am, I offered to carry this board down here for him so that he wouldn't have to carry both of them."

My eyes shifted to Nick, "I never said I wanted you to teach me how to surf."

He grinned at me, "You never said you didn't, either."

I looked at him seriously. "I don't think it's such a good idea. Besides, Chrissy and I are hanging out now and I don't want to leave her alone on the beach."

"Don't worry about Chrissy. I'll stay here and keep her company." Darren grinned at me as he gave Chrissy a flirtatious wink.

"I think you should give it a try, Cami. You might like it." Chrissy smiled sweetly at me, but I could see the mischief in her eyes.

It was useless to try to argue with them. Clearly, I was outnumbered.

"Grab the board and I'll teach you some of the basics before we get in the water." Nick smiled triumphantly at me before walking off towards the water.

After almost thirty minutes of lessons on the beach, Nick led me out to the water.

"We'll paddle out and then try to get some small waves." He called out to me as he paddled further out to sea.

The butterflies in my stomach felt like stones pulling me further down into the water. I was lying flat on my stomach and paddling with my arms the way he'd taught me, but didn't seem to be getting anywhere. Finally, after what felt like hours, I was close enough that I could see him grinning at me.

"What?" I asked defensively.

"Took you long enough," he said with a wide grin and hint of a laugh.

I stuck my tongue out at him and pulled myself upright. I straddled the board and let my feet hang off either side, mimicking his pose.

He smiled at me then looked behind him at the waves coming in.

I followed his gaze and felt the butterflies take off again. "Those waves look kind of big for a first timer, don't you think?"

He laughed and turned back around. "Actually, I was thinking that they seemed kind of tame." He must have seen the panic on my face, because his own look softened. "They aren't as big as they seem from way out here. Trust me?"

It was a strange question. Twelve hours ago, I didn't even know this man existed. I had only had one real conversation with him, yet everything in me knew that I could trust him with my life. Perhaps it was something in the way he was looking at me, or maybe it was just something about him. Either way, I knew there was no doubt that I could trust him. Before I even had time to process my thoughts, I could feel my head nodding.

A genuine smile broke across his face, and then he sprang into action. "Follow me!"

I pressed myself back down on the board and paddled hard to catch up to him. We were much closer to the waves and I could feel the water rising and falling beneath me. I didn't dare look back to see how far from the beach we were. My arms felt like they were on fire, but I kept paddling, anxious to find out where he would lead me. I rode the last crest and came back down, my board just a few feet from his.

"Did I do better this time?" I asked as I pulled myself back up into the sitting position.

"Like a pro," he answered confidently. "Remember what I told you about changing your position?"

I nodded; too excited by the newfound faith I had in this handsome stranger to be nervous anymore.

"I'm going after that one." He pointed at a wave building up behind us. "Watch me carefully. If you think you're up for one after that, give it a try."

Again, I nodded obediently. He paddled off furiously, ready to attack the wall of water quickly rushing towards him. I watched the muscles on his back ripple and flex as he paddled. He'd timed it perfectly, and I watched as he seamlessly pulled himself up onto his feet. Within seconds, he was up and had disappeared behind the curl. Then, just as quickly as he'd disappeared, he emerged from the end of the wave still standing and looking even more like a god.

Years of teaching six-year olds who liked to be celebrated for every minor accomplishment took over and I instinctively clapped excitedly at his success. He turned towards me and bowed in acceptance of the applause then did a flip off his board and into the water. When his head reappeared above the water, he shook the water off and pointed at me. When he was sure I was looking, he pointed behind me at the wave building.

He had made it look so easy. It looked as if he'd put very little effort into it at all, actually. Caught up in the excitement of it all, I stupidly paddled towards the wave and ran through what he'd taught me on the beach.

Surely, it couldn't be that hard! He'd shown me the basics, plus he said the waves weren't that big.

When I'd reached the perfect spot, he shouted at me to stand. And I did! I actually stood up on the board and stayed balanced! For at least three seconds, before the wall of water hit me in the side and knocked me off the board. The expression, 'hit me like a ton of bricks' must have been invented for just that occasion. Struggling to find the surface of the water, and not gasp for air, I waved my arms and legs furiously. A hand came out of nowhere and pulled me up just as I ran out of air. With a loud gulp of air, I grabbed onto the board and held on for dear life.

When I'd gulped air, I'd also taken in at least half a gallon of seawater, and it was pouring out of me as I struggled to breathe. The hand that had pulled me out of the water was now pounding me on the back as I coughed and gagged against the board.

"You alright?" Nick asked with concern.

"What happened?" I choked out between coughs.

"You wiped out," he said with a laugh, "big time!" Apparently, the concern for my safety was gone and he'd moved on to mocking me. "It was quite entertaining, really."

"What happened to my board?" I asked. I'd noticed that the one I was now clinging to was not the same one I'd fallen from just seconds before.

"Don't worry, that kid's bringing it over for you." He gave me a goofy grin and pointed at the adolescent surfer who was now pushing my board towards us.

"That was an epic fail, man! Totally awesome!" the kid shouted excitedly when he reached us. "My buddy got it all on camera, too! Is it okay if we put that up on YouTube?"

"I'd rather you didn't." I said and grabbed the board from him.

He shrugged and shook his head. "Too bad, that totally could have made you famous!" He gave Nick a head nod and paddled back towards the waves.

"Was it really that bad?" I asked as I tried to pull myself up onto the board again. I could already feel how sore my ribs were going to be.

Nick shook his head, but looked away trying to hide the grin on his face.

"It's okay. You can tell me it was bad. I'm kind of known for epic fails, especially the kind that involve me getting injured."

He turned back and smiled so wide I could see all of his perfect white teeth. "It was pretty bad, but I've seen worse."

Exhausted, I laid flat with my back on the board. "I did tell you this was a bad idea."

He laughed, "Yes, you did. I should have listened to you."

"Thanks for saving my life, by the way." I was suddenly too tired even to open my eyes. The adrenaline I'd felt earlier had all vanished, and now I was drained of all energy.

"I thought maybe your drowning would put a damper on our vacation," his voice was full of false modesty and I could tell he was grinning.

He let me lay still for a few minutes, still coughing up water, before he spoke again.

"What's this from?" he asked. He grabbed my leg and pulled me towards him. His hand touched the scar on my inner thigh.

Despite being exhausted, I still felt the zing of electricity as his skin touched mine. My eyes flew open and I sat upright. He pulled his hand away from my thigh and smiled at me, waiting patiently for an answer.

"Another epic fail," I answered timidly and looked down at the scar.

"What sport were you attempting that time?"

"Riding a bike."

"Like dirt bike riding?"

I huffed lightly, "No, just regular bike riding."

He chuckled then asked, "I have to hear this story."

"It was the summer I turned ten. My parents got me a bike for my birthday and I had an accident, or two."

His eyebrow rose in suspicion. "What kind of accident left that scar?"

I hung my head in shame, "I rode my bike into a barbed wire fence."

He let out a quick roar of a laugh, but pulled himself together quickly.

I continued, "I also destroyed Mrs. O'Grady's petunias, ran over my sister's little toe, and dented my dad's car door."

He threw his head back and laughed loudly at the sky. His laugh was infectious and I found myself laughing at him.

"The fence was the last straw. On the way back from the Emergency Room my dad said to my mom,

'Clearly we should have thought harder on a middle name for this child.'" I added between chuckles.

"Wait! What's your middle name?" he asked with a huge grin.

"Grace."

He threw his head back again and I laughed along with him.

After a minute or two, the laughter died down but the smiles stayed put. We both watched silently as the boy who had returned my board expertly rode a few waves close to the shore.

I watched Nick's face as he followed the boy's progress. He looked as if he was longing to be out there with him.

"You don't have to stay here with me. I think I can safely paddle myself back to shore, if you want to surf some more."

He turned to me and looked into my eyes. "I'm okay just hanging here with you."

I smiled timidly at him.

He leaned back and put his hands under his head, "Tell me more about your epic fails."

I spent the rest of the afternoon telling him all about my feeble attempts at sports. As it turned out, running was the only thing I was ever good at. To be fair, I wasn't even good at that, but at least I was less likely to injure myself doing it. He watched me intently as I told him about the time I cracked my front tooth with a field hockey stick, the time I'd broken my pinky in gym class trying to shoot a basket, and even the day in college when I'd fractured my wrist bowling.

I watched his face as he listened to me. I watched how his eyes seemed to smile just as wide as his mouth when he liked what I said. He looked at me like I was the most interesting person in the world, and he watched me intently. He actually listened when I talked, and when he interrupted to ask me a question, he'd reach out and touch my arm or my leg to get my attention.

I felt like I could stay out on the water for another few hours, just talking to him and watching him listen to me, but the sun was setting and my stomach was starting to growl. We paddled back to shore, and carried the boards on our heads back to the beach house. Only, the quiet, calm beach house we'd left that morning was now littered with unfamiliar faces and pulsating with the pounding beats of music.

"What's going on?" Nick asked me when we got under the house. I handed him the boards and he put them back in the storage closet.

"I don't know. It kind of looks and sounds like a party." I shrugged.

"Chrissy?" he asked me with a suspicious look.

I shook my head at him. "No, she told me she was going out on the boat with the guy she met this morning."

He sighed loudly, "Darren."

I raised an eyebrow, "Is this the kind of thing he does?"

He nodded.

"Is this why you two needed to get out of LA for a while?" I asked with a smile.

Nick looked up and nodded.

"Well, as long as I can take a shower, get something to eat, and then be left alone in my room, I don't care what's going on in the rest of the house." I smiled and started up the stairs.

"You're not going to join the party?" Nick asked and followed behind me.

I tried hard not to focus on the fact that his face was practically even with my ass as we climbed the stairs to the first floor of the house.

"I'm not the party type. I'm much happier curled up in bed with a good book." I stopped and turned around to face him. When I did, I caught him by surprise, and he quickly looked up at my face with a blush on his cheeks. Obviously, he had been focused on my ass just as I'd feared. "Actually," I continued, deciding to ignore the reddened cheeks, "my idea of a party involves board games and bowls of snacks."

He cleared his throat and smiled guiltily at me. "That sounds like fun."

4.

After my shower, the party seemed to be even louder. I wandered down to the kitchen and found that most of my food had been left alone in favor of what appeared to be trays of catered goodies. I made myself another peanut butter and jelly sandwich, snagged a couple of cream puffs and headed back upstairs to my room.

An hour later, the beat of the music was still pulsing through the house and even the delicious indulgence of my favorite chick lit novel wasn't enough to drown it out. When we'd put the surfboards away, I'd spotted a comfortable looking hammock hanging under the house. Figuring that the noise was more likely to rise up to the third floor than fall down to ground level, I grabbed my book and pillow and snuck down the stairs. As I passed the second floor, I caught a glimpse of Nick, showered and shaved, shooting pool with a few men. The crowd of adoring half-naked women standing around watching them seemed to be holding his attention as well as the game, so I didn't bother to speak to him.

Down on the ground floor, the noise from the party was muted and a gentle breeze was blowing. Carefully, for fear of falling flat onto the concrete floor, I sank into the hammock. I positioned my pillow behind my head. With my book in hand, I let the breeze blow across me as I swayed back and forth in my netted bed. The memories of the day's events played back as I read the words on the page. The pounding music drifted away, and I relaxed into my own little world. I was perfectly content in my summer vacation spot.

The sound of sea gulls crying in the wind frightened me awake and I nearly tipped out of the hammock. Steadying myself just before I hit the concrete floor, I crawled out of the net and stood up. The hammock had seemed comfortable as I lay in it the night before, reading and enjoying the cool, night breeze. But this morning, my body was aching from the lack of a firm surface. My ribs hurt from yesterday's near drowning, and my neck ached from the awkward position I'd slept in.

I tried to roll my neck to ease some of the discomfort, but it was no use. I was going to have to take something to loosen those muscles. Just as I bent to pick up the book I'd dropped onto the floor at some point in the night, the sound of a guitar filled the morning air. I stood up and listened to the opening chords to one of my favorite songs. I smiled as a male voice quietly joined in with the instrument, singing the words that always made me smile.

I picked my book up and struggled up the stairs. The gentle music a contrast to the pounding beats from the night before. I opened the front door and headed in towards the kitchen. I could smell the freshly brewed coffee, and even though I knew it wouldn't do anything to ease my pains, I had to have some. I looked at the state of the house. It was a mess.

"Well, well, well! Look what the cat dragged in!" Darren greeted me with a sly smile. He was standing shirtless in the kitchen. A giggle escaped from the skinny blonde standing behind him, who had obviously spent the night, and stolen his shirt apparently.

She gave him a playful swat on the arm. "Be nice, D! She didn't do anything you and I haven't done on occasion."

"Yeah, be nice D!" I said in a sarcastic chipper voice. It hurt to do it, but it had been worth it so I stifled the wince of pain. "Besides, I didn't do anything. I slept in the hammock under the house to try and avoid all the noise your party was making."

Darren looked me up and down then gave me a nod of acceptance. The skinny blonde gave me a pitiful look and handed me a cup of coffee.

"Who is out on the deck playing a guitar?" I asked after my first glorious sip of coffee.

"Nick. He takes that damn thing with him everywhere." Darren shook his head dismissively.

"He's pretty good," the skinny blonde added and wiggled up against Darren. "Do you have any secret talents you'd care to reveal?"

He grinned mischievously at her, "What? I know you picked up on my talents last night?" He wrapped his arm around her waist and ran his hand up her back, lifting his shirt to reveal her naked ass to me.

"Ugh! I'm going outside. This house is a mess. I hope you don't think I'm going to have any part in cleaning it up." I hopped off the stool I'd only occupied for a few brief seconds and headed towards the deck.

"Relax; I've called the cleaning service. They should be here within the hour." Darren managed to get out while the skinny blonde placed kisses over his chest. "Actually, would you mind letting them in. I think I'll be a little preoccupied with something else when they get here."

I didn't turn around to see what they were doing. The squeal of delight that the skinny blonde made was descriptive enough. I walked faster and slammed the French door behind me.

Nick stopped playing and stared at me as I walked over to the swing I'd occupied yesterday.

"Good morning," I said as cheerfully as I could.

He eyed me suspiciously, "Good morning." He drew the words out, making them sound like a question.

"What?" I asked.

"Where have you been? I looked for you last night, but I never could find you." He was still giving me a strange look, but his voice was back to normal.

I looked back at him confidently, "Really? You didn't seem to be looking for me when you were playing pool while all the beach blanket bimbos were watching you." I smiled sweetly at him and took another sip of coffee.

The corner of Nick's mouth curled up. He stood up and came to sit next to me on the swing. He pushed the guitar to his side and turned to face me, stretching his leg up to take over most of the swing. With the same crooked smile on his face, he leaned forward and looked directly at me.

"Where did you sleep last night?"

I watched him intently before I answered, "Downstairs, why?"

He narrowed his eyes, "Where at downstairs?"

I tried hard not to think about how close his face was to mine and how good he smelled. I cleared my throat, but didn't flinch back from his proximity.

Before I could answer, he added, "You didn't happen to sleep in a hammock did you?"

I shrugged my shoulders, but didn't break the eye contact. "Maybe, so what?"

He smiled and laughed lightly. He reached up and touched my face gently, "Because you have a waffle pattern imprinted onto your cheek."

Yesterday, when he'd touched my thigh, I'd felt an electric buzz. Today, when his hand brushed against my cheek, it felt like a thousand volts of electricity hit me. Even the embarrassment of realizing that my face looked like a meal at IHOP wasn't enough to distract me from the electric current pulsing through my body.

When I didn't respond, or shy away from his touch, his hand caressed my face and rubbed against the pattern. Neither of us moved, and for a few seconds we sat staring into each other's eyes as his hand stroked my face. The electricity from the contact was almost visible as it built between us.

The sound of footsteps coming up the stairs pulled us both back to reality. I stood up with my coffee cup in hand and leaned over the railing. An army of cleaners was travelling up the stairs, each armed with a plastic tub full of supplies.

"Thank you for coming on such short notice." I called out to them. "The house is a mess, something which I had no part in doing, by the way."

The cleaner in the lead gave me a less-than-pleased smile and continued up towards the front door.

"If you could just get the first and second floors done, that would be great. Don't worry about the bedrooms." Nick, who had joined me at the railing, added to my shouts.

After the women disappeared inside the house, Nick sat back down on the swing and picked up his guitar.

"I heard you playing earlier, you're not that bad." I smiled sweetly as I sat down on my spot on the swing.

Nick laughed, "Wow! 'Not that bad'? What a ringing endorsement! I'm glad I have a day job."

I blushed, "I didn't mean it to sound quite so snotty. Sorry."

He laughed again, "It's okay. I have no musical aspirations. I just like to play, that's all."

I pulled my feet up onto the swing and sipped my coffee. Nick pushed off with his feet, making the swing sway gently back and forth. He positioned his guitar and began to strum it quietly. I watched the sea gulls swooping down over the sandy beach and skimming over the top of the water as his music filled the air. It was a very peaceful way to start a day, and a smile spread across my face. I held the coffee cup up to my mouth to hide my smile, but it was too late.

"What's so funny?" he asked without stopping the strumming.

"Nothing," I said quietly against the ceramic cup and shook my head slightly.

"Why are you smiling?"

Caught in my serene moment, I turned to see him smiling while he watched me.

I lowered the mug to my lap and sighed, "I was just thinking that this is a great way to start a day, that's all."

His smile widened, "It is, isn't it?"

As much as I didn't want to, I turned my gaze from his face and back to the beach. It was far too early in the morning for so much electricity. I pretended not to hear Nick's low chuckle as he continued playing and pushing our swing.

When my coffee mug was empty, I leaned down to place it on the deck floor. I thought I'd timed it perfectly, but as usual, I was off balance. I started to topple, head first, towards the floor. I heard the guitar hit the floor as a hand grabbed ahold of the back of my shirt, pulling me back against the swing. Once again, Nick had been there to pull me to safety.

"You have an incredible knack for danger, don't you?" he said as he pushed me back onto the swing.

After I'd secured my position on the swing, I sighed, "My dad always told me, 'Cami, you may have beauty and style, but you most certainly do not have grace. Please put down that knife.'"

Nick laughed.

"I'm sorry about your guitar. It's not broken is it?" I stared down at the instrument, now lying underneath the swing.

He shrugged, skillfully leaned down, and scooped it up. "It's seen worse, trust me."

I waited for him to start strumming again before I trusted that the guitar really was okay. When it didn't sound any different than it had before, I relaxed. Content to just sit and listen to his music and swing, I stared at the beach in front of us. A few people had started to run past, and a couple of teenagers had already staked their claim on a prime spot in the sand.

"Can I ask you something?" Nick asked without stopping the music.

"Sure."

"Was that a hint of jealousy I heard earlier when you mentioned the beach blanket bimbos?"

I shot him a quick look. He smiled sweetly back at me.

"No, it wasn't jealousy. I was just stating a fact."

He laughed, "If you say so."

I didn't look at him.

After a minute, he said quietly, "I did try to find you. I went upstairs but you were in the shower. When I went back downstairs, I got wrapped up in the game. I looked for you everywhere. I just didn't think to look under the house."

I smiled and shrugged, "Next time you'll know better."

He chuckled then asked, "What do you have planned for the day?"

"Nothing, unless Chrissy wants to hang out, I guess."

"I never saw her come home last night."

I shrugged, "Oh, well then I guess I'm free to do what I want today."

Nick stopped playing and set the guitar down on the deck. "Would you like to hang out with me today?"

"That depends," I turned to him with a smile. "If you're planning on surfing some more then I'm afraid I'll have to say no."

He smiled back at me, "That's probably for the best."

I leaned back against the swing but turned my head so that I could see him, "What did you have in mind?"

This time he flashed a mischievous smile at me, "Don't you trust me?"

I raised an eyebrow at him, "The last time you said that to me, I ended up swallowing half of the Atlantic."

He grinned but I could tell he was suppressing a laugh at the memory of my sad attempt at surfing yesterday.

"What did you have in mind?"

"Meet me down by the storage shed in thirty minutes and you'll find out."

He didn't give me a chance to ask any more questions. He scooped up his guitar and headed towards the French doors.

"What should I wear?" I called after him before he could reach the inside of the house.

"Shorts and a t-shirt will do," he shouted back and kept walking.

"Don't you remember the story I told you yesterday about the summer I was ten."

"Oh, come on! You're telling me you haven't been on a bike since you were ten?" Nick had pulled two big bikes out of the shed and was trying to coax me onto one.

"After I scratched and dented my dad's car, he pretty much forbid me from ever riding a bike again." I admitted freely to him.

"Well, he's not here and I promise I won't tell him." Nick put his hand over his heart as he promised. "Besides, I have an insurance policy in place." He grinned and ran back into the shed. When he came out, he was holding a bright pink bike helmet. He held it out for me and I took it with a quick glare in his direction. "It's more about keeping you safe than anything else. I can't promise you won't have an accident, but I am confident you can't put a dent in your father's car, run over your little sister's toes, or massacre Mrs. O'Grady's petunias."

The fact that he'd remembered all the details from my clumsy confession impressed me. If I'd had any doubt that I could trust him, it was now gone. I put the helmet on my head and fiddled with the straps. He walked closer, took the straps from me, and began adjusting it to fit me. His face was just inches from mine and I could see the edges of a smile forming on his lips. I couldn't help but notice that he smelled fantastic, a mixture of deodorant and sunblock that was steadily becoming irresistible.

When he'd finished with the straps, and the helmet was securely fastened on my head, he looked right at me and smiled.

"Aren't you going to wear a helmet?" I asked as I stared back at him.

He smiled and shook his head.

I put my hand on my hips, "I'm pretty sure it's the law."

He leaned forward, getting as close to my face as the bright pink helmet would allow, and whispered, "I'm a rebel."

A shudder of excitement and electricity traveled down my spine causing me to shiver. A soft sigh escaped my lips at the same time. He leaned away with a grin and I tried to cover up the sigh with a cough. It wasn't very convincing. In fact, it almost sounded like he was laughing as he hopped onto his bike.

Pulling myself together, I grabbed hold of the handlebars of my bike and said, "Well, just so you know, when you crash and you're lying on the ground with a gaping head wound, I will say I told you so as I stand over your mangled body."

He smiled at me and replied, "I would expect nothing less."

With my usual amount of grace, I finally managed to get myself situated on the bike and with a wobbly start rode the bike out from under the house. Nick was kind enough not to laugh at me as I struggled to coordinate my feet and balance myself on the bike. After a few minutes, I seemed to be getting the hang of it and we rode away from the house.

"Where are we going exactly?" I asked and almost crashed into a mailbox. Clearly, I wasn't ready to ride and talk.

Nick shook his head at the sight of me, but answered, "I just thought we could ride around and see what's in the area. It's not supposed to be as hot today as it was yesterday."

I nodded my head slightly, not wanting to knock myself off balance again. My hands kept a firm grip on the handlebars and my eyes stayed glued to the road ahead of me. I was going to try my best not to have any incidents on the bike, at least not any major incidents.

Thankfully, the breeze was blowing Nick's scent away from me. I didn't need that distraction while I was trying to be careful.

"You're not doing so badly!" Nick rode up beside me, causing my path to wobble just a little.

"I'm concentrating very hard on staying balanced and straight." I responded quickly. My wheels didn't stray from their trajectory and I silently congratulated myself for successfully talking and riding.

"Do you think you're up for some dirt biking? I think I saw a course somewhere around here on our way to the house the other day." Nick's voice had a hint of mischief in it when he asked.

I risked a glance at his face, and sure enough, he was grinning from ear to ear.

"If that's what you had in mind for today, then I'll just turn around and go back to the house. Dirt bike riding seems like something I should stay far away from."

He laughed and took his hands off the handlebars. "I'm just joking with you Cami."

"Good."

"I was curious about something." He paused and waited for me to nod him on. "Is Cami short for something?"

"Camille."

"And, what's your last name?"

"Harris."

"Camille Grace Harris," he said my name slowly, as if he was letting it sink in.

When he said my name, a rush of excitement ran through me. I'd heard my name millions of times and never had it caused such a reaction. Somehow, hearing him say it made it more beautiful, more desirable, and much more significant.

"Does anyone call you Camille?"

Another, smaller, rush shot through me.

"My grandmother used to, and my dad does when I'm in trouble."

He smiled, "How often does that happen?"

"Not too often, lately. I'm the oldest, so they have their hands full with two college kids right now. They mostly just ask me the same four questions every time I talk to them." I smiled, thinking about how true that statement was.

"What are the four questions?"

"Have you heard from your sisters lately? How's work? Who are you dating? When are you going to get married and have babies?" I looked over at him and rolled my eyes at the last question. "That last one always comes from my mom, and it's usually shouted from the living room as my dad talks to me from the kitchen. I basically have the same conversation with them every week."

Nick smiled and I shook my head in frustration.

Every week, I called home and those four questions, in one form or another, were the basic outline of our entire conversation. Only occasionally would I be treated to an update on an elderly family member, or the neighborhood gossip, but that was only if it was really juicy. The monotony of it never bothered me. I'd just grown used to it. Although, since my relationship with Jack had ended eight months ago, the questions about when I was going to get married had started to grate on my nerves.

"What are you thinking about right now?" Nick pulled me out of my thoughts.

"Oh," I blushed, realizing that I had been thinking about my ex.

"You kind of spaced out for a few seconds there." Nick smiled warmly, "I was just wondering what you were thinking about."

"Honestly," I scrunched my nose in embarrassment at being caught, "I was thinking about my ex."

"Oh," Nick drew out the word and raised his eyebrows as he did.

"Not like that." I didn't want him to think I was pining over the guy. "I was just thinking about how since we broke up eight months ago, I hate having to answer the last two questions from my parents."

"The dating and marriage ones?"

I nodded.

"How long were you together?"

"Almost six years."

"Wow!"

"We met at Columbia our senior year and we moved in together after graduation."

"So you lived together?"

"Until eight months ago, yes," I sighed.

I really missed the old apartment. It wasn't huge, but at least I wasn't confined to one room. The place I rented now wasn't awful. It was cheap. It was close to work, and the people in the house were all friendly. It's just that, I didn't actually have any space of my own. My bedroom was the space where I felt the most comfortable, and even there it wasn't the same as it had been in the apartment with Jack.

"Why did you break up?" Nick asked, but then quickly added, "If you don't mind me asking."

I took a deep breath. "We grew apart, I guess. When we first got together, we were so young and we didn't really have a plan for where things were going. But after a while, I started to want more than just a boyfriend and roommate. I was ready for marriage and kids, and I thought he was too."

"He wasn't ready?"

"No. In fact, he didn't want it at all."

"With you or with anyone?" Nick asked timidly, obviously trying not to offend me.

"Apparently not with anyone," I clarified. "His parents went through a nasty divorce when he was twelve, so he was afraid of putting his own kid through that."

Nick nodded silently for a few seconds then added, "Our parents' relationships can really screw things up for us as we get older."

I glanced over at him and saw a strange expression on his face. It didn't look like something that he was ready to talk about, so I didn't press.

"Anyway, I tried changing his mind, but that never works. In the end, he just said it wasn't going to work out and asked me to move out."

"Where do you live now?"

I sighed again, "I rent a room in a house."

"Do you have roommates?"

"They're not really roommates, per se. I rent a room in a house, run by two sisters in their sixties, and two other people rent rooms there. We all share the house, but it's not like we live together." I tried to make sense of what I was saying, but even I was confused by the description.

Nick, obviously, was just as confused as I was. He was giving me a raised eyebrow.

"When I had to move out, I needed to find a place quick. My mom knew the sisters from her old church and she knew that they rented out bedrooms in their house." I glanced over to see if he was looking less confused, and he was, but I could tell that he still had questions. "Their parents died and left them a huge townhouse in the city. Neither of them ever married, so they decided to rent out the other three bedrooms. I rent a bedroom, there's another girl, and a young guy rents a room there. Our rent pays for the exclusive use of our bedrooms, common use of the living room and kitchen, and for part of the utilities."

"But you don't really live with them?" he furrowed his brow as we rode on.

"We share a residence, and occasionally the sisters will host a sit down dinner for all of us, but for the most part we just keep to ourselves." I shrugged nonchalantly.

"You couldn't have afforded a place of your own?" he asked and pointed me towards a new road.

I'd been so busy talking to him that I hadn't noticed how far we'd ridden away from the beach house. In fact, I couldn't see the beach at all, much less our house. I hoped he knew where we were, because I was clueless.

"Do you know where we are or where we're going?" I asked nervously.

"Not really, but I think there's a little collection of shops at the other end of this road." He looked over and smiled confidently.

His smile put me at ease, but I asked with a smile, "You think?"

He just shrugged and asked me again, "Tell me why you couldn't just get a place of your own?"

"My salary isn't exactly what you'd call plentiful," I smiled.

"What do you do?"

"I'm a teacher."

Nick smiled, "Ah! That certainly explains it! What do you teach?"

"First grade," I couldn't stop the smile from coming to my face when I thought about all the little faces I'd worked with over the last five years.

"You must really like your job," he said with a short laugh.

I looked quizzically at him, "What makes you say that?"

"Well, for one you just broke into the biggest smile."

He smiled at me and I blushed.

"And, secondly," he continued, "you live in a house with four people you barely know or, I suspect, even like. If you didn't love your job you wouldn't stay at it and make sacrifices like your unpleasant living situation."

"I do love my job," I smiled, "but the living situation isn't that bad. It's just not ideal, that's all."

"How long will you stay there?"

"I don't know. I hope to get out of there before a year is up, but rent isn't getting any cheaper."

As we rode further, I could see the outline of a few buildings in the distance. I didn't know how he knew there'd be shops there, but apparently, there were. He must have known what I spotted because when I looked over at him, he smiled triumphantly.

Nick didn't gloat long, instead he said, "Isn't there someone you can share a place with? What about Chrissy? Can you share a place with her?"

I laughed then looked sideways at him. "Chrissy offered to let me move in with her, but her social life conflicts with my sleep and work schedule. Plus, she was just a few months away from being a kept woman by some married stockbroker she met at one of her mom's dinner parties. I don't think he'd want me staying in their love nest."

Nick's eyebrow rose at the news of Chrissy's love life. "I figured she was a party girl, but I had no idea she was a home wrecker, too!"

I laughed again, "That's what brought us here to the Outer Banks. We normally stay at the house in the Hamptons. Mr. Money's wife found out about Chrissy and threw a fit. She kind of spread the word around the Hamptons, so Chrissy figured we should lay low for the next few months."

"Mr. Money?" Nick asked with a smile.

I smiled mischieviously, "That's what I call her married boyfriend. I've only met him once, and he spent the entire time talking about money."

He smiled some more, "It sounds like you don't exactly like him."

"Honestly," I sighed. "He's probably not that bad, but I don't approve of their relationship. He's married, and not to Chrissy."

"Are they in love?"

I put my feet down and stopped the bike. Nick skidded to a stop as well. He gave me a questioning look.

"It doesn't matter if they're in love or not. He's married. He has a wife and a child. If he doesn't want to be married anymore then he should be man enough to admit he's made a mistake and get a divorce."

Nick nodded his head, "I agree."

I stared at him for a few seconds then asked, "Are you married?"

He stared back at me, "No."

"Are you divorced?" I maintained eye contact with him as I asked.

"No," he said and smiled. "I'm not engaged, either."

A smile crept to my face, "I was just checking."

He shrugged, but kept the smile on his face, "No problem."

Suddenly embarrassed by the awkward turn our conversation had taken, I blushed and looked away. "Where are we going again?" I got back up on the bike and started off in the direction we were heading in before. Nick did the same.

"There's a restaurant up here. I thought maybe we could grab some lunch." He kept his eyes forward as we rode closer to the buildings.

When I'd come down stairs to meet Nick, I had no idea what he had planned. I hadn't brought any money or cards with me.

He must have read my mind. "It's my treat. I owe you lunch from yesterday."

Relieved, but still hesitant to agree to lunch, I said, "Do you think we can find a place that serves peanut butter and jelly sandwiches?"

He grinned, "It can't hurt to ask."

A few minutes later, we'd parked our bikes on the side of a small restaurant and found ourselves seated on an outdoor patio. It was a beautiful day and the ride had been wonderful, but I couldn't help but be happy to be sitting still on a soft cushiony chair.

"Can I get you two something to drink?" the waitress asked us. She looked to be about forty, with a mop of dark curls plastered on the top of her head. She smiled warmly at us and waited for our response.

"Do you have sweet tea?" I asked with a childlike smile.

She lowered her head and put her hand on her hip. "Sweetheart, this is the south! Sweet tea practically comes out of the spigot here!"

I smiled, "Good. I'd love a sweet tea with lemon."

She gave me a wink and turned to Nick.

"I guess I'll have the same." He smiled at us both. Just before the waitress walked away he asked, "You don't happen to serve peanut butter and jelly sandwiches here do you?"

The waitress flashed Nick a seductive smile, leaned over the table, and whispered in a husky voice, "Cutie, you can have whatever your heart desires. It doesn't even need to be on the menu."

I suppressed a laugh as the color rose up from Nick's neck to his hairline. The waitress tweaked his nose, gave me a wink, and walked away.

When she was gone from view, I giggled and said, "Wow! That was quite a proposition you just got. Does that happen to you a lot?"

Nick was still blushing, but a big grin lit up his face. "That was a bit much for me."

I laughed at him. "I think that if you play your cards right, you could have one hell of a night with that hot dish bringing our drinks over."

Nick shook his head and laughed.

"Did you get a chance to think about what you might want?" the waitress asked when she set our drinks down on the table.

I grinned across the table at Nick, who was trying very hard not to blush again. To save him, I ordered my lunch. "I think I'd like to have the Caesar Salad, please."

She turned and gave me a smile. "That's a good choice. I make the dressing myself. It's one of my favorites." She turned her attention back to Nick. "What about you, sexy? Decided what you want yet?"

Clearly flustered, but trying hard to ignore her, Nick submitted his lunch order, "I'll have the bacon cheeseburger, no onions, and extra pickles."

"Are you going to want fries with that?" she asked with a hint of sass.

Nick nodded and handed her the menus from the table. She grinned at him and left us alone at the table again.

I suppressed the laugh that was building up inside me and said, "I have to say, I'm surprised. I never really pictured you as the shy type."

He shook his head, "That woman frightens me. I think she might be serious about her advances."

"She seems harmless enough to me." I grinned at him.

"Can we talk about something else, please?" he begged then reached for his sweet tea. I watched him take a drink and look out of the corner of his eye for the waitress.

I grinned, "Fine. You asked me all kinds of questions about my life on the ride over here, so now it's your turn."

He raised an eyebrow at me.

"Tell me about your family." I started with what I thought was a simple question.

"I'd rather not," he replied sharply.

If the tone of his voice hadn't been enough to deter me from the topic, the look on his face definitely did the trick.

After what felt like forever, he sighed. "I didn't mean to snap at you. I didn't grow up in a family like yours, so I'd really rather not talk about it."

I nodded and took a sip of my tea.

He sighed loudly. "I live by myself in a big apartment. The last girl I dated was named Cheyenne. She was twenty-two, had a fabulous set of fake breasts, but not much in the way of brains. We dated for three months before I couldn't take it anymore and dumped her." He spit out facts about himself quickly, hardly giving me the chance to digest it all.

He took a quick breath then continued, "I've never lived with a woman I was dating. I've never had a heart-wrenching break up and I'm not particularly clumsy so I've never ruined anyone's paint job, toes, or flower bed."

I smiled at him, "Well, thanks for the information. I feel like I know you so much better now."

"What else would you like to know, Cami?" He was obviously trying to make up for the harsh tone from earlier.

I took a deep breath then smiled coyly at him. "So you're a breast man, huh?"

He grinned back at me, "Who isn't?"

"I guess I just had you pegged as a butt man, that's all."

He grinned some more, "Is that because you caught me staring at your butt when we were heading back up to the house yesterday?"

I blushed, "Maybe."

"Well, that wasn't my fault. What else was I supposed to do, not look directly ahead of me as I walked up the stairs?" He grinned, "Besides, I had to keep an eye on you just in case you tripped and came tumbling back on me as we walked up the stairs."

I glared at him and he laughed.

"Although, to be honest," he flashed a sheepish smile, "I was checking out your butt when you were trying to pull yourself back onto the surfboard."

My mouth flew open in mock horror and I tossed my napkin at him.

He caught the napkin, laughed, and shrugged, "I couldn't help it! It was right there in front of me and you just looked so funny trying to pull yourself up."

"Well if there is a more ladylike way to pull yourself onto a surfboard, I've never been taught it, and since you were my teacher, I blame you."

"Glad to see you two getting along again," the waitress said as she refilled our tea. "For a minute there, I thought my flirting had caused a fight between the two of you lovebirds."

Without missing a beat, I said, "Oh, you can have him. He's not much of catch once you take him home and look at him under different lights." I flashed Nick a sweet smile and took a sip of tea.

"She's sassier than I thought she'd be," the waitress said to Nick with a nod and wink in my direction.

Nick eyed me as I smiled back at him. "Don't listen to her. She's crazy about me, has been since the day she met me." Nick said and cocked his eyebrow in my direction as if passing the ball to me next.

"How long have you two been together?" the waitress, who was still hanging around our table, asked.

Obviously, wanting control of our little game, Nick spoke first. "Three years."

"Three years and you haven't put a ring on that finger, yet?" the waitress put her hand on her hip and gave him a stern look.

Seizing the opportunity to take over, I laughed and said, "Oh, he did. Last week actually, except being the genius that he is, he bought me a ring two sizes too big. It's back home at the jewelers getting sized."

Nick smiled.

"How did he do it? I bet it was very romantic. He seems like the romantic type." The waitress was getting into our story now.

Nick, still smiling, watched me intently.

"No romance. He's a straightforward kind of guy. I came home one night last week and he had the ring and asked me. We don't need all that sappy romance stuff, right, honey?" I smiled at Nick across the table.

"Nope. No romance for us. We keep it simple," he smiled back at me.

The waitress, who clearly looked disappointed in the turn our story had taken, asked, "What about the ring? What did it look like?"

Figuring I'd throw her a bone, I sighed and put a dreamy look on my face. "Now that is a different story. See, he may not be the sappy romantic type when it comes to saying how he feels, but he can pick out a nice piece of jewelry."

"I didn't pick it out. I designed it and had it made." Nick corrected me.

The waitress seemed much happier with the new direction of our fake love story.

"It is beautiful. It has a round cut diamond in the center, surrounded by a circle of diamonds. The band is platinum with diamonds along the sides. It has a very vintage look to it. Words cannot describe it, really." With a mischievous smile, I said to Nick, "Don't you have a picture of it on your phone, babe?"

Nick stared back at me for a second then patted himself down, pretending to look for his phone. "I must have left my phone back at the beach house."

"That's too bad," the waitress said in a disappointed voice. "That ring sounds amazing. Well, you two seem like you'll be very happy together."

"Thank you," I said politely, suddenly feeling bad for lying to her.

"Your food will be out shortly." She smiled at us again then left our table.

"So is that really what you'd want your ring to look like?" Nick asked when the waitress was far enough away that she couldn't hear us.

I shrugged, "I don't know, maybe. I guess it's kind of up to him to decide."

"You don't want to have a say in what your ring looks like?" He seemed to be surprised.

"No. I want him to pick out what he thinks would look good on me. He's paying for it, why shouldn't he get what he wants?"

"What if he picks out something that you hate?" Nick asked with a smile.

"If he doesn't know me well enough to know what I'd like then maybe we shouldn't be getting married."

"You make a valid point."

"Okay, I've got one Caesar salad and one bacon cheeseburger." The waitress put our food down in front of us. "I put the dressing on the side for you sweetie. I know how you bride-to-be types are. It's a shame though, isn't it? You spend months starving yourself to fit into a wedding dress and he eats whatever he wants and still manages to look fantastic." She smiled warmly at me.

"Thanks for keeping an eye on me."

Nick smiled at her and laughed as she walked away. I picked up the dressing and dumped it all over my salad.

"What's that they say? A moment on the lips, a lifetime on the hips," Nick said over the top of his burger.

I glared at him as I reached across the table and stole a fry off his plate. "Who said I was planning on fitting into some stupid dress, anyway?"

"What? No big family wedding for us?" he pulled his plate out of my reach, preventing me from taking another fry.

"No way! I have absolutely no desire to force my friends and family to suffer through a wedding on my behalf." I picked up my fork and dug into my salad.

"So, you don't really want to get married?"

I finished chewing most of the food in my mouth and held my hand in front of my face. "No, I want to be married. I just don't want to have a wedding."

He lowered his hamburger from his mouth, "Are you serious?"

I nodded and put another forkful of salad into my mouth.

"Won't your family be upset?"

I swallowed my food and said, "Are you kidding? My dad would be ecstatic! He's got three girls, one of which he already knows is going to be a bridezilla making ridiculous monetary demands for her wedding. Nothing could make him happier than knowing that I plan to sneak off and elope without spending a dime of his money."

Nick shook his head, "I don't think I've ever met a girl who didn't want a big fancy wedding."

"Can't say that now, can you?" I grinned and stole another fry.

He grinned back at me and shook his head.

We had fallen back into our playful banter, and something was buzzing around in my head. "So, I was wondering something."

"I wouldn't want you to hold anything back, so please ask away."

"Would you say that all your exes could be described like the last one?"

He tilted his head to the side, "What do you mean?"

"You know, big tits, small brain. Have all your exes fallen into that category?" I shrugged and took a sip of tea.

"No, not all of them," he answered. "Wait, did you say tits?"

"Yes."

He broke into a wide grin, "That's awesome!"

"When they're real, they're breasts. When you pay a doctor to make them bigger than God intended any woman's breasts to be, they're tits."

He laughed and shook his head, "I can't believe you keep saying tits."

Watching him laugh at something I'd said, and not something ridiculous I'd done to embarrass myself, was intoxicating. Before I could stop myself, I'd joined him in laughter.

We spent the rest of the meal, chatting and laughing at each other. The waitress checked on us a few times, but left us to enjoy each other's company. When we were both stuffed, he picked up the check and led me out of the restaurant.

5.

"What would you like to do next?" he asked when we'd said our goodbyes and received another round of well wishes from the waitress.

"I don't know, but I'm not ready to get back on that bike." I made a face at the thought of being on the bike again. "I like the feeling of having my feet on solid ground. Plus, that seat is not comfortable. It made my butt hurt."

Nick grinned, gently put a hand on my butt, and leaned close to me. "Would you like me to massage your butt?"

I swatted his hand away and squirmed out of his grip.

"What?" he said with a big grin. "I'm just trying to be a supportive fake fiancé!"

I glared at him, "I'm giving you a real no, thank you."

He grinned, "Sorry, I couldn't help myself. Turns out I'm a butt man after all." He smacked me on the butt and took off running towards the row of shops. I followed behind him, struggling to keep up.

When I reached him at the end of the street, he was smiling and waiting for me.

"No fair! You didn't give me a warning that we were racing. You got a head start!" I huffed between big gulps of air. I ran regularly, but I wasn't used to sprinting quite so quickly.

"That was the point. I had to cheat to win."

"What now?" I asked with a steadier breath.

"Can you paint?" he grinned and pointed at the storefront we'd stopped in front of.

I turned and studied the window. "Paint your own pottery? I think I can do this."

He led the way and leaned forward to open the door. Before he opened the door, he turned back to me and said, "Are you sure this is safe? You don't have some kind of freak childhood pottery accident to tell me about, do you? I wouldn't want to risk life and limb just to paint a piece of ceramic."

I gave him a face that said I wasn't amused. He opened the door and held it for me. As I walked past him, I punched him in the gut causing him to double over to catch his breath. When he stood up again, he was laughing and rubbing his stomach.

"Hi! How can I help you?" the girl behind the counter asked. She looked to be about sixteen, with long straight blonde hair. She smiled at me and I smiled back. She turned her smile towards Nick, but suddenly became flustered when she took him in. He smiled at her and a blush immediately formed on her cheeks.

"I can't take you anywhere," I mumbled as the girl cleared her throat and pretended to fix something on the counter.

"What?" he said with a grin.

I shook my head at him and turned to the girl. "How does this work? We pick something out, paint it, and then what?" I jumped in and saved the girl from the awkward moment. She looked up at Nick, but then quickly turned her attention to me.

"Yes ma'am. You paint the pieces, we fire them then you can come back the next day, or for a few extra dollars we can send them to your home." She managed to get through her answer without looking at Nick once.

"How much does it cost to do this?" I asked. I felt bad for mooching off Nick for lunch, so making him pay for the pottery seemed too much.

"Don't worry about it. It's my treat." Nick said sweetly from across the store. He'd wandered off during the girl's initial explanation. "Just pick out something that you want to paint and I'll pay for it."

"I'll pay you back when we get back to the beach house," I added politely and smiled at the girl.

Nick turned and gave me a stern look, "I said I would pay for it, Cami. Don't be difficult."

I was about to say thank you and flash him a smile, but he spoke again before I could open my mouth.

With a mischievous grin, and a quick look at the girl next to me, he said, "Besides, I can think of some ways you can pay me back. No money need change hands."

This time it wasn't just the sales girl who blushed. I could actually feel the heat of embarrassment radiating from both the girl and me as we stood there staring at Nick's wide grin.

"That was uncomfortable, thank you!" I said sarcastically a few minutes later when the girl had left to answer the phone in the back. "That poor girl was as red as a lobster when you made that comment."

Nick laughed, "She wasn't the only one."

I swatted him across the arm. "Don't do that again!"

He laughed some more.

"What should we paint?" I asked and looked around for something that interested me.

"What about these turtles?" Nick picked up two ceramic turtles.

"No, too boring! What about these surfboards?"

Nick shook his head, "No, that's just a flat piece of ceramic. It's not worth the money just to paint a flat piece."

"What about these?" I picked up two figurines. Each was a sculpture of a beach goer, one male and one female, dressed in bathing suits and carrying various beach accessories.

"They're cute," Nick shrugged.

"How about you paint this one," I handed him the girl figurine, "and I paint this one." I took the boy figurine for myself. "We'll paint them for each other and then have them sent to each other's address."

Nick looked confused, "You want me to paint this one but give it to you?"

I smiled and nodded, "Yes. You paint that for me and I'll paint this one for you."

He grinned, "Okay, so is it alright with you if I put little turquoise dots on the ankles of this one?"

I smiled at him. "You can paint it however you want, as long as you understand that I'm going to do the same."

"Is that a challenge, Ms. Harris?"

I took my figurine and sat down at a table across the store from him. When he started to follow me, I stopped him.

"I don't think so! You sit over there!" I pointed at a table on the other side of the store. "I don't want you peeking at my designs."

"Seriously?" he asked with a sad look. "Are you really not going to let me sit with you?"

I shook my head at him. "No. You have to sit over there."

He huffed and stomped off to the table I had pointed him towards. With another loud huff, he collapsed into his chair. I pretended not to notice, but had to lower my head so that he couldn't see me smile. We each sat at our tables, working silently on our figurines.

After five minutes of silence, Nick slammed his paintbrush down on the table. "Are you at least going to talk to me while we paint?"

I laughed at him, but didn't look up. "What do you want to talk about, Nick?"

"What are your sisters like?"

"They are very different from each other," I said with a smile then added, "and very different from me."

"What are their names?"

I still wasn't looking up at him, but I raised my eyes enough to see that he was bent over his figurine painting as he asked.

"Victoria, or Tori, is the youngest. She's the baby and never fails to remind us of that every chance she gets. Allison is the middle child and she does not fit the mold of the middle child myth. My parents always say that somehow, Allison and I switched personalities without their permission." I talked and painted at the same time.

"What do you mean?" Nick asked in a genuinely interested tone.

"The middle child is supposed to be docile, a peacekeeper, and a people pleaser. Allison is bossy, she's demanding, and as a child she was very mean-spirited. Actually, she's still kind of mean-spirited." I smiled thinking about my sisters.

"How is she mean?"

I sighed, "When I was thirteen, and she was ten, she told me that my clumsiness was because my brain was actually smaller than average and because of that I wasn't able to balance myself like other people could."

I didn't look up as I waited for his reaction. I expected him to laugh, but to my surprise, he was silent. Curious to know what he was doing, I looked up.

Nick was bent over like he was working hard on his painting. I almost wondered if he'd heard me, but just before I asked, I noticed his shoulders shaking just slightly.

"It's not funny! It was really mean and it took me a long time to get over it."

My outburst didn't help. He lost control of himself and started laughing loudly. "She was only ten. How could you possibly have believed her?" he said between giggles.

"She tested at a genius level! You don't know how smart she is!"

He laughed even harder at that.

"She has a way of saying things that makes you believe that she's right. She's very convincing." I continued explaining myself as he laughed.

"I'm sorry," he said when he'd finally stopped laughing. "I didn't mean to laugh at you, but that was a funny story. Your sister sounds mean, but creative."

I glared at him for a second and went back to painting my figurine.

"What are your parents like?" he asked with a steadier voice.

"They're great. My dad is an accountant and my mom does the books for my grandfather's construction company." I talked and rinsed my brush. "Well, it used to be my grandfather's company but he died last year. My uncle runs it now."

"So both your parents worked when you were growing up?"

"Technically, yes. My mom did most of her work from home so that she could be there for my sisters and me. She only went into the office to do the paychecks."

"Where did your parents meet?"

Nick was staying focused on his art as he asked me questions. Having finished my painting, I sat and watched him without him knowing. He looked adorable sitting hunched over a tiny figurine. Occasionally, a little crinkle would form on his forehead as he worked. Every time the crinkle appeared, I smiled.

Not wanting to raise suspicion about my silence, I answered his question. "They met at the University of Virginia, which is where both my sisters are at."

"So, how did they end up in New York?"

"It's where my mom is from. She told my dad that if he loved her, he'd move back to New York and marry her."

Nick laughed quietly, "And he did?"

"Yes, he did. He said it was the best decision he never had to make."

Growing up in a house with parents who loved each other as much as my parents did was something that I'd always taken for granted. It wasn't until I got to college that I realized how rare that was. Based on Nick's earlier reaction to the question about his family, I was guessing that he didn't have a similar experience as me.

"He never had to make the decision because there was never a question, right?"

I smiled. "No. He said he knew she was the one and if she wanted him to move to Africa with her, he'd do it. He'd follow her anywhere."

Nick looked up at me and smiled. "They sound nice."

"They are," I said and smiled back at him.

6.

After we finished our figurines, we filled out the paperwork to have them sent to each other. I still wasn't ready to get back on the bike, but there wasn't anything else left to do in the little village of shops. We rode back towards the beach house, but neither of us was in a hurry to get back. When I'd told Nick about Darren and the skinny blonde I'd left him with in the house, he'd laughed.

"It's probably best if we give them a few hours alone in the house. Darren can be a little overzealous with his entertaining." Nick said with a wide grin.

"By overzealous do you mean loud or exhibitionist?" I said hesitantly.

Nick laughed, "Both."

We left our bikes on the edge of the grass and walked towards the small sandy beach we'd stopped at.

"I was just wondering. How did you and Darren meet?" I'd taken my shoes off and was carrying them in one hand as we made our way to the water.

"I met Darren when I did my senior internship at D&A. We suffered through that hell together."

"D&A?" I repeated the name slowly, not sure if I'd heard him correctly.

"Davis and Associates," he clarified.

"Wait, doesn't Darren's dad run that company? He's Ned's nephew right? So isn't his dad Ned's brother?" I asked confusedly.

"Yes, Darren's dad runs the company. He's Ned's older brother." Nick dropped his shoes on the sand and held his hand out for mine.

"So if Darren's dad runs the company, why was Darren doing an internship? Don't the ridiculously rich usually just hand things to their offspring?" My voice was thick with bitterness.

Nick smiled, clearly not missing my vitriol. "How much do you know about Ned and his brother?"

I shrugged, "I don't really know Ned that well. He's always been nice to me, but he works a lot so I don't see much of him."

"Ned and Tim Davis grew up in the typical suburban middle class family. Their dad worked two jobs so that their mom could stay home and raise the boys. They weren't poor, but they certainly weren't rich. When Tim graduated from college, he decided to start the business. Ned joined him when he graduated and they worked hard to build the company into what it is today." Nick's voice was full of reverence for his bosses. "Tim wanted his son to know what it was like to start at the bottom."

"You have a lot of respect for him, don't you?" I could tell that he looked up to Tim Davis.

"Who? Darren?" he said in a shocked tone. "How can I possibly respect someone who clearly has no respect for women?"

I laughed, "I meant his dad."

Nick laughed, "I have a great deal of respect for Tim and Ned, both." He took a deep breath and put a more serious look on his face. "I respect anyone who works hard to better themselves."

Something about the way his face had changed and the words he'd said made me think that Nick knew a lot more about what it was like to better oneself than he was willing to share. I smiled politely at him, hoping that he couldn't tell what I was thinking. We walked silently for a minute. The sand beneath my feet started to cool as we approached the water line.

When the water began to wash over my feet, Nick stopped and looked at me.

"I didn't make friends with Darren so that I could advance in the company. I didn't even know who he was until the second week, and we'd already hit it off by then. I know it sounds like I zeroed in on the boss' kid, made friends with him, and then found myself in a favorable position a few years later, but I didn't." He stared intently at me. "I worked hard to prove myself and I work hard to stay where I am. I earn my keep, and if I don't, I would expect to be let go."

He kept his eyes on me after he spoke. I could tell by the look on his face that he needed me to acknowledge what he'd said. For some reason, he needed me to know that he wasn't a climber.

I smiled, "You don't have to explain to me. I know all about the things people can say about you when you are friends with someone who's not your social equal."

His shoulders relaxed and a small smile formed at the corners of his mouth.

"I know the things people say behind my back when they meet me. I actually hate going to functions with her because of it. Plus, she's absolutely gorgeous, so not only am I Chrissy's poor friend, I'm also her homely looking one too."

"You are definitely not homely," he said sweetly.

"Thanks, but I wasn't fishing for a compliment." I nudged him with my shoulder. "I just know that I can't compete with women who have plastic surgeons on speed dial, and spend thousands of dollars on hair and makeup products and services a month." I shrugged and started walking again. He walked beside me as I continued, "Of course, I'm not trying to compete with them because I actually don't want their life. It all seems so pointless and shallow."

Nick smiled, "There's no competition, Cami. You are on a totally different level than they are, you know that don't you?"

His comment made the blush rise on my cheeks. It also made me realize that there was something that had to be said before we went any further. I exhaled loudly and started.

"I have to tell you something." I didn't look up when I said it. It was much easier to be confident if I didn't have to look at him while I said it.

"Okay," he said the word slowly and hesitantly.

"This is never going to happen." I waggled my finger back and forth between us, indicating the two of us. "You live in LA and I live in New York. We're only here together for a few days, and we'll probably never see each other again. I'm not that kind of girl, so I'm not going hook up with you while we're here. Okay?" After the last word was out, I finally looked up at him.

"Okay," he said with a nod. I could tell he wanted to say something else, but was holding it in.

Feeling slightly embarrassed for being so bold, I stammered out more of an explanation. "I just wanted to be upfront with you about that, because if you're investing all this time in me just for sex, then you should know that it's not going to happen. I don't have sex with guys I'm not dating. I don't go to bars or clubs and pick up guys and I didn't come here to have a summer fling. I'm here to spend a week at the beach before I go back to work. I'm not looking for any type of sexual escapade."

Nick smiled and put his hands up, "Okay, I got it. You're not interested in having sex with me."

Blushing, and feeling bad about how he'd interpreted my meaning, I stupidly kept talking. "It's not that I'm not interested in having sex with you. I'm not interested in having sex with anyone I'm not dating."

He grinned even wider, "So you are interested in having sex with me, but only if we date first?"

Still blushing, I started backtracking again. "I don't hook up, okay. That's not who I am, and I just thought I would tell you that to potentially avoid any awkward moments later."

"Because this isn't awkward at all?" he laughed.

I laughed nervously.

"Don't worry, Cami. I know what you're saying, and I respect it." He flashed a friendly smile.

Relieved, I sighed loudly.

"For the record, though, I was never investing time in you just for sex. If that's all I was looking for, I would have gone for Chrissy." He shrugged apologetically at me, but continued. "I like talking to you. I also like getting to know you. You're not like the girls I usually spend time with."

"Because I have breasts, and not tits, and I can carry on an adult conversation? Is that what you mean by different?" I said teasingly.

"Can I just say that I love the fact that you use the word tits in conversation without even the slightest bit of shame?" he laughed lightly and shook his head.

"I noticed how you skirted around the issue of your lack of taste in women. Clever," I teased him again.

"Tasteful women are a lot harder to pick up," he shrugged nonchalantly.

"Oh, so you're a lazy lover?" I wiped my brow, "Phew, I really dodged a bullet with you, didn't I?"

He stopped walking and looked sternly at me. "Okay, now you've done it! I'm going to give you a head start, and a warning this time, because when I catch you I will throw you into that ocean with absolutely no regard for your dry clothing. You better get running!"

I laughed at him until he lunged at me. I took off running in the opposite direction and ran as hard as I could while still laughing. It only took him a few seconds to catch me, but he didn't have a firm grip on me. I wiggled out of his grip and double-backed on him. He chased me down and wrapped both arms around me, picked me up by my waist, and carried me towards the water. I screamed and laughed, but he repeated his warning.

"Please don't!" I screamed and laughed.

"You insulted my abilities as a lover and since you've already declared you won't sleep with me, I have no other way to defend my honor!" he yelled over my pleas.

"Okay, okay! I'll have sex with you!" I shouted back in response.

"Too late! You missed your chance!" he said and tossed me into the waist deep water.

When I came back up, I jumped onto his back and dragged him down into the water with me. We wrestled in the water for a few minutes, laughing and splashing water in each other's faces. Finally, he grabbed me by the waist and tickled me until I couldn't breathe.

"Truce! Truce!" I screamed breathlessly.

"Take back what you said," he growled at me. He still had his hands on my waist, but he'd stopped tickling me for the moment.

"Fine, I take back what I said," I groaned at him, "Even though I have no way of knowing this, you aren't a lazy lover. There, are you happy?"

"I am," he said and let go of my waist.

I turned around and glared at him, "I can't believe you threw me into the ocean fully clothed!"

He grinned, "I would have stripped you naked first, but I figured that would go against the whole not hooking up thing you just finished telling me about."

I blushed at the thought of being naked in front of him. "Thanks," I muttered sarcastically.

He laughed and turned back towards the beach. I followed behind him, trying my best to put my clothes and hair back in place.

"We should probably dry off a bit before we get back on the bikes, don't you think?" Nick asked when we were only ankle deep in the water.

My shirt was clinging to me in an unflattering way, so I had to hold it out to try to keep it off my skin. The thought of not being able to stop that from happening while I was riding a bike flashed through my mind.

"Yes. Too bad someone didn't think to bring a towel."

He laughed, "I can't think of everything! I found the restaurant and the pottery place, didn't I? Don't I at least get credit for that?"

I shook my head and smiled. "How did you find those places anyway?"

He shrugged, "I looked them up online last night."

"Was that before or after the beach blanket bimbos and the billiards?"

He grinned, "After. I couldn't sleep, so I did a little searching."

"Couldn't sleep, huh? More like wanted to leave the room so that when the bimbo woke up, she would leave the house without a scene." I mumbled and giggled.

"No," Nick said loudly. "I couldn't sleep last night because there was too much noise in the house, what with a party going on and all." He nudged me and pushed me sideways. "Plus," he added quietly as I stumbled back to my position, "I don't really sleep much."

"Why don't you sleep much?" I asked and wrung out the right leg of my shorts. We'd made it back to the sand, but were now strolling along the edge of the water.

He shrugged again, "I don't know. Ever since I was a kid, I've been a restless sleeper. Most nights, I only get about four hours of sleep."

"So what do you do at night, then?"

"Play my guitar, work on work things, surf the internet, you know time filler things." He bent down and picked up a shell then skipped it across the water.

I grinned, "Is that all you do? Are you sure you don't go trolling the bars and clubs for other things to do?"

He stopped and looked at me, "I didn't hook up with anyone last night, Cami. Why do you think that's what I'm interested in?"

I cut my eyes at him, "You're a guy, aren't you? Isn't that what all guys are looking for all the time?"

"I'm not going to lie to you, Cami. I've done my fair share of hooking up, but I don't go out every night looking for someone to bring home with me. I didn't sleep with anyone last night," he grinned at me, "I didn't even try, so don't go thinking that I struck out."

I shook my head, "I wouldn't dream of it. I seriously doubt that you would have heard a no, if you'd have asked."

Nick grinned at me and cocked an eyebrow, "What do you mean?"

"Oh come on! Don't act like you didn't notice how that girl in the pottery place acted when she saw you." I laughed at his false modesty.

His mouth flew open and a loud wail of laughter escaped. "What are you talking about? That girl was like fifteen years old! Women don't have the same reactions, trust me!"

"Right, like one flash of that gorgeous smile, or one peek at your six pack abs, and women aren't throwing themselves at you."

Nick laughed, "Remind me again, didn't you just tell me that you and I weren't going to be hooking up?"

"Yes, so?"

"If I'm so damn irresistible to women then how are you able to control yourself in my presence?" he wiggled his eyebrows at me.

With a laugh, I answered, "I have superhuman self-control. That and I don't happen to find gorgeous smiles and six pack abs all that attractive."

Nick grinned and nodded dramatically, "Oh, I see. I bet I know what your last boyfriend was like. What was his name?"

"Jack," I answered.

"I bet Jack was the artsy type, wasn't he? Probably had a pair of black rimmed glasses that he wore to poetry readings and jazz concerts, right?" Nick grinned as he described what he thought Jack would look like.

"No," I said defensively. "Jack hated Jazz, and his glasses were silver."

Nick laughed. "Have all your boyfriends been that type?"

"Have all your girlfriends been the same type?" I threw the question at him again. He'd never bothered to answer it the first time I'd asked.

"They may have had some similar characteristics," he said slowly through a grin.

"I bet I can guess exactly which two characteristics," I held my hands out in front of my chest to indicate large breasts.

"You know, you keep bringing up breasts. It's starting to get a little suspicious." He lowered his eyes and looked at me.

"Hey, you are the one who brought them up initially. You told me that your last girlfriend had, 'a fabulous set of fake breasts'. So, if anyone is to blame, it's you!"

"That may be true, but you keep bringing them back up. If I didn't know any better, I'd think that you thought your own breasts were somehow inferior." He gave me a very serious look.

"I can't believe you said that!" I said in surprise. "There is absolutely nothing wrong with my breasts. They are exactly the size they're supposed to be!" Just to emphasize my point, I grabbed my breasts and gave them a squeeze.

Nick's eyes widened at my action and a big grin spread across his face. "I would have to agree with you on that. Your breasts are definitely proportionate to the rest of your body. I don't think them inferior at all."

I dropped my hands and put them on my hips. I knew what he was up to. I stopped walking and stood in place, with my hands still resting on my hips. After a few more steps, he realized that I wasn't with him anymore and stopped. When he turned around, I was giving him my best teacher look.

"What?" he said with a grin.

"I'm on to you, Nick whatever-your-last-name-is!"

He grinned, "Fletcher, my last name is Fletcher."

"Okay, I'm on to you, Nick Fletcher!"

"What are you talking about?" he started walking back towards me.

"You keep changing the subject when the conversation turns back to you. I've spent the last two days spilling my guts to you about all my embarrassing moments and my family. But every time the topic turns to you, you skillfully change the subject." I glared at him and held the look as he walked closer.

He sighed heavily, "You caught me. That's what I've been doing." The grin was replaced by an apologetic smile.

My face softened, "Why?"

He shook his head slowly. "I don't really like to talk about myself."

I studied his face as he answered. He looked different as he stood there looking back at me. The confident attractive man was gone, replaced by a vulnerable and scarred man. Sensing that the tough approach wasn't going to get me anywhere, I took pity on him and went the humorous route.

"Is it because you're so uninteresting?" I gave him a look of pity. "I suspected that about you."

He laughed. "You really want me to throw you back into that ocean, don't you?"

"You wouldn't dare," I said as I walked towards the dry sand, leaving him standing at the water's edge.

I bent down and picked up a shell then plopped down on the dry sand. I put the shell down on the ground next to me and picked up another one.

"What are you doing?" Nick asked and sat down next to me.

"I'm collecting shells."

"Why?"

"A lot of my students have never been to the beach, so when I go to beaches I like to collect shells for them. Sometimes, when it rains, or if they have had a particularly good week, I'll put out bins with sand in them. They like to make sand sculptures and dig for shells." I shrugged my explanation.

"Do you let them keep the shells?" He asked and handed me a shell he'd picked up.

"Sometimes," I smiled in thanks and took the shell. "They really like the tiny conch shells and those little spiral ones."

"Like this?" he handed me a shell.

I smiled, "Yes! They love these. They call them shark's teeth."

He laughed and searched around for more shells.

"Sometimes, I'll give each student a shell and have them write a story about the animal that used to live inside it." I held my hand out and he placed a few shells in it.

"I don't remember doing things like that in school," he searched and talked.

"Most people don't remember much about first grade, but I like to do things that aren't necessarily in the state's plan." I looked at the pile of shells that was quickly building. "I wish I'd brought a bag or something to put these in. I'm not sure how I'm going to get them back to the house."

"Use this."

I turned to see him pulling his t-shirt off. While the shirt was covering his head, and his arms were up in the air, I noticed a series of small circular scars under his arm. He moved too quickly for me to get a better look and when he was free from his shirt, I averted my eyes so he wouldn't see me staring. I smiled weakly at him.

"You can put the shells in this and we'll tie it up when we're done. I can carry it on the ride back."

"Thanks."

We collected shells in silence for a few minutes. Eventually, I got up from my spot on the sand and walked around looking for more shells. When I thought I had enough, I brought my bounty back to his shirt. He scooped the shirt up and tied it into a bundle.

"Shall we head back?" he asked as he stood up with the bundled shirt in his hands.

"Sure," I nodded and walked next to him. My eyes kept wandering over to his shirtless torso. I wondered if he had any other scars. He walked ahead of me, and I tried to be subtle as I studied his back for more scars.

Suddenly, he stopped walking. "Is everything okay?" he turned and asked me.

I nodded my head and tried my best to smile like my mind wasn't racing with ideas about him. It was one thing for him not to talk about himself, but add that to the scars, and I was starting to get a picture of his past.

He smiled, "Are you getting nervous about the bike ride back?"

I laughed, "No. I managed to get here in one piece, so I'm feeling confident in my skills now."

7.

Back at the beach house, after the bikes had been put away and my helmet had been hung back up in the storage shed under the house, Nick and I headed up the stairs and into the house. I let him walk in front of me this time.

"Is this so you can check out my butt?" he said with a grin and started up the stairs.

"Well, it is right in front of me," I grinned in reply.

He turned around and started walking up the stairs backwards. He flashed a wry grin at me.

"Now you're just showing off because you know if I tried that, I'd end up in the hospital." I smiled and looked up at him. Of course, since he'd turned around I was no longer staring at his butt. Instead, I found myself staring directly at his crotch. Feeling suddenly embarrassed and flustered, I lost my footing and tripped up the stairs. I put my hands out to catch myself, and when I did, I smacked him in the groin.

He groaned as my hand made contact with his crotch.

My knee banged against the step I'd missed and my head knocked against the railing, but despite my own pain, I still tried to mutter an apology. "I'm so sorry!" I spit out and crumbled to the stairs in pain.

"Are you okay?" he asked in a strained voice.

I rubbed my head and inspected my leg. A bruise had already started to form on my leg. "I'm fine. I didn't mean to hit you, especially not there. I'm so sorry!"

Nick adjusted himself and gingerly walked down the stairs to inspect my wounds. "It's nothing a little ice can't fix."

"Same here," I said with a blush. He was holding my leg and rubbing the bruised spot gently.

"It looks like you are already starting to bruise, and you've got a little scratch. Let me see your head." He leaned forward and inspected the small bump from where my head had made contact with the wooden railing. As he did, his bare chest was just inches from my face.

I shifted my eyes enough to get a better look at the scars I'd seen earlier. Just as I'd suspected, they looked to be cigarette burns. There were about a dozen of them, with some of them looking as if there were burns on top of burns.

"I think as long as we get some ice on it, you'll be okay." He moved and lowered his face down to mine. He smiled at me, "I should have known you wouldn't make it through an entire day without some sort of injury."

I rolled my eyes at him and smiled.

We sat looking at each other. I expected him to move away, to stand up and walk away, to do anything but just sit there and stare at me. I swallowed hard as the electricity that had buzzed between us that morning started to hum again.

He cleared his throat and whispered, "Thank you."

"For what?" I whispered back.

"For telling me that we weren't going to hook up," he sighed and the heat of his breath against my skin sent a tingle of excitement through me. "If I thought it would lead somewhere, I would totally kiss you right now."

Another tingle ran through me. I couldn't deny that there was definitely a physical attraction between us, but attraction didn't change the facts. He lived in LA, I lived in New York, and in a few days, we'd never see each other again. All of those factors made for a bad idea.

His face was still just inches from mine.

I looked into his eyes and sighed. "You're welcome."

He smiled, shook his head, and stood up. He held his hand out to me and I took it. I let him pull me up, but dropped his hand when I was upright.

"I certainly hope there's plenty of ice in the freezer," he said with a hint of humor in his voice.

"I'm sure it won't take that much ice to heal our wounds." I bumped into him and smiled.

"Probably not, but maybe to conserve ice we should use the same ice pack, just in case." He grinned at me mischievously.

It took me a few seconds to figure out why he was giving me that look. I had to think back for a second to realize what he was saying. I pictured the two of us sharing an ice pack, me with the head wound and him with his wounded crotch.

"Oh!" I said loudly and with a blush. "Pervert!"

Nick laughed and held the door open for me.

The smell of cleaning fluids greeted us as we walked through the front door of the house. The cleaners had done a great job of putting the house back together. There were no signs of the wild party from the night before. All the furniture was back in place, the carpets were freshly steam-cleaned, and the kitchen was spotless.

I headed for the freezer and put a few ice cubes in a paper towel. I handed it to Nick before making one for myself. He sat down on one of the stools and put the paper towel bundle in his lap. I put my own bundle against my head and leaned on the counter across from him.

He smiled at me and I smiled back.

"Does your head hurt?" he asked softly.

"Not too bad. How's your crotch?" I asked with a grin.

He grinned back at me, "There might be some swelling going on down there. Would you mind checking it out for me?"

"Those jokes and cheesy lines aren't going to make me change my mind."

"I know that." He got up from the stool. "I wouldn't dream of making you do something you didn't want to do." He put the paper towel bundle on the counter and left the kitchen.

When he was gone, I dropped the ice package on my head and exhaled loudly. I'd never admit it, but the argument against hooking up was getting weaker by the minute. The electricity between us was intense and only getting heavier. But the distance between our lives wasn't the only obstacle now. The mystery of who Nick Fletcher really was seemed to be an even more impossible block in our path. I knew enough about him to know that I wanted to know more.

An hour later, after I'd taken a shower, put on fresh clothes, and transferred my shells from Nick's t-shirt to a plastic bag; I headed down to the second floor and collapsed on the couch in front of the television. I curled up on the couch and settled on a marathon of an old sitcom.

I must have fallen asleep, because when I woke up it was almost dark outside and the television was off. I stretched my arms and feet out and felt a blanket slide off me onto the floor.

"Finally!" Nick's voice called out to me in the dark. "I was worried that you'd given yourself a concussion and then fallen into a coma."

"How long did I sleep?" I yawned loudly and stretched some more.

Nick got up from the chair across the room and came to sit on the end of the couch. He put my feet in his lap. "You've been asleep for about three hours."

"Has Chrissy come home yet?" I tried to sit up and pull my feet away, but he grabbed them and kept me still.

"She did, but she left again. She told me to tell you that she took the emergency stash so you shouldn't worry about her."

I couldn't see his face because it was too dark in the room, but I could hear the suspicion in his voice.

"She wasn't talking about drugs, was she? You definitely don't seem like the type to be involved with drugs, but I'm not so sure about Chrissy." He kept my feet in a firm grip, waiting for my answer.

I laughed, "No, we're not into drugs. She means condoms. I always bring some because she never remembers to."

His hands dropped from my feet. "Condoms? I thought you didn't hook up?"

Free from his grip, I sat up. "I don't!"

"Then why do you bring condoms with you?"

"I bring them for Chrissy. The last thing this world needs is for her to be procreating. I'm doing the world a favor by packing those condoms."

"But you never use them?"

"Not for hooking up, no."

He sighed loudly and stood up. "I'm hungry! Let's go to the store and get something for dinner."

Nick called a taxi to come pick us up and I ran upstairs to freshen up. He chatted with the driver on the way to the store and I watched the sun setting over the water on the horizon. It had been a great day, and I was looking forward to a nice quiet evening.

Once in the store, I headed off to the medicine section to pick up some more ibuprofen. My head was aching a little and the bottle of ibuprofen in my bag was running low. I'd just picked up a generic bottle when Nick appeared at the end of the aisle.

"You eat meat, right?" he asked.

The old lady standing next to me gave him a strange look then looked at me.

I don't know what I was thinking, or even why I was thinking it, but suddenly something completely inappropriate popped into my head.

"Cami?" Nick called out to me.

"What?" I said with a blush.

He walked over to me. "I asked you if you eat meat and you didn't answer. Do you?"

"You mean like chicken and beef?" I asked stupidly. As soon as the question was out of my mouth, I knew I'd made a mistake.

His eyebrow rose. "What else would I mean?"

I blushed again, "Nothing."

He cocked his head to the side and grinned, "Cami?"

I blushed and looked away from him, "Okay, so like maybe for half a second my mind went somewhere else."

He laughed loudly, "You know, for a girl who says she's not interested in hooking up, you certainly do think about sex a lot."

The old lady next to me gave Nick a once over then looked me up and down too.

"Oh come on! You're telling me that if I said something harmless to you like, 'Hey, how do you feel about going downtown tonight?' that your mind wouldn't go there?" I smiled at him.

"Of course not," he said with a smile for the old lady. "I would assume that you were inviting me out for a night on the town in the main district of a city."

"Whatever!" I said and laughed at him. "To answer your question, yes, I am a carnivore."

He smiled, "Good." He turned and walked back to where he'd come from. Just before he left the aisle, though, he turned around and said, "Oh and by the way, I'd love to go downtown. In fact, I've been told that I'm very good at going downtown." He flashed a wide smile then disappeared.

Too embarrassed to face the old lady next to me, I started to walk away from her.

"Hold on to that one, sweetie! Not many men like going downtown and even fewer are good at it!" the old lady shouted after me.

"Why did that old lady just wink at me?" Nick asked as we stood in the checkout line.

My cheeks burned again and I turned away from him. “Probably because you bragged about your oral skills in front of her and now she thinks we’re going home to have sex.”

Nick laughed, “That’s awesome!” He gave the old lady a wink and a big grin.

“Stop it!” I said and handed him a potato.

After the embarrassing incident with the old lady, I’d been too distracted to pay attention to what he was putting in the cart. Now, in the checkout line, I was inspecting what he’d chosen.

“Wine?” I questioned him as I handed him the bottle.

“I thought it would be nice with the meal.” He shrugged and put the bottle on the counter.

“I hope it’s not expensive because I have to confess that I don’t know enough about the stuff to be able to tell the difference between the good stuff and the cheap stuff.” I tossed the other potato onto the counter.

“Good, then I’m glad I got the five dollar bottle.”

“Will you please let me pay for at least part of this stuff?” I begged him politely.

“No! I told you when we got in the car that today is completely my treat.” He flashed a cheesy smile. “If it makes you feel better, you can pay for everything tomorrow.”

Back at the house, Nick started the grill and I pulled everything else together. We ate at the table by the pool and stuffed ourselves with the delicious food. The bottle of wine added to the meal and helped me to relax a little.

“So, I have to ask,” Nick said after we’d both pushed our plates away and refilled our glasses. “Why exactly won’t you hook up with me?”

“I told you, I don’t hook up.”

“Okay, well, let’s say you did do hook ups. Would you hook up with me then?”

I smiled at him, but shook my head, “No.”

“Why not?” he said it with a hurt voice, but the smile never left his face.

"I just wouldn't, that's all." I didn't want to admit the truth to him or myself.

He sat up and leaned across the table, "Is it because you think you're not pretty enough to be with a guy like me?"

I put my glass down and lowered my eyes at him. "That statement is wrong for three reasons. First, it's insulting! I don't think I'm not pretty enough to be with you."

A panicked look flashed across his face, "I don't think that either! I just thought maybe you thought that and I was going to tell you that it's not true! I think you're pretty, you're beautiful actually."

I put my hand up to stop him. "Whatever! Secondly, I've seen enough chick flicks, and read enough chick lit, to know that even if I am just slightly less attractive than you, if this was a movie or book, I'd totally get you in the end!"

He relaxed a little and laughed. "And what's the third reason?"

"The third reason is that you aren't exactly the grand prize winner in the greatest man on earth contest!" I took another big sip of wine.

"What's that supposed to mean?" he asked with a grin.

"Well, you obviously choose to enter relationships that you know will never work out, which means you have commitment issues. Plus, you don't like to talk about yourself, or your family, something which I suspect is the main reason you have commitment issues." I shrugged and took another drink.

He smiled, "You do realize that hooking up means that there is no commitment involved, right?"

"Don't kid yourself! Very few women hook up without even the slightest hope that it might lead to something more than just one night."

"Even Chrissy?" he grinned and poured more wine into my glass.

"Chrissy is the worst kind of hook up! She acts like the flighty party girl but what she really is, is a girl desperate for someone to love her. All she wants is for a man to tell her that he loves her, but what she doesn't realize is that it's never going to happen if she keeps going after men like Mr. Money." I shook my head at the state of Chrissy's love life. I'd told her a thousand times that she needed to stop what she was doing, but she just couldn't help herself. She was broken and always would be.

"What about you?" Nick cocked his head to the side. "You aren't desperate for a man to tell you he loves you?"

"No," I said confidently. "I've had that and it felt good, but what I want now is for a man to tell me that I'm it. I want him to tell me that I am the only woman he will love for the rest of his life. I want to hear him say that there is nothing else in this world that he wants more than to be by my side as we build a life and a family together. You can't get that from hook up."

"No, you can't," Nick said softly.

I took another sip of wine and tried to avoid meeting his gaze. I could feel his eyes on me, but I refused to look over at him.

He finally broke the silence between us. "How would you feel about a bonfire on the beach tonight?"

8.

I filled a cooler with bottles of water and beer while Nick went down to the beach and started the fire. By the time I made it to the beach, the fire was blazing and Nick had a towel down for us to sit on.

"I brought you some beers," I gave him a smile and parked the cooler by the towel.

"Thanks," he said and grabbed his guitar. He sat down on the towel and started playing. I sat down next to him and watched the sparks flying off the fire and into the night sky.

I listened to Nick playing the guitar and watched the flames, feeling completely content. It reminded me of when I would visit my grandparents at the farmhouse in Virginia. They would sit together for hours on the front porch and not say a word to each other. Grandpa Harris would carve and whittle, while Grandma Harris would knit. They were content just being near each other. They didn't feel the need to fill every second with idle chatter.

"I thought that was you," Darren's voice boomed from behind us.

Nick stopped playing and we both turned around to see Darren walking towards us with a gorgeous redhead on his arm.

"We were going to go for a swim, but Ginger heard a guitar and saw the fire, so we thought we'd come check out what was going on down here." Darren flashed his pearly white teeth at us. "Are we interrupting something?"

"No," Nick said with a shake of his head. "We were just enjoying the night with a fire and some tunes. Would you care to join us?"

"This is so romantic!" Ginger, Darren's redhead, exclaimed and plopped herself down across the fire from me.

Darren sat down next to her and stole a kiss.

Nick leaned closer to me and whispered, "That's a different girl from this morning, isn't it?"

I opened my eyes wide and nodded. Nick shrugged and started playing again.

At first, everything was the same as it had been before Darren and Ginger arrived. Nick played a few songs and I watched the flames. Unfortunately, Darren and Ginger started to get a little more enthusiastic in their enjoyment of the ambience. The soft giggles and moans started to become distracting, and I found myself looking up at the stars instead of the flames that only partially hid the loving couple from my view.

The sounds and sights must have been distracting for Nick too, as he started to stumble over the notes of his songs more frequently than he had earlier.

I cleared my throat, hoping it would help, but it didn't do any good.

"They know we're still here, right?" I whispered to Nick when he stumbled over his song for the fifth time in the last minute.

"I don't think they care," he whispered back.

A loud moan broke through our conversation, causing Nick and I to stare uncomfortably at each other.

"Hey, uh, we're going in. Can you make sure to put the fire out before you head inside?" Nick stood up and asked without looking at the couple.

"Yeah, sure, whatever man," Darren said breathlessly.

Nick pulled me up from my seated position and pushed me towards the house. We left the towel and the cooler of drinks on the beach and practically ran back up to the house.

"That was uncomfortable," I said when we'd reached the house.

"Just a little," Nick held the door open for me. "Are you too tired, or are you up for a movie?"

"I might be able to handle a movie."

"I'll get the drinks and snacks and meet you upstairs on the couch. You pick out whatever you want." Nick walked off in the direction of the kitchen and I headed up to the second floor and over towards the media cabinet.

I picked out an action flick, hoping it would be a safe choice. Nick handed me a bottle of water and sat down next to me on the couch with a bowl of popcorn. The blanket he'd put over me for my nap was on the back of the couch and he pulled it off and spread it over our laps as the opening credits of the movie began to play.

Halfway through the movie, we heard the downstairs back door slide open and closed. Next, we heard two voices, one high and one low, as they traveled up the stairs to the third floor. We glanced at each other then turned our attention back to the movie. Within five minutes though, it was nearly impossible to focus on the movie. The moans, groans, and screams coming from the third floor filled the house.

There were no more glances. In fact, we were both trying very hard to act as if nothing at all was happening. Nick continued to munch on the popcorn and I played with my water bottle. I thought we were pulling it off quite well, but then the banging started.

I put my hand over my mouth to stifle the giggle escaping. The banging got louder and faster and was soon joined by even louder moans. The louder they got, the louder my giggles got.

Nick put the bowl of popcorn down on the coffee table and stood up, "Wanna go for a walk?"

"Yeah, that would be good," I said and jumped up from the couch. In less than a minute, we were out the door and headed back down towards the beach. The fire Nick had built earlier, and left in Darren's capable hands, was out but still smoldering. The lights from the back of the beach house were bright enough that we could see all the way to the water. We walked silently for a minute.

"Do you think they have any clue at all how loud they were being?" I asked as we walked along the water's edge.

"I think they were probably a little preoccupied."

We both started laughing uncontrollably.

"Does he do that a lot?"

Nick grinned, "I've never actually studied his technique, but I would assume that if it gets favorable reviews then he probably does do it often."

I smacked his arm. "That's not what I meant! I meant does he pick up a lot of girls and have sex with them in public?"

"Technically they weren't in public. They were in a private residence and in a closed bedroom."

"Okay, let me rephrase that. Does he often have sex with random girls when he knows other people can hear him?"

Nick shrugged, "It's not the first escapade I've had to listen to."

I nodded and we walked in silence for a minute.

"She was faking it, by the way," I said quietly.

"I don't think she was faking that, Cami."

"Trust me," I looked over at him and continued, "She was faking that."

He smiled at me, "What makes you say that?"

With a grin, I looked away and said, "Years of practice."

He laughed but suddenly stopped and got quiet, "Wait! That was what fake sounds like?"

I smiled, "Don't worry, we only fake it because we don't want your feelings to be hurt." I gave him a sympathetic look. "Or, we fake it because we just want it to be over so we can roll over and go to sleep without you poking at us all night."

Nick's brow furrowed, "But you're saying that when a girl makes those noises, she's faking it?"

I laughed and grabbed his hand reassuringly, "I'm sure that when a girl makes those noises with you, they are completely genuine."

"Thanks, but your sarcastic reassurance is not needed. I've never received any complaints, so I'm confident that I can please a woman."

I dropped his hand and put my own up in defense. "Okay, no need to get defensive. I'm sure you're a love machine!"

Nick looked at me intently, "Shall I remind you what happens when you insult my abilities as a lover?"

Just as he threatened me, a wave rolled up on shore pushing cool water over my feet. It felt nice, but I did not want to be soaked with it. Instead, I put up my hand and said, "Truce?"

He smiled and nodded. "Tell me more about your family."

"What do you want to know?"

"What year are your sisters in college?" he bent down and picked up a shell as he talked. He handed me the shell and smiled.

I held my hand out for the shell and smiled back at him. It amazed me how much he heard when I spoke. I don't think there was a thing I said to him that he didn't remember. I put the shell in my pocket and answered his question.

"Tori just started her sophomore year and Allison is getting her Graduate degree."

He laughed, "So how is it that everyone in your family ended up at Virginia, but you went to Columbia? I thought Allison was supposed to be the stubborn independent one."

"She is!" I said with a laugh. "I applied and got accepted to UVA, but when it came time to make the decision I knew there was no other choice for me but Columbia."

"Why? Didn't you like UVA?"

"I love it there, actually. My dad's parents live around Charlottesville, we go down there all the time, but I just couldn't see myself there. Honestly," I shrugged embarrassedly, "I couldn't see myself anywhere but New York."

"Why not?" he asked and watched me intently as we walked.

"I guess it just didn't seem worth the hassle to go all that way just to end up back home in the city."

"Why do you love New York so much?"

I smiled and shook my head. "I don't know that I can explain it."

He smiled back at me, "Can you try?"

I nodded and walked silently trying to collect my thoughts. "You know how when you grow up with someone and they know everything about you, good things and bad things, but you don't care because you know they'll always be there for you? You know that no matter how much things change in your life, or between you, that you'll always have those memories and times together.

Your interests and hobbies might change, but you always have the same moments to fall back on. I guess New York is like that friend for me."

Nick grinned, "New York is your best friend?"

I laughed, "Yes, I guess so. No matter what I go through, it's always there for me. When I was little, nothing made me more excited than getting to go into the city with my mom on a trip, or go to work with my dad. Seeing all the people, the buildings, the billboards, it was all magical to me. When I was fourteen, my parents let me go into the city by myself for the first time, and even though I only went to the library, it was the biggest adventure of my life! The city was there for me and it was a living, breathing being sharing that moment with me."

"You really do love that city, don't you?" he smiled, but there was a hint of sadness in his voice that I couldn't quite understand.

"Men might come and go, my family might move on and move out, but for me, New York City will always be where my heart is." I shrugged and smiled sweetly at him.

"Your family doesn't live in the city?"

"My parents raised us in a three-bedroom apartment about fifteen minutes outside of the city. It only took one short train ride to get us to the best city in the world, but" I sighed dramatically, "last year when my grandfather died and left them some money, they sold the apartment and bought a little house an hour or so out of the city."

"What about your sisters? Don't they want to live in the city?"

"Allison will probably end up living somewhere in Europe. She's got her heart set on a fellowship in Spain or something, and knowing her, she'll get it. Tori, on the other hand, is the all-American girl."

"What does that mean?" Nick asked with a laugh.

"That means, that by the time she graduates with her degree she'll also have a ring on her finger. She and her perfect husband will settle somewhere in Virginia, move into a perfect house, and raise their perfect children."

I made a face at the sickness of her perfection, but smiled despite myself. Things always had a way of working out for Tori. I had learned just to accept it without any bitterness.

"Sounds like the life you thought you'd have by now," Nick flashed me a wry grin.

I laughed, "I never thought my life would be perfect."

"Why should your sister get the perfect life if you don't get it?"

I grinned at him, "If you met Tori, you'd get it. She's perfect, always has been." I laughed, "It's not her fault and she's not arrogant about it or anything. For her, perfection is like my clumsiness. She can't help it any more than I can."

"Who says your clumsiness is an imperfection?" Nick said with a laugh and nudged me as we walked.

"You'd think someone whose crotch was on the receiving end of one of my accidents would classify it as an imperfection."

"You mean my crotch is not your first victim?" he continued with a disappointed voice. "I was really hoping that we had something special in that moment."

I laughed, "Don't worry. We still have two days together. Perhaps I'll accidently stab you or break a bone then we'll have that memory to bond us for life."

He laughed, "That would make for a great story."

"If either of those things happened, I would totally drive you to the hospital. Of course, with my luck, I'd take a wrong turn and end up driving us straight into the ocean killing us both."

He laughed at me and I joined in. We'd made our way back towards the house and were headed up towards the back of it.

"Do you think the coast is clear?" I asked hesitantly.

"Probably, it sounded like they were almost done when we left." Nick grinned.

"Well, it sounded like he was almost done," I said with a wink.

Nick chuckled and led the way up to the house. The lights were off in the house, so that seemed like a good sign. We headed for the doors by the pool, but before we could get there, Nick put his hand out to stop me.

"Did you hear that?" he whispered in alarm.

"No, what did it sound like?"

He didn't get the chance to answer because the noise happened again. At first, it was just the sound of someone making waves in the pool, but then it was joined with a soft moan.

I made a disgusted face at Nick, "I'm glad that pool is chlorinated. Gross!"

Nick put his hand over his mouth to keep from laughing aloud.

"Yes! Todd!" a female voice moaned from the direction of the pool.

Nick and I looked at each other in confusion.

"Todd?" I mouthed the name in question to Nick, who in return shrugged.

"You like that, Chrissy?" a male voice called out.

"Are we the only ones in the house not having sex?" I whispered and stood up to try to get a glimpse of the action in the pool.

"Hey, I offered," Nick put his hands up and grinned.

I caught a glimpse of Chrissy's back as she sat atop her partner, Todd, on the steps in the shallow end of the pool. That little scene was enough for me.

"Let's go in the front door. I don't need to see that." I grabbed his hand and pulled him back down towards the bottom of the house. He laughed and followed behind me.

"Are you sure you don't want to just sleep in the hammock again?" Nick asked as we reached the bottom of the stairs leading up to the house.

"If we get upstairs and the sexcapades are still going on, you can bet I'll be back down here for the night!"

We were halfway up the stairs before I realized that we were still holding hands. "Sorry!" I said and dropped his hand from mine.

"No problem."

When we entered the house, it was dark and silent. The intimate noises from earlier were gone and the French doors managed to muffle the noises coming from the pool. Just to be on the safe side, though, I wanted to get to the safety of my bedroom.

"I think the action has subsided, if you're interested in finishing that movie," Nick whispered in the dark foyer.

I'd already made it up the first few steps, but turned around to answer him. "I think it's probably best if we just go to bed."

Even in the dark, I could see the grin on Nick's face as he spoke, "I thought you'd never ask."

"You know what I mean! I don't think either of us is likely to encounter any more sex fiends if we head to our bedrooms."

"Speak for yourself!" he chuckled in response.

I turned back and headed up the stairs. "What? Do you have a big breasted blonde packed away for emergencies?" I whispered back to him as I walked.

"No!" he said and leaned closer to me, "She's a brunette."

I laughed at him.

At the top of the stairs, I turned to say goodnight to him and ran right into his chest. I hadn't expected him to be so close, but he was. To try to play it off, I wrapped my arms around him and gave him a hug.

"Thanks for a fun day," I said nervously against his chest.

I must have caught him off guard because he hesitated before wrapping his arms around me. "It was fun. Thanks for hanging out with me."

We stood in the hall holding each other for a few more seconds. It felt good to make physical contact with him. He felt warm and smelled amazing. I could have stayed like that for a few more minutes, but it was starting to feel a little too intimate, so I pulled away. He released me from his arms and took a step back.

"Have a good night," I whispered awkwardly and tried to walk backwards away from him.

"Cami," his voice sounded hoarse and strained.

When he said my name, I instinctively took a step towards him. "Yes?"

"Don't walk backwards that close to a staircase. Knowing you, you'll trip and end up rolling all the way down to the bottom of the stairs." He grinned at me and added, "Save some excitement for tomorrow."

I laughed at him, "Good night, Nick."

"Good night, Cami."

9.

When I woke up the next morning, the sunny, breezy summer day had been taken over by a heavy downpour and grey skies. I could hear the rain hitting the roof of the house and against my window. I always moved a little slower on rainy days, so I took my time pulling myself out of bed. By the time I made it downstairs, the whole house seemed deserted. I made myself some toast and stood in the kitchen as I ate it.

With no one else around, I had first choice in how I wanted to spend the rainy day. I thought about curling up on the couch and watching some television or a movie, but the sound might draw people out from wherever they were hiding. I considered going back up to my room and lying in bed with my book, but that didn't suit me either. I watched from the kitchen as the rain poured down from the sky and hit the deck floor. The silence of the house amplified the beat of the rain. Listening to it gave me an idea.

I gathered what I needed and made a mad dash out the door and down the stairs. By the time I got down to the bottom, I was soaked but smiling. The hammock, my hammock, was free and waiting for me. I spread the blanket over the netting and fell into the middle of my makeshift cocoon.

I stayed wrapped up in my sanctuary undisturbed for almost an hour. The rain was still coming down and I put my book down so I could just sit and listen to it pound the ground around me. The last time I'd found myself in the hammock, I was content in my solitude, but this time it felt like there was something missing. I sighed deeply and closed my eyes as the rain picked up.

"I found you," Nick's voice pulled me out of my sanctuary.

I kept my eyes closed, but couldn't stop the smile from forming on my lips.

"I didn't know I was lost," I said in response. I opened my eyes and smiled at him.

He was standing at the bottom of the stairs, dripping wet, but smiling at me.

"Where have you been?" I asked with a laugh.

"Nowhere," he shrugged.

"Why are you so wet?" I pointed at the water dripping off his head and onto the floor.

"I was looking for you."

"In the rain?"

"I found you, didn't I?" he grinned at me. He walked closer to where I was hanging in the hammock. "I see you got smart and put a blanket down over the netting this time."

"No more waffle face for me!"

"Scoot over," he waved at me and tried to get into the hammock with me.

"No way! This is my hammock!" I pushed him away.

"Come on! Let me sit with you," he pouted at me.

"First, you are soaking wet, and secondly, hammocks aren't made for two people."

He pulled his shirt off and used it to dry his hair. "Now will you scoot over?"

"Are you serious?" I tried not to stare at his chest as I questioned him. "There is no room for both of us."

"Yes there is! Just scoot over and we'll fit." He leaned down and pulled the hammock towards him.

"Nick!" I grabbed onto the sides of the hammock and held tight as he sank down next to me, causing the hammock to swing back and forth.

"Scoot!" he ordered me.

I wiggled around and made room for him next to me. We ended up sitting against each other in the middle of the hammock, with our feet hanging off the side. Nick's legs were long enough that he was still able to push us with his feet.

"I told you we could fit," he said triumphantly as he pushed us off, making us sway back and forth.

I was trying very hard not to think about how close I was to his bare chest.

"I hate the rain," he grumbled and threw his head back.

"Really? I love the rain," I said with a smile.

"How can you love the rain?"

"It reminds me of my childhood. When it would rain my sisters and I had to stay inside and play, and we always had a great time." I smiled at the memories that were now flooding my mind. "Sometimes, my mom would let us build a fort in the living room and we would spend hours under those blankets pretending to be in all kinds of fantastical places. When we got older, we'd play board games together and gossip about boys. I loved those rainy days."

Nick was silent for a few minutes, and I debated whether to say something or not. I wasn't sure what he was thinking, but I could tell something was on his mind. The rain pounded the ground, creating a rhythm to our silence.

After a long silence, he said quietly, "Rain reminds me of my childhood too, only I didn't get to make forts in the living room or play board games with my family. In my house, rain meant that I needed to find somewhere to hide and be silent."

"Why?" I asked softly.

He answered without looking at me. "My dad worked construction, so when it rained he didn't get to go to work. When he didn't work, he drank."

"Why did you have to hide?"

"It was always best to stay away from my dad when he was drunk."

"Was he a mean drunk?"

"He was an abusive drunk."

I finally had him talking, so I didn't want to scare him off, but I had to know about the scars. I took a deep breath and went for it.

"Is that where you got the scars?" I whispered.

"What do you mean?" he said defensively.

I shifted to see him better, lifted his arm, and used my fingers to trace the outline of the circular scars under his arm.

"Cigarette burns?" I asked quietly while my fingers rubbed the scars gently.

He nodded and took a deep breath. "That was his favorite way of waking me up."

"What do you mean?"

"If he came home at night and one of my toys was left out, if the house wasn't neat enough, or if he just wanted to wake me, he'd come into my room and put his lit cigarette against my skin." Nick watched my fingers playing against his skin.

My hands stopped moving and I looked up at him. "Is that why you don't sleep well?"

He nodded. "When you spend the first fifteen years of your life having your flesh burned until you wake up, you start to dread the night."

I settled back against him. "What happened after fifteen years?"

"I couldn't take it anymore. I ran away." He wrapped an arm around me and pulled me into his chest.

The intimacy of our contact sent a shiver through my body. I knew we shouldn't be sitting so close, but he seemed to need it, so I didn't fight him.

"Where did you go?"

"I stayed with friends when I could. I spent a few nights in shelters, slept on the beach a lot actually. Then I met Mitch and he let me stay in the backroom of his surf shop." He pushed the hammock and started us swinging again.

"What did your friends say when you told them you had run away?"

"I didn't really tell them."

"You didn't tell them that your dad was abusive?"

"I didn't tell anyone."

"Why not?"

He took another deep breath and long pause before he answered. "I've never told anyone."

Another shudder ran through me. I didn't know what to say to him. His arm was still around me and he was still pushing the hammock gently.

After another minute of silence, I sighed, "If we'd been friends, my parents would have let you move in with us."

Nick laughed lightly, "I hardly think your father would let a teenage boy move into an apartment with his three daughters."

I smiled, "You don't know my dad." I laughed and added, "Of course, he never would have let you out of his sight and probably would have installed deadbolt locks on the bedroom doors."

Nick laughed.

"But you would have been part of the family," I added softly.

"I think I would have liked that."

Silence fell over us again. The rain still hadn't let up and I watched it run off the edge of the floor above us.

"Nick?"

"Yes?" his voice was almost too soft to hear over the rain.

"Do you always have trouble sleeping, even when you're not alone?"

"Always," he answered quietly.

"Tell me about Mitch," I whispered and rested my head against his chest.

For the next hour, I listened as Nick told me about the man that took him in, gave him a job, and helped send him to college. I asked questions when they popped into my head and he answered them all. He kept the hammock swaying and I stayed resting against his chest.

"Do you still talk to him?" I asked after he'd finished talking.

"Not as often as I should, but I send him money every month."

"To pay him back for everything he did for you?"

"Yes," he said through a yawn.

I smiled, "Do you know what else I love to do when it rains?"

He laughed, "No."

"Take naps," I said with a grin.

"That sounds good to me." He pulled his arm from around my shoulders and started shifting in the hammock. He pulled his feet up into the hammock and stretched out lengthwise. I wiggled and matched his pose. I rested my hand against his chest and placed my head back on his shoulder. He put his arm around my waist and held me.

We didn't speak for a long time, and after a few minutes, I heard his breathing shift into a deeper rhythm. I watched his chest rise and fall as he lay sleeping next to me. I closed my own eyes and let myself fall asleep in his arms.

I woke up a few hours later. We hadn't moved positions and I could tell that he was still asleep. There didn't seem to be anyone else in the world but the two of us. There were no sounds coming from the house above us, and the normally busy beach was deserted. The only sounds that filled the air were the rhythmic sounds of his breath, the sound of thunder rumbling in the distance, and the rain that was still beating down around us.

I looked over at his face and watched him sleeping. He looked peaceful and content and I tried to imagine what life must have been like for him. I couldn't understand how anyone could be so cruel and heartless to a child. I put my head back down and took a deep breath. Nick had shared something with me that he'd never told anyone. Not for a single moment did I doubt that he was telling me the truth when he said that. We'd only known each other for a few days, but I knew he wasn't the kind of guy who would make something up just to get a girl to sleep with him.

Besides, he knew I wasn't interested in that.

Despite my confidence in who I was and what I wanted, I found myself in a vulnerable position. I wasn't going to lie to myself and pretend like my heart didn't skip a beat when he smiled at me, or that my pulse didn't race when he touched me. I couldn't even hide the fact that while I'd been happy in the hammock alone, I didn't feel content until he came down and found me. Something was definitely happening and I was powerless to stop it. I couldn't allow myself to compromise who I was, but I couldn't stay away from him either.

I lay there in his arms in that hammock, for another hour, trying to convince myself that what I was really feeling was loneliness. I told myself that I'd been missing the companionship I'd had with Jack, and that for the moment, Nick was filling that void. It was a good argument. After all, I was cuddling with a stranger in a hammock as I thought of it. Nick and I may not have been having a sexual fling, but there was definitely an emotional affair happening.

Since I'd moved out of the apartment with Jack, I'd been living a solitary life. I was social, but I wasn't connecting with people like I had when I was with Jack. I found myself on the edge of things, never really a part of what was happening around me. Nick's attention made me feel a part of things again. He was bringing me back into a social life.

A loud clap of thunder suddenly boomed throughout the beach and Nick's eyes flew open.

"It's just thunder," my voice soft against his skin.

"How long was I asleep?" he whispered huskily.

"I don't know, a few hours maybe."

He stretched his legs out and groaned. "I might have to put one of these in my apartment in LA."

I smiled, "Why?"

He pulled me closer to him, "I haven't slept that hard in years. If that thunder hadn't woken me up, I think I could have slept for another few hours."

Another rumble of thunder hit and we both listened to the storm around us for a minute.

"Are you hungry?" he whispered.

"I don't know if I'm hungry enough to risk getting soaked on the way up the stairs."

He laughed, "I'm definitely hungry, but I don't want to get wet either."

"Wait!" I said, suddenly realizing something. "I brought my phone down with me!"

Nick laughed, "Are we supposed to eat it? What can the phone do for us?"

I pulled the phone out of my pocket and pushed a few buttons. I held it up for Nick to see what I'd done.

"Pizza!" he said excitedly.

"Pizza!"

"What do you want on your pizza?" I asked as I pulled the phone back and pushed more buttons.

"I like pepperoni, sausage, and ham." His stomach growled as he spoke, punctuating his statement.

I grinned and looked slyly at him, "You sure do like a lot of meat."

He pinched my waist and snatched the phone from me. "You have a filthy mind, Ms. Harris. What do you want on your pizza?"

I laughed, "I don't care. I'll eat whatever. If I don't like something, I'll just pick it off."

"That's not what I asked, Cami. What do you want on your pizza?"

"I said I don't care. That pepperoni, sausage, and ham combo sounds fine." I shrugged and reached for my phone.

Nick held the phone out of my reach. "If you were ordering pizza for yourself, what would you order?"

I sighed, "Pepperoni and pineapple."

"Fine, pepperoni and pineapple it is. How are we paying for this?" he asked as the phone dialed the local pizza shop my phone's web browser had directed him to.

"I have my credit card number memorized, so it's my treat today." I insisted and took the phone from him. I ordered our pizza, which proved to be a lot more complicated than I realized since neither of us actually knew the address to the beach house.

"Why did you have your phone down here with you, anyway? I thought you weren't supposed to be making important phone calls when you were on vacation." Nick asked with a reproachful look.

"It's my sister's birthday and I was going to call her."

"Which sister?"

"Allison."

Nick grinned, "Can I talk to her?"

I laughed, "Definitely not."

He chuckled, "Why not?"

"It's not happening, Nick, so you can stop trying."

He grinned and snatched the phone from me again. He skillfully rolled out of the hammock and took off across the concrete, holding the phone up over his head as he scrolled through my contacts.

I, of course, tumbled out of the hammock and onto the concrete floor. When I tried to stand up to chase him, I tripped on my own feet and fell back to the concrete.

"You okay?" Nick asked with a laugh. He had the phone up to his ear, as if he was waiting for someone on the other line to pick up.

"I'm fine, thank you. Also, you're not fooling me. I know there isn't really anyone on the other end of that phone line." I rolled my eyes at him and pulled myself up from the floor.

Nick smiled at me. "Hi, Allison? Happy birthday!"

"I'm not buying it!" I shouted at him doubtfully.

He smiled and kept talking, "Nick, I'm a friend of your sister. She's right here, actually." He paused then held the phone away from his mouth and spoke to me. "Allison doesn't believe that we're friends. She says I sound too hot to be your friend."

I laughed, "You're not that hot!"

Nick smiled and talked into the phone, "Did you hear that? And she says you're the mean one?"

Suddenly afraid that he might actually be talking to Allison, and that he just told her that I said she was mean, I lunged at him in an attempt to get my phone back.

He was quicker, though, and stepped out of the way before I could get the phone.

"No, she really said that. Of course, she provided me with proof." Nick grinned at me. "No, she didn't tell me about that one. She did however tell me your theory about her clumsiness." He started laughing.

"Are you done? Can I have my phone now?" I put my hands on my hips and tried the teacher look on him.

He looked at me, but kept talking. "She's giving me the teacher look right now! How did you know?"

I shook my head and gave up. He, obviously, wasn't going to relinquish the phone to me. I plopped back down in the hammock and listened to his end of the conversation.

"No, we're in the Outer Banks."

"LA, actually."

"Just met her the other day."

"No!"

"Really, I promise!"

"I know all about him."

"I swear that is not my intention."

"Yes."

"I suspected as much."

"I promise."

"Okay, I'll tell her."

"It was good talking to you, too!"

He ended the call and walked over to the hammock. He motioned for me to scoot over and fell into the hammock next to me.

"I don't know why you think she's so mean, she seemed just lovely," he said as he settled into his position next to me.

I didn't bother to look at him, but I could hear the smugness in his voice. I didn't answer him either. I just sat in the hammock with my arms crossed over my chest.

After a full minute of silence, Nick said with a giggle, "So, are you really mad at me or are you just trying to look mad because you think you look adorable when you're mad?"

"I don't think I look at adorable when I'm mad," I said with an eye roll.

"So, you're really mad then?"

"I'm never going to hear the end of that, you know? She's really mean, and she has a big mouth!"

He laughed, "She was actually quite protective of you. She told me that I'd better think twice before I try anything with you, because you don't do that sort of thing."

I made an exasperated huffing noise, but still didn't look at him.

"Of course, I neglected to tell her that we'd already slept together."

I sat up and turned towards him. "We did not!"

He grinned, "May I remind you about that three hour nap we just woke up from?"

"That's different! Literally sleeping together is very different from what you would be implying if you'd told my sister that!"

"I know," he grinned, "that's why I didn't say anything."

"I'm still never going to hear the end of that."

"You are, you know?"

I settled back into my spot in the hammock, "What?"

"Adorable when you're mad," he chuckled.

I elbowed him in the ribs, "Still think I'm adorable?"

He laughed and said in a pained voice, "Maybe not so much." He pulled my phone out and started scrolling through my photos. "Do you have any pictures of Allison in here?"

"What kind of big sister do you think I am?" I asked sarcastically.

"Show me," he said and handed my phone back to me. "Oh, by the way, she said thank you for the flowers. They were beautiful."

I smiled and continued scrolling through the photos until I got to the one I wanted to show him. I figured he'd want to see Tori too, so I pulled up the picture my dad had taken of us, as we got ready to go out to dinner as a family. It was taken at my parents' house a few weeks ago, before Allison and Tori went back to school.

"Here," I said and handed him the phone. "That's all three of us."

He smiled, "I see what you mean about Tori being the perfect all-American girl."

"I know, and the even more annoying thing is that it only takes her minutes to achieve that perfection. She's not like one of those fake perfect girls who have to spend hours forming that façade. Tori pretty much just wakes up and rolls out of bed perfect."

"I also get why Allison is so mean to you," he looked at me and grinned.

"What do you mean?"

"Well, if Tori is the perfect one, and Allison is the smart one, which one are you?" he raised an eyebrow at me in question.

"I don't know. The nice one maybe? The oldest?" I shrugged.

"No, look at this picture again, Cami." He held the phone out for me. "You're the pretty one!"

I blushed, "I am not. Tori is much prettier than I am!"

He shook his head, "No, Tori is the perfect package. You, you're the pretty one. You are the one that is going to catch someone's eye right away. When a guy looks at Tori, do you know what he thinks?"

I shook my head.

"He thinks, 'Wow! She looks like a lot of work!' It may not be true, but that's what it looks like at first." He pulled the phone back and looked at it again. "But when a guy looks at you, he thinks, 'How can I get her to notice me?'"

I watched him as he stared at the picture some more. He smiled at the girls in the photo, but didn't turn to look at me.

"You're just trying to make up for that comment you made last night," I finally said with a smile.

"What? What comment?"

"The one about me thinking that I wasn't pretty enough for you," I grinned some more.

He blushed, "I told you last night that I didn't mean that. I just didn't want you to think that."

"And I told you that I didn't think that," I bantered with him.

He put the phone down and looked at me, "Yes, you do."

His stare had me feeling slightly self-conscious, but I tried to answer confidently. "No, I don't."

He held my gaze as he spoke, "You know you aren't ugly, Cami, but I don't think you really know how beautiful you are. You don't know what a man sees when he looks at you. You don't know what he's thinking when you smile at him, or the way he feels when you talk to him. You are that rare combination of beautiful and genuine."

"What do you mean?" I asked quietly. I don't know where the voice came from because I felt like I couldn't breathe, much less form words.

He smiled, "You make a man feel like a man, Cami. You're the kind of woman a man would fight for, the kind of woman a man would risk his life for. You're the kind of woman a man would work eighty hours a week to provide for, as long as at the end of a hard day he got to come home to you. You're the kind of woman a man can talk to and tell all his secrets to and not feel the least bit threatened in his masculinity."

My head felt scrambled and dizzy. I was having trouble processing what he was saying, but somehow found myself speaking. "It's a good thing I don't hook up."

His smile widened, "Why?"

"Because if I thought it would lead somewhere, I would totally kiss you right now." I repeated his words from the night before. I seemed to be having some sort of out of body experience, because I couldn't understand what was happening. I didn't know how I was able to speak, much less think rationally enough to form the words.

Nick leaned forward and grinned, "First off, don't steal my lines." He reached up and touched my neck gently with the tips of his fingers. "Secondly, it would lead somewhere." He leaned even closer to me and I responded with a lean of my own.

"Uh, did you order a pizza?" the cracking voice of a teenage boy broke through our moment.

Embarrassed, I quickly pulled away from Nick and stood up out of the hammock. "Yes, we, I, uh, ordered a pizza."

The delivery boy smiled at me, "I'll need you to sign this."

I signed and handed the receipt to him in exchange for the pizza.

"Uh, sir? Would you mind if I borrowed that line?" the pizza boy said to Nick with an appreciative stare.

10.

We ate in silence for several minutes. The rain had let up slightly, but it was still pouring down from the side of the house. I'd found a spot on the floor, far away from Nick and any temptation to pick up where we'd left off. If the pizza boy hadn't showed up, there's no telling what we might have done. I'd known while it was happening, that I needed to stop it. Unfortunately, my body had not responded to the persistent shouting from the voice in my head.

"Are we going to talk about it or act like it never happened and just move on?" Nick asked as he sat back in the hammock with his second slice.

"That second option sounds good to me." I stared out at the rain instead of looking at him.

"Okay, that's what we'll do then." Nick shrugged and took a bite of pizza.

I glanced over at him and he looked completely content as he ate his pizza. He didn't seem to be the least bit bothered by the shift in our relationship. Watching him casually eat his pizza, as if he wasn't having any trouble at all moving on, made me angry. Was he just trying to hook up with me? Was he saying all those things just to get me to trust him and let my guard down? If he wasn't feeling anything then why did he keep saying exactly the right thing to make me feel for him?

Fed up and unable to hold it in any longer, I groaned loudly and stood up.

"Something wrong?" he asked with a grin.

"Okay, here's the deal," I said with a frustrated sigh. "I don't think that all men feel that way about me. To be honest, I don't think there is a single man on this earth who looks at me and thinks the things you said he thinks. If there was, then why am I single? If men really thought those things when they saw me, then why have I been alone for eight months?" I stopped to take a breath. "Also, part of me thinks that you are just saying these things to get me to hook up." I looked down at my feet after the last statement.

Nick started laughing.

"What is so funny?" I asked, irritated.

"I knew you couldn't just let it go. I knew you'd want to talk about it."

I shook my head at him.

He stopped laughing and took a deep breath. "Alright, I'll make you a deal. I'll tell you the truth about what I said and what I meant and, if you want, we can forget the whole thing and never speak of this again. What do you say?"

I glanced over at him. He was waiting expectantly for me. I studied his face carefully. He appeared to be genuine in his offer.

"Okay, I want the whole truth."

He smiled, "The whole truth, nothing but the truth, so help me God!"

"Just say it!"

He smiled quickly and sighed. "I meant what I said about you. Men do think those things when they see you. I don't know for sure why you've been single for eight months, but I'm guessing that it may have something to do with how you feel about yourself. You might think you've moved on from Jack, and to an extent, you have, but you haven't forgiven yourself for making such a big mistake with him. You don't trust yourself with men because you're afraid you are going to make another mistake."

I blushed and stared at my feet. "If that's what you think then why were you about to kiss me?"

He laughed, "I have commitment issues, remember? According to you, I look for relationships with women that I know won't work out."

"Gee, don't I feel special now," I said in a sarcastic voice.

"I wouldn't make you do anything you didn't want to," he said with a grin.

I sighed loudly, "Have we reached the point where we can stop talking about this now?"

He smiled, "Whatever you want, Cami."

I sat back down on the floor and grabbed another piece of pizza. With a loud sigh, I said, "If I feel this ashamed after *almost* kissing a guy, who knows what I feel if I'd actually done more."

"Gee, don't I feel special now?" Nick said with a smile and shoved the last bit of his pizza slice into his mouth.

"Sorry, but I did warn you that I'm not that kind of girl."

"Fair enough," he stood up from the hammock and came to sit next to me. "What shall we do with the rest of this wonderful day?"

"I don't know. It doesn't look like the rain is letting up."

"It's a shame, isn't it? I know you were really hoping to get back out there on the waves." Nick nudged me playfully as he teased me.

"I have an idea." Looking at the rain suddenly inspired me. "There is a wall of board games upstairs." I turned to face him and flashed a cheesy smile. "How about we race up the stairs in the rain then sit down to a game marathon?"

Nick jumped up and said, "Last one in is a rotten egg!" He took off up the stairs, leaving me behind.

When I finally made it up the stairs and into the house, with my blanket and the leftover pizza, I was soaked to the core.

"What took you so long?" Nick said with a laugh when he met me at the door.

"I had to grab the blanket and the pizza since you took off without helping me!" I dropped the crumbling and dripping pizza box on the floor. My blanket fell limply to the floor at his feet.

He laughed, "Sorry! I was starting to get worried, though. I thought maybe you'd slipped on the stairs on your way up and knocked yourself out."

"Ha ha!" I bumped into him on my way to the staircase. "I'm going to put on something dry and more comfortable."

"Just out of curiosity, why didn't you just wrap the blanket around you so that you wouldn't get wet?" he grinned at me.

"Shut up!" I shouted at him and kept walking.

Up in my room I pulled my wet clothes off and slipped into the most comfortable thing I had. Rainy days were meant for comfortable clothes, and I was ready to enjoy the feeling. I headed back down to the second floor, where I knew Nick would be waiting for me.

"Oh," he said with a disappointed voice when I plopped down on the couch next to him.

"What?"

"Nothing," he said with a shrug and a bit of a blush.

I peered at him suspiciously, "What, Nick?"

He sighed, "It's stupid. Don't worry about it."

"Just tell me, because you looked kind of disappointed. So, what were you thinking?" I tilted my head to the side.

He blushed, "Fine. I guess part of me hoped that when you said you were going to put on something more comfortable that it might be something a little sexier in its comfortableness. That's all."

I looked down at my outfit and laughed, "So, you were hoping that I would come down the stairs in something lacy and revealing? That seemed like a logical choice of clothing to sit down and play board games in?"

"I just said that I was *hoping* that you would come down in that."

"Why would I come down in something sexy? We've clearly established that this isn't going to happen." I pointed between us again, like I had the day before when I brought the topic up. "Besides, I don't care what those stick-thin models say. None of that lacy stuff is as comfortable as these old sweats and my favorite Columbia t-shirt."

Nick laughed.

"What are we playing first?"

We played board games for the next few hours. While we played, we talked some more about our childhoods. He told me more about Mitch. He told me about the different beaches he surfed, and why Manhattan Beach was his favorite. He told me about working three jobs to put himself through school at UCLA. I told him about my classroom and the school I work in. I also told him about all the little things that I secretly hate about my job.

"Want to play Operation now?" he asked when he came back into the room with a new game.

"You keep asking me that, and I keep telling you no."

"Why? What do you have against this game? Look at it." He held the box up for me to see. "Doesn't it look fun to you?" He flashed a cheesy smile from behind the box.

"Don't even act like the only reason you want to play it is because you know you'll win. You're counting on my clumsiness to give you an easy victory." I laughed at him.

"That sounds like something a person who is trying to hustle me might say, you know?"

I rolled my eyes at him, "Just bring the damn game over here and let's play it."

He shook the box happily and brought it over to the coffee table we were playing on. "I always wanted this game, but my dad wouldn't let me have it because he said it made too much noise." He talked while he pulled the game out and put all the pieces together. He was smiling from ear to ear and watching him made me smile too.

Just to make him happy, we played the game three times. We ate the leftover pizza while we played and continued talking about anything and nothing at all at the same time. He'd just cleaned up the pizza when Chrissy walked in.

"What's up? What are you doing?" she asked and plopped down on the chair across the room.

"Just playing a few games," I shrugged. "Where have you been all day?"

"I was out with Todd."

Hearing her say his name brought back the memory of last night. I was about to make a comment when I heard a snicker from behind me.

"Todd? The swimmer?" Nick asked.

I giggled and Chrissy eyed me suspiciously.

"What does that mean?" she asked him, with another glare in my direction.

"We saw you in the pool last night." Nick said with a smile. He sat down next to me.

"Pervert!" Chrissy said half-heartedly.

"We didn't mean to see you, Chrissy. We had to escape the house because Darren and his redheaded friend were making too much noise, so we went down to the beach. On our way back to the house, we stumbled upon you and Todd in the pool." I explained with the hint of a blush.

Chrissy smiled, "Sorry. When he brought me home last night, we thought everyone was asleep because all the lights were off and the house was silent."

"Where is everyone?" Darren's voice boomed from the first floor.

"We're up here!" Nick shouted back in response.

"What are you doing?" Darren shouted and ran up the stairs to join us.

When he appeared in the room, I answered him. "We were playing board games."

Darren turned to Nick with a strange look, "Are you telling me that I left you alone in the house with two beautiful women and all you've done is play board games with them?"

Without missing a beat, Nick said casually, "Chrissy just got here, but I did sleep with Cami earlier today."

Chrissy sat up in her chair, "What?" she shouted at me.

I elbowed Nick in the ribs. He laughed and gasped for air at the same time.

"We were sitting in the hammock downstairs and fell asleep. We *literally* slept together." I clarified for our audience.

"What the hell?" Darren looked at Nick. "Are you kidding me? What are you, twelve?"

"It's not his fault," Chrissy said with a giggle. She'd settled back into the chair. "Cami's not that kind of girl. She doesn't hook up."

"That's just nonsense!" Darren exclaimed and left the room.

"He can't even begin to understand that concept." Nick, who was still struggling to take a full breath, commented as his friend left the room.

"Forget these kids' games, let's play something dirty!" Darren shouted as he walked back into the room. He had four shot glasses and a bottle of tequila from the house's liquor cabinet.

"A drinking game?" Chrissy said with a giggle. "I haven't played one of these since college. What are we playing?"

"How about 'I never…'?" Darren grinned at her.

"I'm pretty sure that the object of that game is to find the sluttiest person in the room and get them drunk so someone else can take advantage of them," I said with a suspicious grin.

"Don't worry," Nick leaned forward and gave Darren a comforting look. "I won't let either of these girls take advantage of you."

Chrissy laughed and got up from the chair. She sat on the floor across from me, and in front of the couch. Darren put the glasses and bottle on the table, and plopped down next to Chrissy.

"What do you say? Shall we play?" Darren asked us all.

"I'll start!" Chrissy smiled and poured tequila into all four glasses. "I've never been to Disneyland."

Darren groaned, reached for his shot glass, and threw back the drink. Nick grabbed the glass in front of him and did the same.

Darren was up next. "This isn't exactly what I had in mind, but we can start slow. I've never been to the Statue of Liberty."

Chrissy and I both took a shot.

Nick was next. "I've never eaten oysters."

Darren and Chrissy took shots.

"I've never owned a car," I smiled as both of the men took another shot.

Darren slammed his glass down on the table, "That's enough of the G-rated game. Let's spice this thing up, shall we? You're up, Chrissy. Make it a good one."

She smiled at him. "I've never had a threesome."

Darren tipped his glass at her and took a shot. Nick slowly leaned forward and picked up his glass. I didn't look at him as he took that shot. I knew it shouldn't bother me that he drank to that, but I couldn't help but feel a tingle of jealously.

"I've never kissed a man," Darren grinned at us.

"That's not fair!" I said back at him.

"Okay," Darren conceded. "I'll change that to I've never kissed someone who is the same sex as me."

Chrissy took a drink.

"I've never had sex with three different people on the same day." Nick said with a head nod in Darren's direction.

Darren glared at him and took a shot.

I was up next, but had to think for a minute about what I wanted to say. "I've never cheated on a partner."

All three of the others took a drink.

"Wow! Does anyone have morals anymore?" I asked jokingly as Darren refilled their glasses.

"My turn!" Chrissy said excitedly. "I've never worn a French maid costume in the bedroom!"

My face immediately turned red as both Nick and Darren turned to look at me. With absolutely no pride left, I leaned forward and picked up my glass. I took the shot and slammed the glass back down on the table.

"A French maid costume? What, no sweats and t-shirt that night?" Nick said with a grin.

I didn't look at him, but responded quietly. "There are supposed to be no explanations necessary."

"This is getting good!" Darren said with a laugh. "Okay, I've never met someone at a bar and taken them back to a friend's house because I didn't want them to know where I live because I secretly knew they were crazy, but I really needed to get laid."

I turned to look at Nick. Darren's statement seemed extremely specific and detailed. Nick avoided my gaze and did his shot.

"Best four hours of your life though, right? Isn't that what you said when you brought my keys back?" Darren laughed loudly.

"Something like that," Nick said shyly. He cleared his throat and started, "I never."

I didn't let him finish though. "Wait," I said quickly. "By four hours you mean the four hours you spent with her all together, right? You mean that it took four hours to meet her, convince her to come back to Darren's with you, drive to his house, have that awkward make-out session on the couch, have sex, and then take a one hour nap before driving her home, right?"

"Not exactly," Nick grinned. "It was more like four hours from the time we got to Darren's until the time we left his house."

"Okay, moving on," Chrissy jumped in.

"Hold on," I put my hand up to indicate for her to stop talking. I looked at Nick with a disbelieving look. "Four hours, really? Are you sure you weren't just exaggerating that timeline to brag?"

Nick laughed, "No, it was four hours."

Chrissy tried to speak again, but I shushed her before the words could come out.

"Seriously?" I stared at Nick, still disbelieving what I was hearing. "Did you take a pill or something? What do you even do for four hours? I don't think you're doing it right if it takes that long." I shook my head then stopped and looked at him again, "Maybe I'm not doing it right. I was lucky if I could get a solid twenty minutes out of Jack."

Darren and Chrissy laughed.

Nick smiled, "No pills."

"Rethinking that I-don't-hook-up policy?" Darren asked with a smile.

I nodded, "Yes, but for research purposes only."

Nick laughed, "Okay, moving on!"

We played a few more rounds, but my head wasn't in it anymore. I played along, but couldn't seem to get the four-hour thing out of my head. I tried not to picture it, but the fact that Nick was sitting close enough to me that our legs were touching, made it very difficult to not imagine it.

When it got to me again, I panicked and said the first thing I could think of. "I've never had a pregnancy scare." I looked around to see if anyone was drinking, but all the glasses stayed still.

"Um," Chrissy's quiet voice drew my attention to her. "Does an abortion count as a scare?"

"What?" I asked slowly.

"If I had an abortion, does that count as a pregnancy scare?" Chrissy asked again with a hint of shame in her voice.

"When did you have an abortion?" I sat forward, leaning across the table.

"Six months ago," she said and looked down at her hands. "Clark didn't want his wife to find out about us that way."

"Why wouldn't you tell me about that, Chrissy?" I scooted even closer to her.

She shrugged, "I guess I was afraid you'd judge me."

"Chrissy, I don't have to agree with every decision that you make, but I will always be there when you need me."

Chrissy looked shamefully at me. "I wanted to tell you, but Clark said that if I told you then you might tell someone else. He didn't want me to be embarrassed or ashamed of it.

Darren made a loud huffing noise and we all turned to look at him. "What?" he said.

"Just stay out of it," Nick said quietly to Darren then they exchanged a look.

"What does that mean? Why did you make that sound?" I asked Darren then turned to Nick. "What did you mean by stay out of it?"

Darren sighed, "I don't know what I was thinking."

"Whose turn is it?" Nick asked, trying to lighten the mood again.

"It's me this time," Chrissy said with a smile.

"Hit us with it, Chrissy!" Darren said and reached for his glass.

"I've never been in love," Chrissy said cheerfully.

I leaned forward and grabbed my glass. I threw the alcohol back and slammed the glass down on the table. I looked around at everyone else, expecting the guys to be doing the same, but everyone else was just sitting still.

"None of you have ever been in love?" I asked in disbelief.

They all shook their heads at me.

"Wow! That's just sad. All that sex and no love," I shook my head at them. "What's the point?"

Chrissy suddenly broke into sobs, filling the room with the sound of her crying. Nick and Darren both froze in place, not sure what to do next.

"Chrissy, baby, are you okay?" I crawled around the coffee table and over to where she was sitting. "What's wrong?"

"He's never going to leave her, is he? I'm just kidding myself by thinking that he's going to leave her for me." Chrissy whimpered to me through her tears.

I rubbed her back and tried to comfort her. "You know you deserve better than him, right? That's why you're not in love with him. You just said you've never been in love."

Chrissy just sobbed some more and fell back against the floor.

Darren sighed loudly, "Game over, I guess. As soon as someone starts crying it's time to stop the game."

"Is she going to be okay?" Nick asked with a concerned voice.

I nodded, "I think so. I think she's probably just tired and kind of drunk. I think I should take her up to her bed." I stood up and tried to pull Chrissy up off the floor, but she wasn't doing much to help me.

"I'll take her," Nick got up from the couch and walked around to where Chrissy and I were. With little effort, he scooped her up and carried her away and up the stairs.

I sat back down on the couch and threw my head back against the back of the couch. Darren plopped down next to me.

He turned to me with a smile. "You're not like other girls, at least not the girls I'm used to meeting."

"I'm not hooking up with you, either, Darren."

He laughed, "I know that, Cami. If you were going to hook up with anyone then you and Nick wouldn't be hanging out down here with us tonight."

I smiled at Darren and spoke confidently. "That's not going to happen and he knows that."

"You're not that type of girl, I know." Darren smiled at me. "He's a great guy, though."

"I know," I nodded and stared straight ahead of me.

"He saved my ass at work last week." Darren leaned forward and poured another shot of tequila. "I made a huge mistake and nearly cost the company a billion dollar client. I don't know how he did it, but he somehow managed to fix it all before it cost us the client."

"Is that why you're here?"

"My dad told me to get out of town for a few days so he wouldn't kill me. Nick volunteered to come with me, though I think he came to chaperone me more than anything."

"So you're here on punishment and he's your prison guard?" I smiled and looked at Darren.

He laughed and nodded. "It's too bad you're not that kind of girl, because you could do a lot worse than hooking up with Nick."

I smiled, "You're quite the wingman, aren't you?"

He laughed again, "I swear he knows nothing of this conversation."

"Well, it's not going to happen."

"I know. You're not that kind of girl. You're one of the good ones." Darren smiled at me.

I grinned, "I'm not that good."

"I think I'd like to hear some more about the not so good things you've done." Nick's voice reached us before we could see him. He walked around the couch and sat down in the chair across from us. "Let's start with that French maid outfit, shall we?" He grinned at me.

I laughed, "It was a birthday gift! I swear!"

"For who? You or him?" Nick asked with a grin.

"I don't think it matters, we all know who really got the gift that night!" Darren joined in with a chuckle.

"Alright boys, I'm also not the kind of girl who sits up alone with two drunken men. I'm going to bed. I'll see you in the morning." I stood up from the couch and picked up my empty shot glass. "Try not to get too drunk, don't leave the house, and keep it down, okay?"

"Yes ma'am," Nick and Darren said in unison.

I put my shot glass on the bar and headed up to my room. It didn't take me long to fall asleep, even though I'd taken a nap earlier. With my arm tucked under my pillow, I slept comfortably in my big bed.

11.

Since my room didn't have a clock, I had no idea what time it was when I was awakened by a soft, but persistent knock on my door. At first, I thought it was something outside, but the longer it went on the more I realized it was someone at my door.

I got up from the bed and stumbled to the door, nearly tripping over my suitcase on the way. I opened the door slowly, not sure of who or what would be on the other side.

"Did I wake you?" Nick said with a smile.

"What time is it?"

He looked down at his bare wrist as if he was reading a watch. "Three or four o'clock, I think."

"You can tell that by looking at your arm?" I said sarcastically.

Nick smiled, "Can I come in?"

I raised an eyebrow at him, “I don’t think so, Nick.”
His face fell, “Why not?”
“Because you’re drunk and because I’m not stupid,” I answered with a shake of my head.
“I promise I won’t try anything, I just want to talk to you.” He smiled persuasively at me. Then he leaned forward and said with a grin, “Besides, it’s not like we haven’t slept together before.”
“What do you want, Nick?” I asked him with a cocked eyebrow.
“I just want to talk, I swear.”
“Talk out here, Nick. What do you want?” I asked again.
He sighed and a wave of tequila hit me in the face.
“I just wanted to say that your ex-boyfriend, what was his name again?” he looked to the side like he was trying hard to remember something.
“Jack.” I helped him out.
His face lit up, “Right, Jack. I just wanted to say that your ex-boyfriend, Jack, was a fool. He was a fool for letting you go.” Nick stumbled on his words and even slurred a few, but continued. “I wouldn’t let you go. I would give you anything you wanted, even if I was scared out of my wits. I would fight against everything in me, just to make you happy and give you what you want.”
My heart skipped and my pulse raced. I took a quick deep breath and exhaled loudly.
“That’s all I wanted to say,” he took a step back from my door.
I watched him walk away, knowing that I should have said something, but was unable to make myself speak. Just like I had earlier in the day, I could feel myself struggling with the decision to give in. Yes, I’d felt ashamed of myself for almost kissing him earlier, but that shame was nothing in comparison to the thrill it gave me. The almost kiss with Nick earlier that day, was more exciting than anything I’d ever experienced with another man.

I saw Nick close the door to his bedroom and disappear from my view. I leaned my head against the frame of my door and exhaled loudly again. My heart and pulse were still racing and I could feel myself being pulled to his door. Despite my apparent physical need for him, my head took over and pulled me back to my own bed.

It took longer to fall asleep the second time, but eventually I did. I didn't sleep peacefully, though, and tossed and turned until the sunlight streaming through my window pulled me out of bed. I dressed slowly and walked quietly down the stairs towards the kitchen. Chrissy was at the table, dressed in a bikini top and very short denim shorts. I couldn't see who she was talking to, but I could tell that there was someone else in the kitchen with her.

"Good morning, sunshine!" Chrissy greeted me with a smile. "We've been waiting for you to get up! Go back up and put your suit on, it's a beautiful day and we're going to spend it on the beach!"

Before I could ask who 'we' was, a strange man appeared at the table next to her and handed her a glass of juice. He gave her the glass then turned to me.

"Hi," the stranger said with a smile. "I'm Todd." He held his hand out to me.

I smiled and shot Chrissy a look, "Hi Todd. I'm Cami."

"It's great to meet you, Cami. This is Mike." He pointed at the other strange man who had appeared at the table after him. "We were just about to head down to the beach."

Mike smiled at me, "Why don't you go back and put your suit on so you can join us."

Behind the guys' backs, Chrissy was waving her hand in front of her face and mouthing the words 'he's so hot' to me.

"I don't know," I said hesitantly. I felt like I should find Nick and talk about what he said last night, but I didn't want Chrissy to know what had happened.

"Oh wait! I forgot to tell you something," Chrissy tapped herself on the forehead like she always did when she remembered something important. "I saw Nick heading out to the beach earlier, and he said he needed to clear his head so he was going to be out on the waves all day."

Blushing, I said quickly, "Um, okay, I don't know why I'm supposed to know that."

Chrissy eyed me, and my reddened cheeks, suspiciously then said, "Great, so go get changed so we can enjoy this beautiful day on the beach!"

After I changed and came back downstairs, the four of us headed down to the beach. We found a spot near the house and camped out. Mike turned out to be a nice guy. He and Todd both lived in the area. He talked to me while Chrissy and Todd played in the water. We didn't have the same playful and easy banter that Nick and I shared, but he was definitely easy to talk to.

When Chrissy tired of playing in the water, she suggested a game of beach volleyball. Knowing my propensity for injury, I tried to wiggle out of the game, but Mike insisted that he would do all the work for our team. Hesitant, I stood across the net from Chrissy and Todd and just tried to stay out of Mike's way. The plan worked until it was my turn to serve. Never having been taught how to do it, I dropped the ball three times before Mike finally came to my aid.

He stood behind me and raised my arm up with his underneath. "All you need to do is hold the ball up here with this hand, make a fist with this one then bring your fist up to the ball." His hands ran down the length of my arms, showing me what my arms needed to do. When he finished his demonstration, his hands slid down to my waist and held me close to him.

"Okay, I'll try not to hit you, but I can't make any promises," I laughed and practiced what he'd showed me.

"I'm tough. I can take it," he said with a smile.

"Alright, but you've been warned!" I laughed and attempted to serve the ball.

I hit it and watched it sail over the net and right in between where Chrissy and Todd stood. They were probably shocked I even made contact with the ball much less made it go over the net. When I realized I'd just made a point, I clapped and threw my arms in the air. Mike's hands were still on my waist and he lifted me up in celebration. I turned around and hugged him, proud of myself not only for scoring, but also for not injuring anyone in the process.

When I pulled out of the hug, I turned to see Nick standing on the beach, dripping wet and looking very upset. I smiled at him but he just glared at Mike.

"Do you know him?" Mike asked when he noticed Nick staring at us.

I nodded, "He's my friend." I smiled at Mike. "I kind of need to talk to him for a moment."

Mike smiled back, "Let me know if you need anything. I'll be the one on the court owning these two!" he pointed at Chrissy and Todd then went back to his game.

I walked away and towards Nick, whose face hadn't gotten any softer since I first saw him.

"How are the waves?" I asked as I approached him.

"Who is that?" he asked without taking his eyes off Mike.

I turned and looked at Mike, who was busy working our half of the court. "That's Mike, he's Todd's friend."

"He's awfully friendly, don't you think?" Nick's gaze shifted from Mike to me.

I smiled, "He was just showing me how to serve. That's all."

"Yeah, I'm sure that's all," he said in a voice heavy with sarcasm.

"I thought you were going to be out on the waves all day. Chrissy said something about you wanting to clear your head."

His brow furrowed, "I was planning to be out on the waves all day, but then I saw you being manhandled by that jerk, so I came in to see what was going on."

I laughed, "I wasn't being manhandled, and he's not a jerk. He's a nice guy, actually."

"So I should just leave and let him put his hands all over you. Is that what you want?" Nick said angrily.

"Whoa! What the hell, Nick!" I put my hands up in defense. "I don't know what you think was happening, but we were just playing a game of volleyball."

"He had his hands all over you, Cami," he said in a quieter voice but with the same intensity as before.

I didn't respond. I just stood there staring at him. As I did, he seemed to calm down. He took a deep breath and closed his eyes.

"I'm sorry," he said quietly. "I don't know what's going on with me, Cami."

"I can take care of myself, Nick. I know he probably thinks he's getting somewhere with me, but you and I both know it's never going to happen." I gave him a small smile and watched him relax even more.

"You shouldn't play with a man's hopes like that," he grinned at me. "It's not fair."

I smiled. "How are the waves today?"

He turned and looked out at the water then turned back to me. "They're okay."

"Is your head clear yet?" I asked with a smile.

He laughed, "I thought it was, but then I saw you and your boyfriend practically making out on the volleyball court."

I pushed him and laughed, "He's not my boyfriend."

"But you were making out?" he said with a smile.

"No!" I pushed him again.

He took a step back to steady himself and laughed.

I lowered my eyes and stared at my feet. "Besides, I was only hanging out with them because you ditched me for a surfboard."

"I brought the other board if you want to try it again."

I looked up to see him grinning at me.

"I think I've probably tempted fate enough when it comes to surfing," I smiled, "but I could just paddle out and ride the waves with you."

He smiled widely at me, "I'd like that." He looked past me then grinned, "Do you think Mike will be upset if you leave him?"

I turned back and caught Chrissy's eye. She had been watching me and Nick intently and when I caught her eye she raised an eyebrow at me. I grinned. The great thing about my relationship with Chrissy was that we'd known each other long enough that we could have an entire conversation without saying a word.

"I don't think I care," I said to Nick and turned back to face him.

We picked up the boards where Nick had left them and paddled out towards the waves. Nick left me long enough to catch a wave and I pulled myself up on the board and watched him. Just like he had the first day, he made it all look so easy, but this time I wasn't fooled into thinking, I could try it. When he emerged from the curl, he turned to look at me. I cheered loudly for him and gave him the thumbs-up sign. He smiled then flipped off the board. He paddled back to me. When he got close to me, he sat up on the board and let it float towards me.

"I get why you come out here to clear your head. It's quiet," I smiled at him as he brushed the water out of his face.

"It's quiet, but it's not silent. There's just enough noise to let you think."

I nodded and let him settle in on his board. "What's got your head so muddled that you needed to spend the day out here?"

He smiled and looked me in the eyes, "You."

"How so?"

He sighed, "I don't know if I can put it into words."

I nodded slowly, "Is it because you find yourself wanting to say and do things that you wouldn't normally consider saying or doing?"

He nodded.

"Is it because half of you wants to do something that the other half knows isn't what you should do?"

He nodded again.

"Is it because even though you've always known who you are and what you want, you find yourself doubting it all?"

He nodded again.

I smiled, "Yeah, I have no idea what that's like."

He laughed and shook his head. After a few seconds, he looked over at me and said, "I'm really sorry about last night."

"Don't be."

"I shouldn't have said those things to you."

"Don't apologize for what you said. I do accept your apology for waking me up to say it, though."

Nick smiled, "Fair enough."

"I'm sorry for not saying anything back to you last night. I was a little caught off guard, and I just didn't know how to respond." I smiled apologetically. "However, I've thought about it, and what I should have said was thank you."

"Thank you?" Nick repeated my words back to me.

"Yes, thank you for making me see that it really is over between me and Jack." I shrugged, "I guess if I was being honest with myself, I thought that maybe it would be nice if he came to me and said he wanted me back."

Nick stared at me, "What would you say if he did come back?"

"What would I say now? Probably 'go to hell', but if he had come back last week I probably would have taken him back." I shrugged.

Nick smiled and looked down at his surfboard.

"So, did you really expect me to let you in last night?" I grinned as I asked him.

"By let me in, you mean into the room, right?" he winked at me playfully.

I splashed him with water, "Yes."

"I don't know what I was thinking last night, actually. After I talked to you, I barely made it to my room before I passed out."

"Even drunk, you should have known that I wasn't going to let you into my room." I gave him the teacher look and he smiled. "Besides, what kind of person would I be if I took advantage of you while you were drunk?"

He laughed, "A guy, that's who you'd be."

"Can I ask you an incredibly intimate and inappropriate question?"

Nick grinned and looked curiously at me, "I suppose."

"How many women have you slept with?"

He grinned, "Counting you?"

I kicked water on him and said, "I meant sex, you idiot!"

He laughed then answered, "Fifteen."

"Fifteen!" I shouted back at him.

"That seems like a lot to you, doesn't it?"

"That seems like a lot to the CDC. How old are you?"

"I'm twenty-nine." He watched me try to process the information he'd shared with me. "What's your number?"

"A lot less," I shook my head in disbelief. "Take your number and divide it by five, that's how much less. Wow! Fifteen!"

It was Nick's turn to look shocked. "You've only had sex with three guys? How old are you?"

"I'm twenty-seven, and there's nothing wrong with my number! I live by the one hand rule." I said it proudly, not at all ashamed of my low number of partners.

Nick cocked an eyebrow at me, "The one hand rule?"

"The number of sexual partners I have in my lifetime needs to be able to be counted on one hand. I'm doing pretty well so far." I held up three fingers to show him.

He grinned, "So that means you've only got two left."

"It's not a countdown, Nick. I don't have to get to five. I just don't want to go over five."

"What happens if things don't work out with you and number five? What do you do then?"

I shrugged casually, "I don't know. I suppose maybe at that point I switch to the two hand rule."

He grinned at me and said mischievously, "In my opinion, it's always better when you use both hands."

I rolled my eyes at him and he splashed me.

"This is going to sound corny, and I freely admit that," he put his hand up to cover his eyes in shame, "but, I kind of admire you for keeping your number so low."

"You're right, that was corny." I splashed him and laughed. "What you don't know is that I wasn't exactly beating them off with a stick during my teenage years. I had glasses, braces, and a lot of very bad haircuts. Trust me, there weren't many desirable offers coming my way for a long time!"

"You certainly grew out of all that awkwardness," he said as he gave me a once over.

"Believe it or not, Chrissy helped make me what I am today. When we met freshman year, I was still a mess. She took me in and made me her little project. A new haircut, some make up tips, and help picking out clothes and she'd transformed me into a normal looking human being." I laughed and added, "Thankfully, I am a fast learner and was able to complete my transformation before Chrissy turned me into what I can only describe as a high society escort. You should see some of the things that girl goes out in!"

Nick smiled, "I'm sure she's quite the scene stealer."

I nodded vigorously.

"Do you go out with her often?" He shifted on his board so that he was lying on his back. He turned his head towards me and waited for my answer.

I stared at him for a few seconds, transfixed by his body. It wasn't like I hadn't noticed it before, but when he stretched out on his board like that it was as if something in my head clicked. Beads of water glistened on his tanned, and toned, chest. His abs flexed as he turned to look at me. When my eyes reached his belly button, I forced myself to stop looking, not sure if I could handle seeing how his abdominal muscles angled down into his trunks. I shook my head, trying to bring myself back to reality.

Feeling hot and flustered, I tipped myself into the water on the other side of my board. When I came up, he was staring at me with a huge smile on his face.

"You did do that on purpose, right?" he asked with the grin still in place.

I nodded, "I was just starting to get a little warm, so I thought I'd hang out in the water for a while."

He gave me a strange look then rolled his head back over to look straight up. "You never answered my question."

"Oh yeah," I suddenly remembered that he had been talking to me before I got distracted by his body. "We go out sometimes, but I'm really not into it. It used to be clubs that she wanted to go to, and I hated that. All those people standing around, drinking, doing drugs, and pretending like they don't care about anyone else but secretly hoping that everyone is watching them. It was exhausting."

Nick chuckled, "That sounds a lot like LA. What does she do now?"

I made a face and said, "It's actually worse now! She's constantly going to these dinner parties and cocktail parties. Half the people there are older than my parents. The other half are their twenty-something wives! It's gross, actually. After a long day at school, I'd much rather just pick up some take out, put on my pajamas, and curl up in front of the tiny television in my bedroom. Who cares if I never meet a man that way? At least I won't be married to someone who has wrinkles older than I am!"

Nick smiled again, "In LA, it's the same. Except that, all the girls are trying to break into the business by sleeping with producers and movie execs."

"Disgusting," I said with a shake of my head. "That's why I'm in no hurry to put myself out there again. Dating as an adult is a lot trickier than it was in college. There are too many questions and expectations now."

Nick turned his head towards me, "So, you haven't dated since you broke up with Jack?"

"No," I shook my head. "I haven't been on a real date in six years."

"What's a real date?" Nick asked with a grin.

I blushed, "You know, the kind where a guy picks you up, takes you to a nice restaurant or to the movies, then brings you back home at the end." I shrugged it off, but it wasn't until that moment that I realized exactly how out of the loop I was. A strange thought occurred to me then. "Wait! Is that how it's still done? Do guys still pick you up for a date or is that too risky with all the freaks out there? Do people still go to dinner and a movie? I am so out of it!"

Nick grinned, "Some people still follow that pattern. Although, if you don't actually know the guy then you would probably be safer just meeting him somewhere. That way if he does turn out to be a freak, at least he won't know where you live. Unless, of course, he's already looked you up on the internet and has all your information before you tell him anything."

My eyes widened, "It all seems so complicated and scary now. I don't want to have to go through all of that. I'm hoping to be one of those lucky girls who happens to bump into some man on the subway, or in line to get coffee, and things just click. I don't think I'm equipped for the fast-paced dating scene that is going on out there today."

Nick grinned, "Maybe you'll meet him on the beach and you'll fall in love with him while he shows you how to play volleyball."

I dipped my head under the water, swam under my board and came up beside him. He had his eyes closed, so he didn't see me coming. I lifted his board, tipping him into the water. I grabbed ahold of my board and tried to pull myself onto it before he emerged from the water. Graceful as always, my wet hands slipped against the board and I couldn't get myself up out of the water. I felt his hands on my waist, pulling me down from what little progress I'd made getting onto my board. I squealed as he pulled me closer to him then pushed my head down into the water.

I came up from the water, still smiling, but gulping for air. He waited long enough for me to catch my breath before he pounced on me again, pushing my head under the water again. Thinking I'd outsmart him, I started swimming away from him. I felt his hands on my feet pulling me back towards him. My hands groped at the water in front of me, but I could feel myself moving backwards.

"Stop fighting me!" Nick laughed and moved his hands up my legs to my waist.

"Promise me that you won't push me under the water again!" I shouted back through laughter of my own. My hands were still struggling in the water, but I wasn't really putting any effort into getting away from him.

Suddenly, we were facing each other as we bobbed in the water. His hands were still on my waist and he was still pulling me towards him. Our feet bumped against each other under the water and the skin contact sent a wave of pleasure through me. I watched his mouth getting closer to mine and felt my body fighting with my head over what to do next. His arms wrapped around my waist and I felt my body melt against his in the water.

Just before our mouths touched, my head took over.

"This is a bad idea," I whispered against his lips.

He inhaled sharply and closed his eyes. A few seconds later I felt his grip on my waist loosen and his body pull away from mine.

I swam away from him and back towards my board. He stayed in place for another minute before turning around and coming back to his board. I watched him out of the corner of my eye as he pulled himself onto his board.

"Sorry," I said quietly.

He took a deep breath, "For tipping me into the water or for teasing me with a kiss?"

I blushed, "Both, I guess."

He lay back on his board and grinned, "Don't be. I enjoyed every minute of it."

12.

Nick and I stayed out on the water for several hours. We talked and laughed the entire time. We also kept a safe distance from each other. Eventually, the horizon darkened as the sun got lower in the sky.

"We should probably go in now," Nick said with a sigh.

"Do we have to? I'm kind of afraid of what might be happening in the house." I looked towards the house, but couldn't tell if there was anything going on there.

Nick laughed, "Come on. I'm starving."

I followed him towards the shore, paddling as best as I could to keep up with him. When we got close, and the water got too shallow to paddle any longer, we both stood up and picked up the boards. Nick shifted his board to his other side and motioned for me to give him my board. Suddenly feeling too tired to fight him I stepped closer and let him take my board. When he did, our hands brushed against each other and a shock of electricity shot through me. I pulled my hand away and took a step away from him as we walked onto the shore. Neither of us spoke as we headed back to the house.

When we reached the house, Nick headed for the storage closet and I went for the stairs.

"Do you want me to make something for dinner?" I asked before going any further.

"Sure, whatever sounds good to me," he gave me a smile and walked on.

The house was eerily quiet and dark. I called out to see if anyone was home, but received no response. Now that I was out of the water, I started to feel the effects of spending the day in the sun. I headed for the kitchen, hoping to find something easy to fix for dinner. The refrigerator was stuffed with leftovers from the party a few days earlier, so I pulled a few things out and set them on the counter.

"What have we got?" Nick asked when he walked into the kitchen.

"There is an entire tray of leftover cheese. I found some fruit left, too. There's also some lunch meat in there, though I don't think there is any bread left." I surveyed the kitchen and the assorted trays I'd set out on the counter.

"We'll just pick off of these trays all night. How does that sound?"

I shrugged, "Sounds okay by me. I think I'm going to go take a shower first, though." I didn't wait for a response. When I left the kitchen, Nick was busy picking off one of the trays.

After my shower, I felt better. When I went to the mirror to comb my hair I realized that I'd gotten a little more sun than I'd intended to. My nose was bright red, so were my cheeks and the skin under my eyes. I searched through my stuff looking for something with aloe in it, but couldn't find anything. My hair was still dripping wet as I walked out of the bathroom.

"Nick?" I called out over the banister of the stairs. I thought he'd be in the kitchen still, so I'd screamed as loud as I could. But when he responded, it was a lot closer than I'd expected.

"Yes?" he said from behind a door across the hall from where I was standing.

"Where are you?" I asked in a much quieter voice.

"I'm in my room. What do you want?" he said in an amused tone.

"What are you doing in there?" I asked and walked towards the door.

"I'm getting dressed!"

I stopped. I'd just spent the day with him, marveling at his toned and half-naked body, and I'd even slept on his bare chest the day before, but suddenly the thought of him naked just on the other side of the door made me blush.

"Did you need something?" he asked and I heard footsteps in his room. He opened the door and stood there looking at me. He still wasn't wearing a shirt, but he had traded his board shorts for a pair of faded jeans. The waistband of his briefs peeked out as he buttoned the jeans.

Another wave of heat rushed over me and I could feel my cheeks getting redder as I stood there. Thoughts and questions raced through my head. Had he always been that attractive? Did he look that amazing yesterday? What in the hell was going on with me?

"Cami, did you need something?" he asked again, this time with a worried expression.

"My face," I started then collected my thoughts a little. "I don't think I had enough sunscreen on and my face got a little burnt. Do you have any aloe?"

He smiled, "I noticed that. That's why I suggested we come in. I didn't want you to get too crispy." He laughed, "Come on. I've got some in here somewhere." He turned back and disappeared into his room.

I didn't move. I couldn't move. Something weird was happening to me. Earlier, when we'd almost kissed, I could actually feel the two halves of me fighting against each other. I could feel my body wanting one thing and my head telling me to do the opposite. I stood in the hall, waiting to feel that fight. But it never happened.

"Cami?" he shouted back at me.

Hearing him say my name made my feet come alive. I started walking and soon found myself standing in his bedroom. He was knelt down over his suitcase looking for the aloe he had offered me. I sat down on the bed and watched him, surveying his body. Yesterday, when I'd asked him about the scars, I had wanted to ask him if he had any others. I searched him over, looking for any evidence of more scars. I couldn't see any, but I had a feeling that there were more.

"Nick?" I asked quietly and kept my eyes on his back.

He was still rummaging around in his suitcase. He didn't turn around when he answered, "Yes?"

"Do you have any other scars?" my voice was still soft.

His hands stopped and the muscles in his neck stiffened, but he still didn't turn around to face me. After a deep breath, he stood up and walked over to the bed. He sat next to me and turned his body to face mine.

"I have one on my head from the time I wiped out and knocked it on my board," he said as he squeezed aloe into one hand. With his other hand, he scooped a dab of aloe and gently applied it to my face.

I watched him as he spread the aloe across my face. He kept his eyes on his own hands as he gently rubbed the cold, soothing aloe into my heated skin. For one brief second, he looked up and we locked eyes.

"That's not the type of scar you meant, was it?" he asked with the hint of a smile.

I shook my head lightly, not taking my eyes off him.

He sighed, "I only have one other scar."

"Where is it?"

He averted his eyes and resumed applying the aloe to me. "It's in a much more private and sensitive area than the others."

I felt my brow furrow as I tried to think it through. When I'd figured it out, I knew my cheeks flushed. "Oh," I uttered. Outrage quickly took over for embarrassment. "Why would he do that to you?"

He smirked, "I told you he was an abusive asshole." He looked at me, "Also, he caught me looking at his skin mags." He smiled, trying to lighten the mood.

I smiled in return. "And that didn't turn you off of big-breasted women for life?

He laughed, "You'd think it would have."

"What do you tell your women when they ask you about the scars?"

"My women?" he laughed. "You make me sound so cheap when you say it like that!"

"Sorry, I couldn't think of a better word to use." I smiled apologetically.

He nodded in acceptance, "They don't usually ask." He shrugged, "The few who have were satisfied when I told them they were just chicken pox scars."

"So you lied to them?"

He nodded.

"Why didn't you just lie to me?"

He dropped his hands from my face, and looked into my eyes. "It was never an option."

I titled my head and asked, "What does that mean?"

He shrugged, "I'm not sure why, but I just never thought of not telling you the truth."

We looked at each other for a few seconds, neither of us sure what to say or do next. The house was so quiet and still that the sound of our breathing seemed amplified.

"Cami," Nick said softly without looking away from me.

I waited for him to continue, but he never did. After a few seconds, he shook his head, muttered something under his breath, and stood up.

"I need to get the rest of this stuff off my hands. I'll meet you downstairs in a little bit." He left the room, leaving me alone on his bed. I heard the door to the bathroom shut and the water turn on.

Something else was on his mind, but he'd stopped himself from saying it. Thinking that it was probably better not to tempt fate any longer, I left his room and headed back down to the kitchen. After five minutes or so, Nick joined me and sat across from me at the table. Neither of us spoke while we ate the leftover meals we'd made for ourselves. A few times, we'd made eye contact, but it was always followed by a nervous or awkward smile.

When he was finished with his food, he carried his plate back to the kitchen. Perhaps feeling bolder with distance between us, he called out a question to me.

"Do you want to finish watching that movie from the other night?" he called out as he rinsed his plate.

I was definitely not ready for bed. It was too early for bed, not to mention that the encounter with Nick in his room had left me too amped up for sleep.

"Sure," I answered. I took my own plate to the kitchen. Nick was still standing near the sink and my arm brushed against him as I placed my plate in the sink. When my skin touched his, every nerve in my body seemed to light on fire. I inhaled sharply and heard him do the same. He quickly slid to the side and put distance between us.

"I'll go get the movie started." He mumbled in a rough voice and left me alone in the kitchen.

I closed my eyes and took a deep breath. I wasn't sure when it had happened, but at some point in the day things between us had changed. The easiness we'd had the past few days had been replaced with an awkward tension. Any time his body made contact with mine, my nerves went crazy. The battle I'd been having with myself was shifting. My head was no longer fighting as hard as it had before. My physical reactions and needs were making stronger arguments than my head.

After a few deep breaths, and a slow walk to the living room, I joined Nick on the couch. I was careful to choose the furthest cushion from him. He flashed an awkward smile as I sat then turned the movie on. I pulled my feet up onto the couch and wrapped my arms around my legs, keeping myself as secure as possible. The movie started where we'd left off, and I settled into my safe corner of the couch.

Twenty minutes later, my legs were starting to cramp up from the awkward position I'd put myself in. I unwrapped my arms, released my grip on my legs, and unfolded myself. Feeling slightly more relaxed, I let my head rest against the arm of the couch and stared at the screen.

Another ten minutes into the movie and I found myself feeling uncomfortable again. However, this time it had nothing to do with how I was sitting. The tension between Nick and I was almost visible as we both worked to look as unaffected as possible by what was happening on the screen. When he'd suggested the movie, I thought we'd be safe from any awkwardness since I'd chosen an action flick. Unfortunately, I'd forgotten about the graphic sex scene.

The sound of the character's heavy breathing, moans, and the sight of their writhing bodies made for a very uncomfortable few minutes on the couch in the beach house. I didn't dare look over at Nick, though I could feel his eyes wandering over to me a few times. He cleared his throat and exhaled loudly.

"Heard anything from Chrissy this evening?" he asked, obviously trying to alleviate the tension.

Hearing his voice made my heart start to race. I closed my eyes, trying to steady myself.

"She sent me a text earlier saying that she was hanging out with Todd and Mike tonight."

Nick cleared his throat again and said with a nod, "Darren sent me a message, too. He said he'd found a friend and he'd most likely see me in the morning."

I nodded, but didn't look over at him. Clearly, we were going to be alone in the house all night. Instead of releasing some of the tension between us, the conversation had actually made the tension thicker. The thought of being completely alone with him was sending my pulse racing again. The battle was clearly not turning back in favor of my mind.

When the movie was finally over, I stood up and stretched. "Well, I suppose I'm off to bed now. I had a nice day with you, again." I risked a look at him and flashed an awkward smile at him.

He stood up and took a step closer to me.

"Cami," he said with a wild look in his eyes. "If you lived in LA, or if I lived in New York, would tonight be ending differently?"

I looked into his eyes. I could tell he was breathing harder, but I couldn't take my eyes off him. With a deep sigh, I answered him.

"Probably."

We stood staring at each other for several seconds before I broke away. I left him standing in the living room and started up the stairs. I didn't stop moving, but I did look back at him a few times. Each time, he was still standing in the same place. He had his eyes closed and he was taking slow, deep breaths.

When I got to my room, I fell down across my bed. It felt like my heart had been racing for the last hour. Just being near him had been enough to make my body react physically. Something had definitely changed. There was no longer a voice in my head telling me not to give in. The voice had gone silent. Instead of shouting at me to be reasonable, it was silent. My body wasn't shouting at me, but it certainly had something to say. It was in total control as I stood up from the bed and reached for the door.

I thought he'd still be in the living room, standing where I'd left him, maybe even with his eyes still closed and breathing deeply. I don't know what I thought I'd say to him when I got back down there, but I expected to find him there.

I didn't expect to see him standing just outside my door when I pulled it open.

"Nick!" I said his name loudly. "What…what are you doing out here?"

He shook his head, "Trying to fight the urge to knock on your door."

"Why?" I asked in a whisper.

He shook his head again, "I don't know what I thought I was going to say, Cami. I just know that you make me feel things that I didn't expect. I don't know if I know what it means, but I just feel like there's so much more that we need to say to each other."

Suddenly feeling braver than I'd ever felt before, I took a step closer to him. I smiled, "I meant why are you trying to fight it?"

It only took him one step to reach me. He reached for me and pulled my face to his in one swift movement. Our bodies melted together as his mouth found mine. My arms wrapped around him and held him tighter to me.

When his mouth finally left mine and moved to my neck, I whispered breathlessly, "This is not a hook-up. This is just a really short relationship that moved at a very fast pace."

Nick laughed gruffly against my skin and said, "I can work with that." His mouth returned to mine and he pushed me back into my room. He slammed the door shut with one hand, while the other slid under my shirt.

It didn't take long before we were both undressed. I fell onto the bed and Nick followed. His hands roamed over my body leading a trail for his mouth to follow. In turn, my hands caressed his body, taking care to pay special attention to the small scars that marked his body.

Afterwards, we lay together in my bed, my head resting on his chest and his arms wrapped around me. My fingers gently traced the roughness of his scars and his fingers ran up and down my back.

"For the record, that was nowhere near four hours," I whispered teasingly.

He laughed, causing me to rise and fall with his chest. "In my defense, that's been building for the last few days."

I chuckled, "So I get four days of foreplay and twenty minutes of actual sex?"

"Come on, that was at least thirty minutes!" he tickled my side.

I wiggled against him and laughed, "I'll give you twenty-five."

He shifted and rolled on top of me. I wiggled into a more comfortable position under him and wrapped my arms around him. He rested his elbows on the pillow on either side of my head and gently brushed the hair out of my face.

"I wish you lived in LA," he whispered softly to me.

"I wish you lived in New York," I whispered in response, looking into his eyes.

He stared back at me. "We could make it work, you know? We could talk on the phone, e-mail, and video message each other during the week. Then on the weekends, we could take turns flying to each other's places."

I smiled weakly at him, "One round trip ticket to LA would probably deplete my account. Besides, I don't have a place you could come to, remember?"

He sighed, "Fine, I could get a place in New York. You could stay there all the time and then I could fly in on the weekends and stay with you."

I reached up and ran my fingers through his hair. What he was proposing sounded a lot like a situation Chrissy would find herself in. I liked Nick. I liked him a lot. However, I didn't think I could handle being in that situation with him.

I sighed, "Let's not talk about it. Let's just enjoy what we have right now."

He closed his eyes and nodded.

I could see the disappointment on his face, but couldn't bring myself to face it. I leaned forward and pressed my lips against his. His body instantly responded to mine, and he kissed me back.

"I have a confession to make," he whispered against my ear when he'd finally broken the kiss.

"What?" I asked breathlessly. I was enjoying the way it felt to have his body pressed against mine again and wasn't exactly looking to make conversation.

"About that four hour thing," he said between planting kisses on my neck. He smiled against my skin and raised his eyes to look at me.

"You were lying weren't you?" I giggled as he gently nibbled the skin on my shoulder.

"No, I wasn't lying," he said with a sly grin. "It's just that it wasn't like one continuous session. It was more like several smaller sessions completed over the course of four hours." He smiled wider, "That girl was insatiable, and she liked to do dirty things, very naughty, dirty things."

"I don't want to hear this!" I said and pretended like I was pushing him off me.

He laughed and pulled me back closer to him. "You're not going anywhere."

I wiggled under him and put my arms back around him. He lowered his head to mine and kissed me softly.

"Nick," I bit my lip and looked shyly at him. "Do you think you could do that thing again?"

He smiled, but asked innocently, "What thing?"

I felt my cheeks redden and closed my eyes. His hand brushed against my cheek and I opened my eyes. He was watching me, with a big grin on his face.

"That thing with your hips, can you do that again?" I asked quietly.

He dipped his head down, pushing his body closer to mine. With his mouth pressed against my neck, he sighed, "It would be my pleasure."

13.

I woke the next morning with a smile on my face, and an aching feeling in every muscle of my body. I stretched through the aching and rolled over, expecting to find Nick there next to me, but found that I was alone. I sat up and looked around the room, hoping that maybe he was just pulling his clothes back on, or maybe just sitting in one of the chairs across the room. But I was alone in the room. I reached for my clothes and dressed quickly. Never having participated in a tryst, I wasn't sure what the protocol was for dressing and leaving, but I needed to find him and talk to him.

I sank back down on the bed and finished dressing. I had just pulled my shirt on when the door flew open, scaring me half to death.

"Guess what?" Chrissy shouted happily, as she burst into the room.

"Chrissy!" I screamed and grabbed my chest.

She looked around the room then turned a suspicious eye back to me. "What the hell, Cami? You look terrible. Your hair is a mess, your lips are swollen, and those sheets look like they've been twisted to within an inch of their life. I'd say you look like you've just woken up after a night of wild sex, but I know you too well to think that." She laughed then added, "That and there are no condom wrappers lying around the room."

Chrissy laughed hysterically, giving me the opportunity to pull myself together before she caught a glimpse of the embarrassment on my face. Not only was I embarrassed by what I'd done and the fact that I'd been caught, but it had suddenly just occurred to me that Chrissy was right. There were no condom wrappers lying on the floor. Neither Nick nor I had stopped to think about protection.

"So, guess what?" Chrissy said as she finished laughing.

"What?" I asked, not caring what she had to say, but desperate to keep the topic off me.

"Clark just called. He's leaving his wife! He's getting a place of his own and he wants me to move in with him!" Chrissy screeched with joy and jumped up and down.

"Wait! What?" I asked in disbelief.

"He's chosen me! He wants me!" she said with a big grin.

"Does he know about Todd and all the other guys you've made friends with this week?"

She put her hand on her hips, "He can't possibly be upset about what I may or may not have done while we weren't together."

I raised an eyebrow at her. She averted her eyes from my gaze. She knew that I knew what she'd been up to, but if she was going to try to hide it from Mr. Money that was her prerogative.

"Get packed. Our flight leaves in two hours," she said and left my room.

I processed what she'd said then jumped off the bed and followed her out into the hall. "Our flight?"

"Yes, I called the airline and had our tickets switched to today. I figured you wouldn't mind. I mean, it's not like you were even doing anything down here." Chrissy smiled, twirled, and disappeared behind her bedroom door.

I leaned against the railing and sighed.

"You don't have to go with her, you know?" Nick said softly.

I opened my eyes and saw him sitting on the stairs, a coffee cup in each hand. He smiled hopefully at me.

"I thought you'd snuck off," I said softly.

He held up the coffee cups, "I went downstairs to make coffee for us. When I heard Chrissy come in, I followed her up the stairs worried that she might find you still asleep in bed." He smiled apologetically, "You weren't exactly decent when I left the room."

I blushed.

"It's true, though. You don't have to go with her." He repeated his earlier statement.

"The ticket is already paid for," I said softly.

He stood up and walked up the stairs to join me on the third floor. "I can pay her back. You can stay here with me for the next two days. Darren and I can take you back to New York on the company jet when we go back to LA."

"She probably used Ned's credit card to pay for the tickets."

He smiled and handed me a coffee cup, "Even better. I can pay Ned back for the ticket."

I sighed and stared at the black liquid in the cup he'd handed me. "It's sort of just delaying the inevitable, though, isn't it?"

His brow furrowed, "So we're not even going to discuss the idea of making this work?"

"Nick," I sighed. "You live in LA. I live in New York."

"I told you I would buy a place in New York. You pick it out and I'll pay for it. You can stay there all the time and I'll fly in on the weekends." He leaned against the railing and watched me intently.

I shook my head slightly.

"Tell me why not?" he pleaded with me.

I stared at the coffee, "I just can't do that."

"Why not?"

"I don't want to be someone's weekend piece, Nick."

He touched my arm, "That's not what you'd be, Cami."

"I can't be that for you. I can't be that for anyone, Nick."

He dropped his hand from my arm. He took a step back and said coldly, "You're better at this than you think."

I looked up at him. "What?"

"Hooking up," he said. "You're better at it than some guys I know. The hardest part is the exit. You've got that down."

I flinched back from him, "I don't know what you're talking about."

He smiled coldly, "You were great. You did really well. You were cold, distant, and unfeeling. Nice job with the walking away part of this." He toasted me with his coffee cup.

"Nick," I shook my head in shame.

"No, take the compliment Cami. You earned it." He tipped his head at me and walked past me. He was down the stairs before I could think of what to say to stop him. I stood there and listened to the sound of his feet as they sped down the stairs. When the front door slammed shut, my whole body flinched at the noise.

Chrissy came out of her room, "Who were you talking to?"

I looked over at her, but couldn't find the strength to say his name.

"Are you packed yet? We need to leave here in the next thirty minutes!" she gave me a warning look then went back to her room.

With our suitcases stuffed into the trunk of the taxi, Chrissy and I drove away from the beach house. I stared out the window as the beach sped past us. I searched the waves for Nick's figure, but we were moving too fast for me to see anything. I'd tried to find him before we got in the car, but he was gone. I thought about leaving him a note, but couldn't think of what the right thing to say would be. Sitting in the backseat of the taxi, I rested my head against the window and closed my eyes.

"Are you feeling okay?" Chrissy asked.

"I'm just tired." I lied to her. I didn't want to spend the next few hours rehashing all the details of my week with Nick, so I gave in and gave Chrissy what I knew she wanted. "So, where do you think Clark will get a place?"

Chrissy talked excitedly the entire trip home. She talked about Clark in the taxi. She talked about Clark as we waited for our flight. She talked about Clark as we flew from North Carolina back to New York. When we landed in New York, Clark was there to meet her at the airport. He was kind enough to give me a ride home in his car, but spent the ride making out with Chrissy in the seat across next to me.

I would have preferred Chrissy's commentary.

The driver dropped my bags at the door to the townhouse and I gave him a small tip as a thank you for the ride. As the car drove out of sight, I took a deep breath and closed my eyes. Ready to be alone in my room, I opened my eyes and opened the door. I dragged my bags upstairs to my bedroom, shut and locked the door, and collapsed onto my bed. All the feelings I'd been suppressing since I woke up that morning welled up inside me and I screamed into the comforter.

I stayed locked in my room for a few hours, trying to work it all out of my system. When I finally emerged from my bedroom, I slipped into the bathroom for a much-needed shower. I washed the last remnants of my vacation, and my encounter with Nick, off me and tried to convince myself that I was done. I'd cried it all out, washed it off me, and was ready to move on.

The next few days were miserable, but I got through them. I still thought of Nick all the time, but I'd finally stopped tearing up every time I did. To try to keep my mind off him, I'd spent a few hours every day working in my classroom. Chrissy had been virtually nonexistent since we'd returned. She sent me a message about how great the place Clark had gotten for her was, but other than that, I hadn't heard anything from her. To be fair, I wasn't sure that I even wanted to hear from her. Listening to her talk giddily about how happy she was with Clark seemed like exactly the opposite of what I wanted to hear.

Midway through the week, the sisters decided that the house needed to have one of its famous family dinners. We all gathered in the dining room, at their old family table, and filled each other in on what was happening in our lives. I kept to myself, not feeling in the mood to share my misery with the rest of the house.

"What's up with you, Miss Cami? You've been awfully quiet since returning from the beach this last time." Henrietta, the oldest sister said teasingly to me from the other end of the table.

I smiled politely, "Nothing new with me, Hen. I'm just trying to get back into the mood for the school year."

Everyone at the table smiled and nodded at me, but Henrietta raised an eyebrow. The conversation continued to flow around me and I let out a sigh of relief. I'd been a ghost around the house since my return. It's not as if I was normally a social butterfly, but I did like to spend time in the shared living space. Lately, however, I stayed in my room and stayed by myself.

Later, when we were clearing the plates from dinner, Henrietta cornered me as I filled the dishwasher.

"So, you met a guy, huh?" she said confidently.

A blush immediately burned my cheeks, "No. What makes you say that?"

"You're not the same girl who left here, so that makes me think that either you met someone or you did something you shouldn't have." Hen winked at me. "Of course, you could have done both, but that doesn't seem like the Cami we've come to know."

When I didn't deny it, or even look up at her, she must have figured she was right. Before I could stop it, she'd grabbed my arm and dragged me into the library. Renters weren't allowed in the library, it was one of the few rooms that were off limits.

"Spill it!" she ordered me when the door was shut behind us.

"It's not that big of a deal, Hen. I just made a mistake, that's all." I shrugged casually.

"Cami," she shifted her weight to one side and looked sternly at me.

I sighed, "Fine! Sit down. It's going to be a long story."

I told her almost everything. I didn't give her any details about our last night together, even though she asked for them repeatedly. I also left out the part about not using protection. She didn't need to know how much of a mistake I'd made.

"He sounds great. Why didn't you stay?" she asked when I'd finished my story.

"He lives in LA. What would be the point of staying for one more day?"

She said quietly, "He did offer to get a place here. That means something doesn't it?"

I sighed, "Hen, he wanted me to be his weekend girl. Who knows what he'd be up to in LA during the week? That lifestyle is just not for me!"

She shook her head at me, "Still, you didn't have to be so cold. You wanted him as much as he wanted you that night."

I grimaced at her. "You're really not making me feel any better, Hen."

She smiled, "Did I ever tell you that I was engaged?"

"No," I said in surprise.

"Yep," she smiled sadly. "For two whole days, I was engaged to the most amazing man."

"What happened?" I asked incredulously. I'd always assumed that Henrietta and her sister Georgia were lifelong spinsters, women who'd never shown any interest in living a different life. Finding out that Hen was engaged was like finding out that your parents used to date other people. It seemed weird and completely out of character.

"He really was an amazing man." She looked dreamily out the window then turned back with a smile. "He was gorgeous, too."

I smiled at her as she continued in a dreamy voice.

"We met on the subway one rainy afternoon. He told me he liked my umbrella then chatted me up the whole ride. When we got to my stop, he got off too. I asked him if he lived nearby and he said no, that he actually lived three stops back but didn't want to end our conversation so he stayed and rode with me. That was it for me! From that moment on, I was hooked on him. We went to fancy dinners. We went dancing. We went for long walks in the park. It was all very romantic. When he got down on one knee and asked me to marry him I didn't even hesitate before I said yes." Hen smiled sadly at her own story.

"So what happened?" I asked, entranced by her story.

She sighed, "He wasn't perfect, but I knew that. He'd told me about his less than virtuous past. He said one look at me had changed him forever." She rolled her eyes. "Being the innocent girl that I was, I believed him when he said he was changed. Georgie on the other hand, she didn't believe a word he said. I thought she was just jealous because someone wanted me and not her, but it got me thinking. I started to wonder if a man really could change that easily. I wondered if he was playing me for a fool. I must have stayed up for two days straight, just thinking about all the what ifs. So, when he came looking for me two days later, I wouldn't come to the door. I sent Georgie out with the ring in a box."

"You talked yourself out of it? Why?"

She shook her head, "Being as headstrong as I was, I just couldn't fathom the idea of someone being able to change. A leopard can't change its spots, my dad used to say that to me all the time, and that's all I could think about when I looked down at that ring. I didn't want to end up like some of the ladies in my mother's tea group, married to a man who couldn't be faithful and was barely around."

"Whatever happened to him? Do you even know?" I was still processing everything, but had to know the outcome.

"He eventually got married to a lovely girl from Jersey. They lived a few blocks from here for many years."

"So he did change after all?"

She shook her head vigorously, "Oh, goodness, no! He turned into a big drunk and notorious skirt chaser! I really dodged a bullet with that one!"

Feeling gypped with the ending, I said, "Thanks for the story, Hen, but I'm not sure it really relates to my situation." I stood up and took a step towards the door, but stopped when she started talking again.

"The point was, dear, that those two months I spent with him were the best two months of my life and I don't regret them for a second." She stood up and walked over to me. She placed a hand on my shoulder and smiled. "If you're going to be a fool for anything, let it be for love, Cami."

I shook my head at her, "I'm not in love, Hen. I only knew him for a week."

"It only takes one spark to start a fire big enough to burn a whole house down to the ground." She patted my shoulder and left me standing alone in the library.

I'd never allowed myself to say the L word, even in my head. I'd been in love before. I thought. I thought I'd been in love with Jack, but that was different from what I felt with Nick. I had chalked it all up to the excitement of meeting a handsome stranger, but at the mention of the word love my heart beat faster and I felt the room start to spin. Needing support, I plopped down on the nearest chair and closed my eyes.

"It figures," I said quietly and threw my head back against the back of the chair. "The one time you foolishly hook up with a guy and you fall completely in love with him."

A miserable week after that, I came home to find Henrietta waiting for me on the stairs leading up to the bedrooms.

"You got a package today!" she said with a big grin.

I reached for it and she pretended to snatch it back from me. Not at all in the mood to play, I gave her my teacher look and she relinquished the package.

"It's from a ceramics place in North Carolina," she smiled as she handed the package to me.

My heart raced at the memory of the day we'd painted the ceramic sculptures. All the tiny details of that day flooded my mind. The way it felt when he'd touched my face that morning, the way his scent drifted over to me with the beach breeze, the feeling it gave me when he smiled at me, all the details of that day replayed in my head.

"Aren't you going to open it?" Hen asked excitedly.

I stared at the box in my hands. I knew what would be in it, I'd snuck a peek at it as he handed it to the girl behind the counter, but I just couldn't bring myself to open it.

"Come on! Open it. I want to see what's in there!" Hen pushed me to confront what was in the box.

I shook my head, "I'll open it later. I have some stuff to do." I carried the box up to my room, set it on the dresser, and sat down on my bed. After a few deep breaths, I stood up and headed for the dresser. My cell phone rang before I could get to it, though. The screen said it was Chrissy calling, and since I hadn't heard from her in a while, I figured I needed to take it.

Three hours later, I found myself sitting in Chrissy's new apartment admiring the view and the expensive wine Mr. Money had stocked the kitchen with.

"So, what do you think?" Chrissy asked with a cheesy and expectant grin.

"It's amazing, Chrissy. The view is spectacular and the place is beautiful." I turned away from the window and grinned at her. "You've got everything you've ever wanted."

She smiled, "I know. It feels good, too."

"How are things with you and Clark?" I asked as I sat down next to her on the fancy couch. I'd decided that I wasn't going to call him Mr. Money anymore, at least not to Chrissy. If he was whom Chrissy had chosen, then I needed to respect that choice enough to call him by his real name.

Chrissy shrugged and took a sip of her wine.

I cocked an eyebrow at her, "What does that mean?"

"What does what mean?"

"I asked you how things were going and you shrugged." I imitated her action. "What does that shrug mean?"

She shrugged again, "You know how it is when you live with someone. At first it's exciting, but then you fall into a routine and things start to get a little familiar, that's all." She tried to make it sound casual, but I knew her well enough to know better.

I put my wine down. "Chrissy, you've been living together for two weeks. The honeymoon period usually lasts a few months, at least. What's really going on?"

She sighed loudly, "He's still seeing her."

"Who?" I asked and studied her face. I should have known she didn't just call me over to check out her new place. She was in pre-crisis mode and she needed me to talk her through it. I'd seen it many times before.

"His wife," she said with a sad look. "He's still seeing her."

I gave her a sympathetic look, "When?"

"She's always there when he goes to visit the kid. She won't let him take the baby by himself, so either she goes with them or he stays over there for the visit." Chrissy whimpered helplessly.

Trying to reassure her, I said consolingly, "I'm sure it's nothing. He just wants to be a good dad and spend time with his daughter."

Chrissy looked over at me suspiciously, "At eleven o'clock at night?"

"Babies keep odd hours," I grimaced as I spoke, not convincing myself of what I said.

Chrissy started crying, "I thought this was what I wanted. I thought that having him in a place with me would make him see that he didn't want her anymore, that he should be with me and not her. I hate this, Cami. Instead of her waiting up for him while he's out with me, I'm the one lying in bed alone and watching the clock for him to come home."

I put my arm around her and she collapsed against my shoulder. "I'm sure it's just a transition period. Things will change, I'm sure of it."

"Do you really think so?" Chrissy sniffed loudly.

"I hope so." I rubbed her arm in support.

"You're a really great friend, you know that? I'm so glad I've got you. I don't know what I'd do if you ever left me alone in this city to fend for myself." Chrissy wrapped her arms around my waist and squeezed me. "How about I treat you to the spa this weekend?"

I laughed, "Sure. I could use a relaxing spa day. I've been sort of tense lately, anyway."

She sat up, "What's going on? Stress at work?"

"No, that hasn't really started yet. The kids haven't come in yet, so it's just the teachers right now." I'd officially reported back to school, but the students weren't due to arrive until next week. Job stress wasn't new to me. I was used to that. "I've just been tired this week and for the first time in a long time I've got cramps. I did not miss those."

"Men are so lucky they don't have to deal with that crap. As if the cramping, bloating, and bleeding weren't enough, then we have to deal with the whole childbirth thing!" Chrissy, clearly feeling better, sat up and grabbed her wine.

"My mom used to say that if men were responsible for birthing children then the human population would have died out centuries ago." I shifted on the couch.

Chrissy and I both laughed and sat back against the couch, settling in for a lovely evening of catching up. I didn't tell her about Nick, and she didn't ask. One of the best things about my friendship with Chrissy was that if I didn't want to talk about something, she was perfectly happy simply to fill the void by talking about herself. If, however, by chance I did want to talk, she'd always be there to listen. She didn't try to pry things out of me. She knew that with three sisters, I grew up without a lot of secrets, so as an adult I chose to keep most things to myself. I appreciated her respecting that.

Of course, it could also just be that she was so self-centered that she didn't even want to know what was happening in my life.

At the end of the evening, I caught the subway back to my place and collapsed onto the bed. It hadn't been a particularly busy week, but it had been exhausting. I'd actually taken a little nap in my classroom at lunch the day before, so it shouldn't have surprised me when I woke up the morning after my visit with Chrissy to find that I'd fallen asleep on my bed fully clothed and with my shoes still on.

The rest of the week was about the same. I went to work, kept busy planning my latest year with first graders, then came home and collapsed on my bed. By Friday, I was ready to spend my whole weekend curled up in bed. I stopped at the store to pick up some vitamin C and other cold preventatives. I figured I was about to get sick, and the first week of school was not the best time to be rundown or ill. My phone rang just as I walked out of the store.

"What are you doing tonight? Come out with me!" Chrissy said in an obnoxiously cheerful voice.

"I don't think so, Chrissy. I'm pretty sure I'm getting sick, so I should probably stay in this weekend and try to nip this in the bud before it gets too bad." I talked to her as I dug through my bag in search of the candy I'd bought myself as a treat. I always bought myself a small treat when I went to the pharmacy. It was a tradition left over from my childhood when my mom would take us all to the drugstore and the pharmacist would give us each a lollipop. I unwrapped the sucker and popped it into my mouth.

"The kids haven't even showed up yet and you're already sick?" Chrissy whined.

"I think I can catch it in time. I've just been feeling achy lately, so I'm going to try to load up on vitamins to fight off whatever it is I'm developing."

"I guess I'll let you stay in this time," Chrissy's voice had a disappointed tone.

"Where's Clark, anyway?" I asked as I headed back towards my place.

"He's away on business. You know, when we didn't live together it didn't bother me that much when he'd go out of town, but now that we do, I've noticed how often he goes away." She sighed, "I don't know, Cami. Sometimes I think I've made a bad decision. Being a mistress is a lot easier than being a live-in girlfriend."

I shook my head. "Perhaps you should have thought of that before you agreed to move in with him."

"I know, but," she sighed again, "the place is amazing! I'd be a fool to let this apartment go, right?"

I laughed at her, "I hardly think a nice apartment is worth all the heartache, do you?"

"It is for now, I guess."

Chrissy said her goodbyes and I finished my walk home, feeling tired but in better spirits. When I got home, I immediately changed into my pajamas. I made myself a mug of tea, popped a vitamin into my mouth, and curled up on the couch with a good book. I'd planned to spend the weekend doing just that. Most of the other house residents had gone away for the weekend, so there were very few of us milling around the house. With less people around, I was able to fulfill my weekend plans of being a couch potato.

Sunday night, still in my pajamas but feeling much better, I picked up the phone to call and check in on my parents. I usually called them on Sunday nights, so they picked up on the first ring.

"Cami!" my dad said cheerfully.

"Hi, dad," I answered him back with a smile. "What's up?"

"Not much. Let me go into the kitchen so that I don't disturb your mother." I heard him say as he carried himself away from distraction in the house.

I smiled to myself. I don't know why he bothered getting up. My mom was just going to shout at him from the living room as he talked to me on the phone.

"She's got me watching some show about girls trying on wedding dresses. It's been on for three hours already! I've got to get a television for that garage." My dad whispered into the phone, just in case my mom might hear him.

Since moving to a house further from the city, my dad had tried to assert his masculinity a little more. Living in an apartment with four women left him in desperate need of man time. For him, the big selling point of the new house was the detached garage where he could keep tools, lawn mowers, and other man stuff. He'd planned to get a television so that he could watch what he wanted, but they'd been in the house a year and he still didn't have the television. My theory was that he secretly liked having to watch all those girly shows.

"It's probably a marathon, dad." I said with a laugh. "What have you guys been up to?"

"We went to the Farmer's Market today and picked up some organic vegetables. That market is great. They have so many things there." My dad said excitedly. For the next ten minutes, I listened as he went through and described the entire stock at the market. A few times, I could hear my mom interjecting loudly from the other room.

"That does sound like a good place to shop," I said when he'd finally stopped talking about the market.

"It is. So, what's up with you? Tori mentioned something about you saying you didn't feel well."

"I'm probably just rundown. I've been really tired and achy, but I spent the whole weekend in my pajamas and I've been taking extra vitamins to try to fight it off. I'm sure I'll be fine by midweek."

"Well," my dad stopped as my mom shouted something from the other room. "Okay, fine! I'll ask her!"

he shouted back at her. With a sigh, he said to me, "Your mother wants to know if you're seeing anyone?"

"No, I'm not seeing anyone." I smiled and shook my head.

"She said no," he shouted back to my mom. I heard her saying something in return, and then my dad was back. "She said what about the guy from the beach, the one that called Allison?"

My body froze. Since no one had mentioned it the week before, I stupidly assumed that Allison hadn't said anything to my parents about Nick's phone call. I should have known better. There was no way Allison was going to keep that to herself.

Before I could answer, my mom's voice came on the line.

"Allison said he sounded very nice. Is there anything between the two of you?" she asked in a hopeful voice.

I took a deep breath and tried to calm myself before I answered. "Mom, he was just a friend that I made at the beach. He lives in LA, so we probably won't ever see each other again."

"Oh," she said disappointedly. "Was he cute? Did you like him?"

I took a deep breath before answering, "My feelings on both of those subjects are moot, mom. He lives in LA, and that trumps cuteness and likability."

She sighed, "I just want you to be happy, that is all."

"I know that, mom, and I appreciate it. It's just harder to meet the right kind of guys now than it was in college. Most of the men I meet aren't really interested in the same things I'm interested in." Whatever I was coming down with must have weakened my defenses against my mom's prying.

"I understand that honey, and I don't want you to compromise. I just think that maybe you could put a little more effort into looking for the right kind of man." She said it sweetly, so I didn't take offense.

"You just want grandkids to spoil," I said with a smile.

She laughed, "I do! I admit it. I can't wait to spoil a little bundle with love and kisses. Sue me!"

"Well, I'm afraid you're going to have to wait for your chance, at least from me."

We talked for a few minutes before I finally got her off the phone. She didn't mention Nick, or any other man, for the rest of the conversation. We talked about the upcoming school year and about what my sisters were up to.

I'd tried hard not to think about Nick for the last few days. Although, if I was being honest with myself, most times trying hard not to think about him only made me think about him more. I missed him and it bothered me to no end to admit that to myself. I'd only known the man for a few days, and yet I missed him. A big part of me wondered if the achy, rundown feeling had anything to do with him. I wondered if I'd somehow managed to fall into depression over a guy I'd known for a couple of days.

When thoughts of Nick seeped into my head, I tried to push them away, but they just kept coming back. On the subway last week, I could have sworn I heard his voice, but when I turned towards it, it was a short bald man. Walking through the store, I was hit by a waft of cologne that smelled like Nick's. I had to leave the aisle; my thoughts were so jumbled by it. I couldn't escape him, no matter where I went.

The package from the ceramics shop that I'd originally placed on my dresser had been hidden in my closet. I hadn't even bothered opening it. I couldn't. I couldn't bear the idea of holding something that he painted for me in my hand. I certainly wasn't going to display it in a place where I'd have to confront it daily. So, hidden in my closet, the little beach girl sat packed away. I hoped that someday the ridiculous feelings I was having for him would join her in the closet. However, until then, I felt a little better knowing I couldn't see her.

14.

The first week of school went off without a hitch. It was as busy as usual, so there was no time to be achy or rundown. I must have been running on adrenaline alone, because by the time I got home on Friday I was too exhausted to eat dinner. I had just enough energy to drag myself up the stairs, change into my pajamas and crawl into the bed. I didn't wake up until the next morning.

When I opened my eyes the next morning, I was greeted by the smell of eggs cooking downstairs. Normally, that was a welcomed thing, but for some reason that morning, it made my stomach turn. I buried my face in my pillow and took a few deep breaths. When I felt like I could handle it, I sat up slowly. A cold shiver ran over me and I wiped a bead of sweat off my forehead. I steadied myself before getting up off the bed. Clearly, not eating dinner before going to bed was a bad idea.

I dressed and slowly wandered downstairs for something to eat. The smell of cooked eggs still filled the kitchen, and I felt my stomach start to turn again. I grabbed my box of cereal and put a handful of pieces in my mouth. When the cereal hit my stomach, I felt a little better. I made a bowl and sat down at the table to finish my breakfast. After breakfast, I called Chrissy to see what she was up to.

"Oh, hi Cami," Chrissy said when she picked up the phone. She didn't sound like her usually cheerful self.

"What's wrong?" I asked and settled down on the bench outside in the backyard garden.

"I think I need to break it off with Clark," she sighed.

"Why?"

I listened as Chrissy detailed everything that had been happening in her relationship over the past week and a half. She'd followed him and seen him out with his wife. They went out for a romantic dinner then headed back to the house they used to share. Despite all that, she was still willing to give him the benefit of the doubt, until he called to tell her he was working late that night and wouldn't be home until the early morning. She took the call as she sat outside his old home.

"I'm sorry to hear that, Chrissy, but how is it any different than what it was like when they were still together?" I tried to be sympathetic, but I wasn't really getting what her problem was. She didn't seem to have any trouble being the other woman before.

"It's different because now I'm the one sitting up waiting for him. I'm the one getting the phone call full of lies. I'm the one alone, and she's the other woman!" Chrissy burst into tears.

"I'm so sorry, Chrissy. Do you want me to come over?" I asked, more out of politeness than real desire to leave my cozy spot in the garden.

"No, mom's taking me shopping."

I smiled, "Well, that should help cheer you up."

"I hope so. Actually," Chrissy said sheepishly, "I hope it puts her in a good mood, because I'm going to ask her if I can move back into her old apartment. She was planning on renting it out, but I'm going to need it again."

I spent my Sunday helping Chrissy move out of her love den. Since Clark had furnished the place, and Chrissy was moving into a furnished apartment, all we had to move were her clothes. It took us seven trips and five hours, but at the end of it all, Chrissy was officially moved out of Clark's life. Knowing that she wouldn't be able to stand her ground if she had to say it face to face, she left him a note explaining it all.

"I've turned over a new leaf, Cami. I'm going to be more like you." Chrissy said after we'd carried the last of her clothes to her new apartment. She was shouting at me from the kitchen, while I collapsed into one of the comfy chairs.

"What do you mean?" I shouted back at her.

"I'm swearing off men. Here, this is for you," she handed me a glass of wine and sat on the couch across from my chair.

"I haven't sworn off men, Chrissy." I argued with her. I lifted the glass of wine to my mouth, but stopped when the scent hit me. "What kind of wine is this?"

"I don't know. It's something Ned sent over for me, why?" she shrugged and sipped at her own glass.

"It doesn't smell right to me." I put the glass on the table next to my chair and hoped my stomach would settle.

"Okay, so you haven't sworn off men completely, but you have to admit that you are very picky. I mean, have you even gone on a date since you and Jack broke up?" Chrissy kept talking, not at all phased by my comment about the wine or my current state of unease.

I took a few deep breaths to steady myself before I answered. "I'm not picky, Chrissy. I just don't go around hooking up with any guy with a cute smile."

Chrissy laughed, "I wasn't that bad!"

I looked sternly at her, "Tell me honestly, how many guys were you with when we were in the Outer Banks?"

Chrissy shrugged nonchalantly, "That was a bad week for me. I was in a vulnerable place."

I gave her a disbelieving look, "Sure you were."

"How many guys did you hook up with that week?" she asked then added sarcastically, "Oh, wait, never mind! You don't hook up. I got you a perfectly good man that you could use for your pleasure, and you ditched him for your surfer boy. At least he was gorgeous."

I blushed out of guilt. Chrissy still didn't know about me and Nick, and I wasn't sure that I should tell her. If Nick had just been a random guy I'd met, then perhaps I wouldn't have been so hesitant to tell her all about it. Since Nick worked for Chrissy's stepdad's company, I didn't want to take any chances that the information would get back to him.

"Let's talk about how you're going to change your ways and be more like me. How serious are you about this? Are you serious enough to stop going out every night? Is this serious enough to not spend seventy-five percent of your day shopping?" I leaned forward and looked directly at her. "Are you serious enough to actually get a job?"

Chrissy shot me a look, "Don't be ridiculous, Cami."

I sat back and laughed.

Surprisingly, Chrissy stayed true to her word. For the next two weeks, she didn't go out, hook up, or even shop. In fact, she'd invited me over several nights and actually cooked dinner for me. It was nice. I really liked the new Chrissy.

"Are you feeling okay?" Chrissy asked as I made my way back to the living room after my third trip to the bathroom.

"Yes," I said defensively.

"You're not turning bulimic on me, are you?" she asked with a suspicious look.

"No! Why would you ask that?"

"Because you've been here for an hour and you've already gone to the bathroom three times. Plus, you haven't been eating like you used to. At first, I thought it was about my cooking, but Ned tells me that my food is good. Also, every time I offer you wine, you tell me no." She put a hand on my arm and looked sympathetically at me. "If you're trying to lose that little bit of weight you've put on recently, I would be happy to let you use the gym in this building."

"I'm not trying to lose weight, Chrissy. I'm not bulimic, or anorexic, for that matter. I haven't been eating much lately because my stomach has been really sensitive. The wine thing is because it all smells funny to me, okay." I stared down at my hands. "I admit that despite all the stomach issues, I seem to have put on a few pounds. However, it's the beginning of the school year and things are a little stressful for me right now. I've also just been too tired to run. I'm sure that now that we're into October, things will settle down and I'll be back to my old self."

"I hope so. We can't both be trying to change who we are. I can't be a good girl who hangs around with a fat chick." Chrissy said with a smile.

I tossed a pillow at her. "I'm not fat!"

Chrissy laughed and dodged the pillow.

Walking home from Chrissy's house an hour later, I thought about what she'd brought up. I'd been busy, so I hadn't noticed all the changes I'd made in the last few weeks. I'd gotten used to babying my stomach, so I'd stopped paying attention to all the problems I'd been having. Putting everything together got the gears turning.

Feeling nervous, and embarrassed, I stopped in at my pharmacy to pick up something I'd never bought before. Standing in line at the counter with the box in my hand, I felt like my face was on fire. The old lady standing in front of me turned around, looked at what I had in my hand, clearly checked my hand for a ring, and looked up at me with a disgusted look. Trying hard not to cry from shame, I ignored her and looked off to the side.

Back at home, I snuck my purchase into the bathroom with me and waited nervously for my results. I sat on the toilet staring at my watch. Five minutes later, I finally worked up the courage to look. Staring at the little white stick, I wasn't sure how I was supposed to feel. The two pink lines stared back at me, waiting for some sort of reaction.

I called in sick the next day, and headed back to the pharmacy. Hoping that I'd simply gotten a faulty test that gave false results, I picked up one of every test available. I bit my nails nervously as I stood in line. When it was my turn, I tossed the boxes onto the counter and reached for my credit card.

"Oh, honey! You can take as many of those as you want, but you're just going to get the same results you got from the first one," the middle-aged woman behind the counter said to me. "Which result were you hoping for, positive or negative?"

"How did you know I'd already taken one?" I asked in mid-chew.

She smirked, "The look on your face, and the way you're tearing up your nails are both dead giveaways. Which result were you hoping for?"

I shook my head, "I don't know." I felt tears start to well up in my eyes.

"Oh, you poor thing!" she said and walked around the counter. "Frank! We've got another one!" she shouted at the pharmacist in the back of the store. She put her arm around my shoulder and walked me back towards the pharmacy window. "It's all going to be just fine. What does your husband think of all this?"

"I don't have a husband," I sobbed against her.

"Oh, dear, well that does complicate things a little." She stroked my hair sympathetically.

"What's going on?" Frank, the pharmacist, asked as he came out from behind his counter.

"She's just a little upset right now, that's all. She was buying four different pregnancy tests." The woman filled Frank in on what was happening. "She hasn't told me what result she got from her first test, but judging by the fact that she's crying, and she's not married, I'd guess she got both lines."

Frank sighed, "If you got a positive then chances are that you're pregnant. Have you had any symptoms?"

I sniffled and shrugged, "Maybe."

"Have you been feeling tired? Had any unusual cramps? Have your breasts been tender? Any morning sickness?" the woman rattled questions off to me.

"More importantly, have you missed your period?" Frank asked me directly.

I counted back in my head as quickly as I could. When my eyes started to well up again, Frank and his coworker exchanged a look.

"I think you should probably call your doctor and arrange an appointment." Frank said then walked back to the counter.

I wiped my face and sniffed loudly.

"Is there someone you can call to take you?" my comforter asked me.

"I'm fine. I can do this by myself." I stood up and sniffed confidently.

"That's the spirit. You've already gotten what you needed from a man! You can raise this baby on your own." She stood up with me and patted me on the back.

I walked away from her and towards the exit of the store. Just before I reached the door, I heard her shout at me.

"Just make sure you stick it to him when it comes to child support! You get your money every month!"

After a shameful confession of what I'd been up to and all that had occurred in the past five weeks, my doctor smiled sweetly at me.

"It happens to the best of us, Camille. Don't beat yourself up over it." She patted my hand. "We'll do a urine test and a blood test just to be sure, but it sounds like you're not going to be surprised by the results. Are you planning on contacting the father?"

I took a deep breath and nodded.

"What do you think he'll say?" she asked as she reached in the cabinet.

"I don't know. I don't even know what I'll say to him. I don't know that I can say it. I'll probably just end up sending a letter and letting him take it from there." I rambled and watched my hands twisting in my lap.

"You need to tell him. How you do it is up to you, but he deserves to know." She handed me a stick to pee on and pointed me towards the door.

I left the doctor's office with yet another positive pregnancy test. She sent my blood test to the lab, and said she'd call me by the next afternoon to let me know what she'd found out. We both knew what the blood test was going to say, but a small part of me was still holding on to the hope that the other two tests were wrong.

I rode home, completely lost in my own head. I tried to think about what I would say to Nick. I knew that a letter was the best option. If I wrote him a letter then I didn't have to hear him. If I wrote him a letter and never heard from him again, then at least I wouldn't have to live with an actual rejection. A letter and no response would give me the freedom to demonize him, and perhaps that's what it would take to get him out of my system.

Of course, I did have another option.

That thought only lasted half a second. As soon as it came up, my head went down, and my eyes focused on my stomach. Tentatively, a hand came up and rested against my stomach. In that moment, I knew what I had to do. I didn't have a choice. I knew that things were going to be difficult, and there were some tough conversations ahead, but I had to go through with it. I didn't know the little creature growing inside me, but I did know that I loved it unconditionally.

15.

I sat down at my desk after the kids had left for the day. I'd spent the last few days since the doctor's visit composing my letter to Nick. I still hadn't told anyone, though I planned to break in easily by telling Chrissy before I told my parents. My sisters were in town for my mom's birthday, so I was taking the train out to their place tomorrow. I figured that telling Chrissy would be a good dress rehearsal for telling my family.

I'd searched online for possible addresses for Nick, and settled on just sending it to him at work in LA. I knew it would reach him if I sent it there. The other addresses were just a guess. I folded the letter, stuffed it into the addressed envelope, and sealed it up. My cell phone rang just as I finished.

"Hi, Chrissy," I said with forced excitement. I was actually dreading telling her, because I knew she would be angry when she knew I'd kept Nick a secret from her the whole time.

"Do you have plans for tonight?" she asked.

"Actually, I was hoping you would call."

"Great!" Chrissy said, cutting me off. "Be at my place by six. Gotta run! Bye!"

She didn't wait for me to say goodbye before hanging up.

When I showed up at Chrissy's place that night, she was waiting for me outside her door. I still had Nick's letter stuffed in my purse. I had stopped at the mailbox, but couldn't work up the courage to drop it in the mail.

"You're late!" Chrissy shouted her greeting to me.

"I'm not late! You told me to be here by six. It's six o'clock." I smiled and shouted back at her.

"I've got a cab waiting. Come on! Let's go!" she said and hopped down the stairs.

"Where are we going?" I asked and followed her into the black and yellow car.

"Mom and Ned's house," she answered then threw me a look. "A few weeks ago, I broke down and told them that I was trying to change. Now, they're both doing everything they can to find me a 'decent' man to settle down with. "

I watched her make a face at their attempts.

"I simply cannot sit through another dinner with some poor sucker my mom and Ned think is perfect for me!"

I laughed then took a deep breath. "I need to talk to you about something, Chrissy."

"Sure, what's up?" she turned to face me and smiled anxiously.

"It's about that week at the beach." I stopped to take a breath. Just as I was about to start up again, Chrissy's cell phone rang.

"I have to take this," she said apologetically.

I waved her on and turned to look out the window. I didn't listen to what she was saying on her end of the conversation. I was too busy planning what I would say. Unfortunately, I didn't get the chance. Chrissy's phone conversation lasted until we got into Ned's house.

"She's always on that phone!" Ned said with a smile as he greeted me in the foyer. "It's wonderful to see you again, Cami."

"Thank you, Mr. Davis. It's good to see you, too." I smiled warmly at him. I had always liked him, but after what Nick had told me about Ned and his brother, I liked him even more. The memory of Nick telling me about Ned made me nervous about what might happen to us all when the truth came out. Would things change, or would everything remain the same?

"Cami! What a surprise! We didn't know you were coming." Chrissy's mom greeted me with a hug. I knew that she hadn't meant that statement as a snide remark. She was always happy to see me. She told me once that she felt better knowing that Chrissy had me around, to prevent her from making every stupid mistake out there.

"Chrissy kind of tricked me into coming. I thought we were just going to hang out at her place, but here we are!" I hugged her back.

"Well, if we had known you were going to be here we would have invited another young bachelor to join us for dinner. You are quite the catch, Miss Cami." Ned said and laughed loudly.

"Don't worry about me, Mr. Davis. I assure you I'm not that much of a catch."

We all laughed politely, and Chrissy finally hung up her phone.

"What's everyone laughing at?" she asked.

"Nothing," Ned said with a smile. "I'm afraid our other dinner guest is running late. He called me a few minutes ago and said for us to start without him."

We all headed to the dining room and settled in for the meal. Chrissy spent the first course being drilled with questions about how her new life was going.

"Enough about Chrissy!" Ned said with a laugh. "Let me tell you ladies about Fletch! He's nothing short of amazing, trust me. I cannot begin to tell you how excited I am to have him on my team now. He's been a godsend to Tim over the past few years, but he's all mine now."

"Sounds like maybe you should date him, Ned." Chrissy cut her eyes at me.

Ned laughed loudly, “Believe me, Chrissy, if I were a woman I would! Not only is he a genius in the office, he’s also quite handsome. When he walked in today, you should have seen the heads turning!”

Chrissy’s mom laughed.

“He’s got this whole west coast vibe that just exudes off him,” Ned added and shook his head.

“Still, a name like Fletch is pretty much a deal breaker for me.” Chrissy stuck her tongue out.

“Actually,” a familiar male voice said from behind us. “It’s Fletcher, and it’s my last name. Of course, if you’d bothered to get to know me at all at the beach, you would know that.”

Everyone but me looked up in the direction of the voice. I didn’t need to look. I knew who was speaking. I’d been hearing that voice in my head for the past five weeks. I felt the familiar tingle run through me.

Chrissy’s face flashed with recognition. She turned to look at me, but I kept looking intently at the food on my plate, and only barely raised my eyes to notice her.

“Rick, right?” Chrissy said with uncertainty.

Nick laughed, “It’s Nick.”

Chrissy shrugged him off and gave him a playful smile, “Sorry, I’ve never been that great with names.”

“Funny, I don’t remember you having any trouble with the name Todd,” Nick quipped back with a chuckle in his voice. He walked into the room further, so that he was now completely visible to Chrissy’s mom.

“Oh my!” Chrissy’s mom sighed as she took in the sight of Nick.

“Fletch! Glad you could make it!” Ned stood up and greeted his employee with enthusiasm. “I didn’t realize you already knew our Chrissy.”

Nick smiled and looked at Chrissy. “How much can someone really know Chrissy?”

Ned laughed and Chrissy glared at him.

“Where did you two meet?” Chrissy’s mom asked Nick with a grin.

"I was lucky enough to share a house with her at the beach this summer," Nick smiled at Chrissy's mom.

"So then you know Cami, too," Ned said and looked at me with a smile.

Nick slowly turned in my direction. With the smile gone, he said softly, "I know Cami."

I couldn't open my mouth to speak, so I just waved and smiled politely. He nodded in response.

"Sit down, sit down!" Ned said and pointed him towards the chair next to Chrissy.

I stared at my plate as he sat down. I couldn't look up at him. I could feel Chrissy's eyes on me, so I looked up at her. She raised an eyebrow at me in question, and I nodded slightly in response. With that one gesture, Chrissy knew about Nick and me. She gave me an apologetic smile.

"So Nick, what brings you to New York from LA?" Chrissy's mom asked, oblivious to the silent conversation her daughter and I were having.

"LA just didn't feel right for me anymore. After that week in North Carolina, I started thinking that maybe the east coast would be a good fit." Even though I couldn't see him, I could tell he was smiling as he talked.

"Well, Ned is certainly pleased to have you here in New York. He was just telling us how great you are." Chrissy's mom spoke in a giddy voice that reminded me of the way the girl in the ceramics shop had reacted to Nick.

"I'm happy to be here. I'm hoping that everyone else is just as pleased to have me here." Nick answered her. I could feel his eyes on me.

A wave of nausea washed over me. I stood up suddenly, causing Ned, and Chrissy's mom, both to flinch back in surprise.

"I'm sorry!" I said quickly. "I'm not feeling well, all of a sudden. Please excuse me." I put my hand over my mouth and ran out of the room. Locked in the hall bathroom, I steadied myself against the sink. The nausea had gone away, but the room was spinning. I took several deep breaths then splashed water on my face. The last thing I wanted was a face-to-face confrontation with Nick. His arrival had put a big kink in my plan for telling him about my situation.

My hands shook as I reached for the door and turned the knob. When the door opened, Nick was standing on the other side of it. It felt like my heart dropped to my feet and all the blood ran out after it. I clutched the doorknob for support.

"I didn't move here for you," he said as he stared at me.

I cleared my throat and looked down. "I didn't think you did."

He took a step forward, "Let me finish, please."

I nodded.

He took a deep breath. "I didn't move here for you. I moved here for purely selfish reasons. I moved here because this job is better for me and offers me more chances for promotion. I'm here because I needed to get away from LA. I'm also here because I need to be near you."

The floor started spinning and I closed my eyes to avoid seeing it.

"I know it's incredibly selfish of me to move here and expect that you're happy to see me. I know that you could quite possibly be with someone now. You could be in love with someone else. I know all of that, but I hope that's not the case. I hope that you want me around." He stopped and I looked up at him. "If you are with someone, please tell me now. I can be just friends with you, if that's my only option."

I shook my head, "I'm not with anyone."

He closed his eyes and sighed loudly. "I missed you so much, Cami. I know it sounds crazy because we barely know each other, but I did. I got back to LA and I hated every inch of that place. I hated every minute of being back there. I'm an idiot, too, because it took me almost three weeks to admit it." He took another step towards me and grabbed my hands, "Cami, I need you. I don't know how you did it, but you got to me. You made me feel things I didn't think were possible. You made me a better person, and I want to be that person all the time now. I need you." He leaned against me and rested his forehead against mine.

I breathed in his scent and felt the warmth of his skin as his hands held mine.

"Cami, say something before I go crazy," he whispered.

"I missed you too," I said softly.

He let go of me and wrapped his hands in my hair. He pulled me to him and kissed me. I felt myself melt into him as my arms wrapped around him.

He broke the kiss. With his hands still wrapped up in my hair, he smiled and looked into my eyes. "I have something for you."

I swallowed hard, "I have something too."

He smiled and stood up. He pulled away from me and reached into his pocket for something. "I looked everywhere for the right one, but couldn't find it. I finally just broke down and had one of the guys in graphic design draw it for me. I took the drawing to the jeweler and had it made. Do you like it?" he asked with a voice full of hope, as he held the diamond ring out for me.

"What?" I asked in disbelief.

"Right!" he said with a smile and shake of his head. He knelt down in front of me and held the ring out to me. "Cami, I know we haven't known each other for that long, but I know that if I love you this much and I barely know you, then I can't fathom how much I'm going to love you in thirty years. You're it, Cami. I want to spend the rest of my life trying to keep you from tripping on things and falling down. I want you, and I want you forever. Please marry me and put me out of my misery!"

"What the hell is going on here?" Chrissy said loudly from the hall.

Nick put his other hand up to silence Chrissy. He was still looking intently at me, though the smile was gone. "Cami, will you marry me?"

"I need to tell you something first," I said with a dry mouth.

He grabbed my hand. "Whatever it is, Cami, I'm sure it can wait." He smiled nervously, "I'm kind of hanging here, Cami."

Before I could hesitate or stop myself, I spit out what I needed to say. "I'm pregnant."

Suddenly, the house seemed to go silent. It was the first time I'd said the phrase aloud and it felt strange, but somehow made it all real.

"What!" Chrissy shouted and started walking towards me. Her mom reached out and stopped her before she could get closer to me.

"This is between them, honey. We should let them handle it." She said as she pulled her daughter back down the hall.

I could hear Chrissy's incredulous voice, even though she couldn't be seen. "I'm her best friend. How could she not tell me that?"

"Are you sure?" Nick asked nervously.

I nodded, "I took a test at home then went to the doctor the other day."

He was still looking at me with a nervous look. "It's mine?"

I nodded, "Yes, and I'm sure about that too."

His eyes closed but he didn't move from his proposal position. I stared at the ring he was holding out for me. It was exactly what I'd described to the waitress our second day at the beach. It was platinum with a round diamond placed in the center around a circle of diamonds. The whole thing was set in a band with diamonds set inside it. My eyes started to tear up as I looked at it.

"I'm still waiting for your answer," he said softly.

I'd been too busy staring at the ring to realize that he was looking at me.

My voice broke as I asked, "Are you sure?"

He grabbed my hand and slipped the ring on my finger, "Are you kidding me? Do you honestly think I'm not going to be there for you and our baby?"

"You don't have to marry me just because of the baby. I don't want you there just because you feel obligated to be there." I could feel hot tears streaming down my face.

He smiled, "I asked you before I knew, remember?"

"I know, but everything is different now."

He stood up and held me against his chest. "You're right. Everything is different." He rubbed my back. "It's better now."

I sighed and leaned into him.

He started laughing.

I leaned away and looked up at him. "What's so funny?"

He smiled at me, "We should have known this was going to happen. You are the most accident prone person I've ever met."

I smiled, "I've never had this kind of accident before."

He leaned down and kissed me on the lips. "This was no accident, Cami. This was meant to be. I love you."

"I love you too."

"Can I touch your bump?" he said sweetly.

I blushed, "It's not really a bump so much as a blip." Carefully, I pulled my shirt up and lowered the waistband of my skirt.

He gently placed his hand on my belly. He smiled and stared at it, "That's our baby." He leaned down and kissed where his hand had been. "I'm going to be a dad."

"I'm sorry I was so cold the last time we talked." I ran my fingers through his hair as he kissed my belly again. "I didn't understand why I was feeling the way I was, and I thought that walking away would make it all better."

"Boy were you wrong, huh?" Nick said with a grin and stood up. "Don't worry about it. I get it. I will accept your apology on one condition."

"What's that?" I asked nervously.

"Accept mine for being an ass and running away," he grabbed my hand and brought it up to his lips. He kissed my hand softly and waited for my response.

"I accept."

He smiled then held my hand up and pointed at my ring. "Do you like it?"

I smiled and nodded.

"I had an inkling that you would," he kissed my hand again. "You never said yes, by the way."

"Yes, of course it's a yes!" I laughed.

He pulled me in for a hug and I hugged him back.

"We're insane, you know that!" I laughed against him.

He laughed, "I wouldn't want it any other way." He kissed me gently then pulled my arms from around his shoulders. "Come on, let's go to our place. I found this amazing apartment that I think you're going to love. I'll give you a tour in the morning. Right now, we've got some catching up to do." He winked at me, grabbed my hand, and started pulling me towards the door.

"Didn't I tell you that guy was amazing?" Ned said in awe as we walked past him, Chrissy, and her mom. "He just swooped in here and got her. Amazing!"

"You better call me! You've got some explaining to do!" Chrissy shouted after me as we walked past.

I laughed and gripped Nick's hand tighter.

"Do you want to go get some stuff from your place, or can that wait until tomorrow?" Nick asked when we were outside.

Suddenly remembering my plans for the next day, my face went red.

"What?"

"Let's go now, because I've got somewhere to be tomorrow."

He looked intently at me, "Where do you have to be?"

"My parents' house," I said hesitantly. "It's my mom's birthday and both my sisters are in town." Telling my parents I was pregnant should have been challenging enough, but telling them that I was pregnant and engaged to a man that I'd only known for five days was probably going to be even tougher.

Nick's face went white. "How do they feel about this?" he pointed to my belly when he asked.

I grimaced, "They don't know."

He sighed loudly, "Oh good! Well, when I meet them tomorrow, we can tell them together."

I shook my head. "I don't think we should tell them yet."

"Why not?"

"I think me showing up with you and announcing that we're engaged is probably shocking enough. Let's take this one step at a time with my family, shall we?" I stepped out to hail a cab. In typical Cami fashion, I misjudged the curb and started to tumble to the ground. Nick caught me before I hit the ground.

"Do you think that for my own peace of mind, and sanity, that you could at least try not to have any accidents while you're carrying my child?" he said as he pulled me back up to safety.

Unfortunately, the quick movements and the adrenaline mixed to form a powerful wave of nausea. I pushed away from him, ran to the trashcan next to the lamppost and leaned over it just in time.

"That's just gross," I heard Nick say behind me. In a second, I felt his hands rubbing against my back. "Are you okay?"

I nodded slowly, "That's the first time I've actually thrown up. I get nauseous all the time, but I've never actually thrown up."

He chuckled, "Well, I'm glad I could be here to experience that with you. Can I get you something?"

"No, I'm okay. I have water, mouthwash, and gum in my purse." I stood up and started digging through my purse to retrieve what I needed. As I dug, the letter I'd written, but never sent, fell out and onto the ground. Nick bent to pick it up.

"You dropped this," he said and handed it back to me. He must have spotted his name, because he pulled it back and looked at it. "Did you write this to me?"

I was swishing mouthwash in my mouth, so I nodded instead of answering.

"Is this how you were going to tell me?" he asked with a grin.

I spit the mouthwash into the trashcan. "Yes, I didn't think I could handle it in person or over the phone."

He smiled, "I think you did pretty well."

I smiled back at him, "Well to be fair, I was offered a ring first. The ring kind of softened the blow against rejection."

He opened the letter and began reading. I watched him as he read the words I'd spent days poring over. It had taken me forever to get it out exactly the way I wanted it, and even then, it still felt like it wasn't enough. I realized that telling him to his face was the best way. That's probably why the letter never felt right.

When he was done, he folded the letter back up and put it in his pocket. "You do know that if I had gotten this letter I would have been on the next flight out here, right?"

I smiled, "I was always hoping for that."

"I love you," he said and pulled me into his chest again.

A cab pulled up just as he finished speaking. We slid in and I gave the driver my address. Nick grabbed my hand and pulled me closer to him.

"Are you sure we need to go to your place tonight? We could just go to our place and I could buy you all new things."

I laughed and rested my head on his shoulder. "I don't have that much stuff. I had to downsize when I moved out of Jack's place. My room is kind of small."

"So you're saying I don't need to rent a truck to move you in?" he laughed and kissed me on the top of the head.

I smiled, "Are you even moved in yet?"

He laughed, "I have some furniture." He leaned down and whispered into my ear, "I have a bed."

I turned and gave him a severe look, "When you said we had some catching up to do, I didn't realize you only meant in the bedroom."

He grinned, "Don't be ridiculous! I fully intend on us christening every room in the apartment."

When we pulled up to my apartment, Nick paid the driver to wait for us and helped me out of the cab. I opened the door and walked in hesitantly, not sure who might be hanging around to meet us. To my relief, the place seemed to be deserted. Nick followed me up the stairs to my bedroom. With one last look down the hall, I closed the door behind us. Finally alone, a sudden awkward feeling swept over me. Seeing Nick standing in my room seemed like a dream, but one of those weird ones where you're not sure what's going on.

"So this is where you've been living?" he asked and surveyed the space.

"This is my room. I also pay to use other parts of the house." I looked around, hoping that I didn't have anything embarrassing lying around.

His eyes widened, "I'm pretty sure the back room at Mitch's shop is bigger than this."

I laughed nervously, "It served its purpose."

He clapped his hands together and looked around, "Okay! What are we grabbing for now? We can always come back tomorrow or Sunday for the rest of your stuff."

I went to the closet to retrieve my suitcase. It was stored on the top shelf and I stretched to reach it. Nick appeared behind me and reached over me to grab it.

"Knowing you, a bowling ball would have come from nowhere and whacked you on the head." He smirked at me as he handed the suitcase over to me.

I shook my head and smiled. "Will you grab my tennis shoes and loafers out of the closet?"

"Whatever you'd like, dear," he said dreamily and went back to the closet.

I grabbed some clothes from the dresser and started placing them in the suitcase.

"So, uh, are you planning on bringing that French maid costume with you tonight, or is that something you're saving for when we're actually married?" Nick chuckled as he rifled through the clothes in my closet.

I laughed, "I don't have that anymore. Besides, why would you want me to wear a sexy outfit that another man bought for me?"

Nick wrapped his arms around my waist, "I wouldn't. I'll buy you a new one." He kissed my neck and leaned against me.

I looked down at his arms around my waist. "Enjoy this now, because soon you may not be able to fit your arms around me."

He put his hands on my stomach, "I can't wait!"

"Something tells me that if it was your chiseled physique that was about to be ruined, you wouldn't be quite so excited."

He laughed, "First of all, I don't have a chiseled physique. I take care of myself, but I'm not some ridiculous gym freak." He put his hands on my shoulders and turned me around to face him. "Secondly, I'm sure that you will be the most beautiful pregnant woman in the world. You're already adjusting well."

"What?" I looked down at my stomach. "I'm not even showing."

He grinned, "No you're not showing there," he pointed to my stomach. "However, up here," he pointed at my breasts, "I can definitely tell a difference."

My mouth flew open.

He smiled widely, "Don't be offended! I like them. Of course, I liked them before. However, I have to admit, the extra oomph looks good on you."

I grinned, "They are never going to be tits, Nick."

A grin broke across his face, "I have missed you so much!"

I turned back around and closed my suitcase.

"Okay, I'm packed and ready to go. Will you carry my bag?"

"I will on one condition," he said and reached around me to grab it.

"What?"

"Say, 'Take me home and put me to bed, baby!' If you say that I'll take your bag for you." He leaned closer to me and flashed a cheesy grin.

"I'm not saying that. It's stupid, and I'll feel ridiculous saying it." I argued with a grin.

"Fine," he stood up and backed away. "If you don't say it then you can carry your own bag."

"Fine," I said with a shrug. "I'll carry it myself, and try my best not to trip down the stairs as I do." I lifted the suitcase off the bed and stumbled back dramatically from the weight of it.

"Give it to me!" Nick said and grabbed the case from me. "Is this what I have to look forward to for the rest of my life? You manipulating me into doing things?"

I smiled, "Isn't that what marriage is supposed to be?" I tweaked his nose and led the way out of the room.

I stopped at the bathroom to brush my teeth before we left. Nick followed behind me as we walked down the hall and down the stairs. When we reached the bottom, I caught a glimpse of Henrietta sitting in the living room. She spotted me, raised an eyebrow, and nodded in Nick's direction. I smiled back at her. Nick stepped ahead of me and opened the door. While his back was to me, I lifted my hand to show off my ring to Hen. A huge grin broke across her face and she winked at me.

"What was that all about?" Nick asked when we were back in the cab.

"What?"

"The exchange you just had with that old lady? What was that all about?" he had a grin on his face, so I knew he had seen everything.

I smiled in response, "Henrietta called me out for my sullen behavior after returning from the beach. I told her about you, and I guess she figured that you were you."

"What did you tell her about me?" he wiggled his eyebrows at me playfully.

"Just the facts," I said seriously. "I didn't give her any details, and I certainly didn't tell her that we were careless in our activities and therefore ended up like this." I pointed to my stomach to indicate the baby.

He laughed, "I've been meaning to ask you something about that. Aren't you on the pill?"

I blushed a little, "I was, or I was supposed to be. I don't take a pill, I wear a patch, and I took it off before we went to the beach because I didn't want to get a weird tan line."

He grinned, "So, we're having a baby because you're vain and didn't want to have a tan line."

My mouth flew open in mock horror, "Or," I said loudly, "We're having a baby because you didn't put a condom on!"

"Funny, I don't remember you stopping me and reminding me to do that," he grinned. "In fact, I believe at one point you actually said..."

I cut him off by putting my hand over his mouth, "Okay, you can stop there!" My face felt like it was on fire. I could see the cab driver smiling as he watched us from the rearview mirror. "It's entirely my fault. Let's just acknowledge it and move on. I don't think we need to keep bringing it up, especially in front of strangers."

He pulled my hand from his mouth and held it in his own. He leaned down and kissed me softly on the lips. "I agree. Besides, it's not like things would be different if you weren't pregnant. I still would have moved here, and you still would have been happy to see me."

"True, though I'm curious to know what your plan was." I snuggled against him as he wrapped his arm around my shoulders.

"What do you mean?"

"You showed up at Ned's with this ring, so were you expecting me to be there?" I played with the ring as I asked.

"No, but I knew that Chrissy would be. I was hoping to pry your information out of her and then rush off to get you. I figured once I showed her the ring, she'd know I was serious and help me out." He grabbed my hand and held it up to look at the ring. "Of course, I also assumed that you had told her about what happened between us, but obviously that didn't happen."

I shook my head.

He pressed his lips against my ear and whispered, "I'm going to act like I'm not worried that you didn't tell your best friend about us, because I don't want to start a fight or argument. I'd just really like to get you home and show you how much I missed you."

I shuddered as his breath ruffled my hair. "I didn't tell her because I didn't think she would understand." I defended myself for the decision not to tell Chrissy. She didn't understand relationships in the real world, though her recent experience with Mr. Money might have changed that. Explaining to Chrissy how I felt about Nick, after only knowing him for five days would be like trying to explain taxes to a child. It would be pointless. "I was also embarrassed that I'd let myself fall in love with you."

He put a hand under my chin and turned my face towards him. "Why were you embarrassed?"

"I hook up one time and end up pregnant and in love with the guy. That's not reason enough to be embarrassed?" I lowered my eyes so that I didn't have to look at him.

He leaned down and kissed me softly on the lips. "We didn't hook up, remember? We just had a very short relationship that moved at a fast pace."

I smiled at him.

The cab pulled over and stopped.

"We're home," Nick said with a smile.

16.

"Nick, wake up." I tapped him on the chest. "I need to talk to you."

He stirred and groaned. "What?"

After our bodies had cooled and our breathing had returned to normal from our last encounter, I'd stayed awake with my head resting on Nick's chest. My head was full of questions and worries.

"What if we can't do it?" I asked on the verge of tears. Lying in the dark next to him had my mind racing.

"Cami, we just did it like three times," Nick grinned but kept his eyes closed.

"I'm not talking about sex, Nick. I'm talking about us."

He sighed and sat up. "What about us?"

"Are we rushing into this? Are we making a mistake? How do you know that we're doing the right thing?"

Nick put his hands on either side of my face and looked directly at me. "Cami, relax." He watched me and waited until I settled a little. "Do you trust me?"

He'd said that to me on the first day at the beach, and again on the day of our bike ride. Even when I barely knew him, I knew I could trust him. He was still holding onto my face and I reached up and put my hands over his. I nodded and he smiled at me.

"And you love me, right?" he asked with a grin.

I nodded and grinned back.

He took a deep breath, "I don't know how to put it into words. I just know that this is right. I know that we're meant to be with each other. It has nothing to do with the baby, and everything to do with who we are for each other. I feel safe with you. That's something I've never felt with anyone, ever."

"I feel safe with you, too."

He smiled, "You should, I've already saved your life a few times."

I rolled my eyes and pushed him on the shoulder. He dropped his hands from my face and pushed me back against the bed. He crawled up my body until his face was just inches above mine. I wrapped my arms around him and wiggled underneath him.

"I have a confession to make," he said and dipped his head down to kiss me softly on the lips.

"What?"

He rested his forehead against mine and looked me in the eyes, "I'm a little scared, too. I don't know how to be a good husband or a good father."

"You know what not to do," I said quietly.

He closed his eyes and shook his head slightly. "I promise to never be like my dad."

I kissed him on the lips, "You would never be like that."

He shook his head again then opened his eyes. "I never thought this would happen to me."

"Getting a girl knocked up?" I laughed. "Really? Fifteen girls and not one slip-up? I find that hard to believe."

"Nope, not one," he smiled and shifted his weight onto his elbows, "and it's sixteen, now."

My body froze, "Sixteen?" I tried to wiggle out from under him. "Sixteen? Did you sleep with someone when you got back to LA?"

"Cami," he grabbed me by the arm and pulled me back to him, "I was at fifteen and you were at three. Now, I'm at sixteen and you're at four. Think about it."

I did the math in my head and looked away embarrassed, "Oh, sorry."

He laughed, "Don't be. It was nice to see you be the jealous one this time. Well, jealous again, actually."

"Again? When was I ever jealous over you? You were the one who came running out of the water because I was playing volleyball with someone else." I laughed and teased him.

He smiled, "Okay, I'm going to tell you again, that Mike guy was all hands! He didn't need to be touching you that much just to show you how to serve a volleyball."

"Well, you got more than a handful later that night, didn't you?"

"I sure did." He reached down and pulled my legs up around his hips, "Don't change the subject on me, though. Admit it. You were jealous when you saw me playing pool with those girls on the first night."

"Oh! The beach blanket bimbos. No, I wasn't. I barely knew you then." I shrugged nonchalantly.

"I was thinking about you the whole night." He pushed his hips into mine causing a small moan to escape my lips at the contact. "All I could think about was how sexy you looked on the surfboard that day."

"Was that before or after I had my epic run?" I laughed.

He laughed too, "It was when you were hanging off my board coughing up half the Atlantic."

"I'm sure that was a very sexy scene. I bet you couldn't wait to get me back to the house and tear my clothes off after that."

"Actually," he said as leaned down and kissed me, making me forget all about the conversation.

When I woke up the next morning, Nick was still lying next to me. I blinked the sleep out of my eyes and said gruffly, "Good morning."

He smiled at me, "This is my new favorite way to wake up."

I smiled, "Naked and sticky?"

He smiled back, "No, next to you." He scooted closer to me. "Although, waking up next to you naked and sticky is pretty damn good, too." He pulled me into him and kissed me on the nose.

"You know, if you hadn't snuck out that first morning then you would have known how great it could be."

"I was getting you coffee. I thought I was doing something nice for you. How was I supposed to know that you were going to wake up, or that Chrissy was going to come in, before I could come back?"

"I know," I said sweetly at him. "I'm just teasing you."

"Would you like some coffee now?" he asked with a smile.

"Unfortunately, I'll have to say no. Coffee is one of those things that I think I'm going to have to give up for a few months." I put my hand on my belly and gave him a pitiful look.

A pained expression grew on his face. "I never asked you this, but the baby is healthy, right?"

"I guess so. The doctor didn't really do much on that first visit. She said that at my next appointment she'd do an ultrasound to check that everything was fine."

"When is that appointment? I'd like to go, if that's alright with you?" he said softly. "I don't want to miss anything, if I can help it."

I smiled at him, "I'd like that."

"You don't know yet what you're having, do you?"

"No, it will be a few more weeks before that can be determined. But," I hesitated before I finished. "I kind of don't want to know." I gave him a cautious look.

"Why not?" He stared at me quizzically. "Don't you want to know what kind of clothes to buy and what color to paint the nursery?"

"It's not that," I shrugged. "I just think it would be great to not know. I think it might be nice not to have any expectations about what he or she might look like, or be like. I don't want our child to feel like there's a mold that they need to fit into."

He smiled at me. "I like that. I'm with you on this one. Let's not find out. What do you say we spend all day tomorrow shopping for nursery stuff?"

"That sounds tiring and expensive."

"Don't worry about the money," he said with a smile. "How do you feel about a beach theme for the nursery?"

I laughed, "I can't imagine why you'd think of that?"

He pulled himself up and out of bed. "I'm taking a shower, would you care to join me?" He winked at me seductively.

I sat up slowly and laughed, "No, thank you. I think I've had enough for a while. I'll just wait my turn."

Nick leaned down, kissed the top of my head, and said, "I'll save some hot water for you."

When he was gone, I pulled some clothes on and snuck out of the room. When we'd arrived at the apartment last night, we were both too distracted to think about anything but getting to the bedroom. Now, I was curious what the rest of the place looked like. I crept down the hall and into the front of the apartment. He didn't have much furniture but what he had looked nice. Actually, it looked expensive and not at all baby-proofed. The coffee table had sharp pointy edges, and the couch was covered in a non-washable fabric. Clearly we'd need to shop for more than just baby furniture.

I headed back down the hall to the other bedroom, the nursery. It was much smaller than the master bedroom, but still bigger than the one Tori and I had shared growing up. There was a window with a view of the garden, and a small closet on the opposite wall. I tried to picture what the room would look like filled with all the assorted baby needs.

"So, what do you think?" Nick said from the doorway. "Did I do okay picking out a place?"

I nodded, but didn't turn around.

"I was thinking that we could hire someone to come in and paint a beach scene on this wall," he came up behind me and wrapped his arms around my waist. He pointed at the wall to our left. "Maybe put the crib over there," he said and pointed to the opposite wall.

I leaned back into his chest, "That sounds nice."

"Maybe we could put a hammock in that corner," he said and rested his chin on my shoulder. "That way we could both sit in it and rock the baby to sleep." He started swaying as he held me by the waist.

I nodded and rested my head against his.

"What time are we expected at your parents?" he asked quietly.

A soft laugh escaped, "I'm expected at two. They're never going to be expecting you."

"Why not? You didn't tell them about me either?" he said teasingly.

"Oh no, they know about you. I told you Allison wouldn't be able to keep her mouth shut about that phone call."

He laughed, "Did I get you in trouble?"

"No, but I had to explain to my mom that you lived in LA and that there was no chance that we'd ever see each other again." I turned sideways to look at him. He was grinning from ear to ear. "What?" I asked at his Cheshire grin.

"Liar," he said through the grin.

"I am not! I didn't think I would ever see you again. I hoped that I would, but a girl can't sit around and hope for something to happen."

"So did you tell her that I was your number four?" he kissed my cheek playfully.

"No! I don't talk to my mom about that kind of thing. She'd probably be mortified if she knew." I shuddered at the thought of having to tell my mom I'd gotten pregnant from a one-night stand. It was the moment I'd dreaded from the second I'd seen the results on that stick. Telling Nick was scary, but telling my mom was horrifying. I turned around and kissed him on the lips.

"What was that for? I thought you'd had enough?" he wrapped me up in his arms again.

I smiled, "That was for moving to New York and coming to me. Thank you for saving me from having the awkward and mortifying conversation with my parents about all this."

He kissed me again. When he pulled away, a sudden flash of worry crossed his face. "Do you think they'll like me?"

"Are you kidding me? Of course they'll like you."

"How do you know?" he asked in a worried tone.

"Because I love you," I said and wrapped my arms around him for a hug. "If I love you, and I'm happy, that's all that will matter to them."

17.

Our cab pulled up outside my parents' house at exactly two o'clock. We'd taken the train out of the city, and caught a cab to the house. Nick paid the driver and we got out. He grabbed my hand as the cab drove away.

"Ready?" he asked in an annoyingly confident tone.

"No," I answered. "Remember, we're not telling them about the baby. Let them think we didn't know about it until afterwards, okay?"

"Relax! It's going to be fine." He pulled my hand up and kissed it.

We walked up the driveway and onto the porch. He reached for the door, but I stopped him.

"Wait," I said softly. "You don't have to tell them about your family, if you don't want to. I'll just change the subject when it comes up, okay?"

Nick cupped my face in his hands, leaned down and whispered against my lips, "You are my family now."

The minute his lips met mine, I relaxed.

"Mom!" Tori's voice rang out loudly from the other side of the window. "Cami's making out with some guy on the front porch!"

Nick and I both laughed silently.

"Oh God! It's not Jack is it? She's not back with him, is she?" Allison's voice shouted back.

"Girls! Stop that nonsense! I don't believe for one second that your sister is making out with some guy on the front porch!" My mom screamed at my sisters.

"She is so! Come look and see for yourself!" Tori shouted defensively.

The sound of footsteps coming towards the front of the house followed, as my mom shouted, "It isn't Jack is it? I thought they'd broken up for good?"

"I'm so sorry," I whispered to Nick, whose face was still just inches from mine.

"I'm just glad I'm not Jack," he whispered back.

"Oh my! Who is that?" my mom said loudly.

"I don't know, but he's way too hot for her!" Allison said.

"We can hear you, you know?" I turned and shouted at the three faces pressed against the window. "We can see you, too!" I stepped away from Nick. He grabbed my hand and held it tight, though whether it was for my benefit or his I wasn't sure.

All three of them laughed and scurried from the window. Within seconds, the door flew open and my mom greeted us.

"Hello, Camille," she said cheerfully, "Who is your friend?"

"Hi, mom," I said and stepped into the house, dragging Nick behind me. "Happy birthday!" I said and handed her the small wrapped present I'd bought for her last week.

"Wait. Is the gift the box or the boy?" Allison said snidely.

Tori giggled and put her hand to her mouth.

"It's the box," I said dryly and turned to my sisters. "Hi Allison. Hi Tori."

"Hi Cami!" Tori said sweetly and waved.

"You've gotten fat," Allison said maliciously.

"I have not!" I said defensively. "What is your problem?"

She cocked an eyebrow at me then looked at Nick, "I'm the mean one, don't you remember?"

"Hello again, Allison," Nick said with a smile.

My mom and Tori both turned with puzzled expressions to look at Nick then back at Allison.

"How do you know Allison?" my mom finally asked.

Nick smiled sweetly at her, "I don't. I did talk to her on the phone once, though."

My mom looked at Allison again then it clicked. Her mouth flew open in recognition. "You're Nick from the beach?"

"Yes, I am." Nick dropped my hand and stepped forward to greet my mom. "Nick Fletcher. It's a pleasure to meet you, Mrs. Harris."

My mom smiled and blushed, "Please, call me Charlotte." She pulled him in for a hug. "I thought you lived in LA?"

Nick hugged my mom then stepped back before answering. "I did, but I live in New York now."

"What's all the commotion about in here?" my dad's voice reached the room before he did. "I thought I heard something about Cami and making out!" He stopped when he spotted Nick standing in the living room next to me. "Who is this?"

"This is Nick, from the beach," my mom said in that not-so-subtly cryptic way she does when she's trying to tell my dad something without actually saying it.

My dad looked at her then at me. "I thought he lived in LA?"

"I did, sir. But I moved to New York and I live here now." Nick's voice sounded less confident than it had before.

"Well, now, you're not the first man to move to New York because of a girl," my dad chuckled and stepped forward with his hand out towards Nick.

"He didn't move to New York for a girl, dad. He moved here for work," I said as I pulled my jacket off.

"Actually, I did move here for the girl. The job was just an excuse." Nick grabbed my dad's hand and shook it. "Nick Fletcher, sir, it's a pleasure to meet you."

I glanced over and caught my mom making eyes at Tori.

"Nice to meet you Nick," my dad shook Nick's hand. "Tell me, do you like sports?"

"Yes sir, I do."

I watched as Nick's shoulders relaxed. The two men drifted off to one side of the room and I watched them closely, curious to see not only how my dad would react to Nick, but also how Nick would take to my dad. I was so busy watching the men that I didn't notice Allison staring at me.

"What's that?" she said, pulling me out of my head.

I turned to her and followed her gaze. She could have been staring at my belly, or she could have been looking at something behind me.

"What?" I said self-consciously.

She pointed at my midsection, "That!"

"Allison! Where are your manners? Do not point at people!" my mom scolded my sister.

Allison rolled her eyes, "Her finger? What's on her finger?"

Everyone turned to look at me. I hadn't realized that I was playing with the ring as I stood in the living room.

"Surprise! We're engaged!" I said nervously. Despite the nerves about announcing the engagement so quickly, I was happy that Allison hadn't spotted the tiny bump I was hiding under a loose shirt.

My mom gasped loudly and clutched her chest, "Oh my word! What a birthday gift!" She rushed across the room and wrapped me up into a bear hug. "I'm so happy for you!"

I looked across the room at Nick, and then at my dad.

"If I have your permission, of course, sir," Nick said nervously as he looked at my dad.

Everyone in the room turned to watch my dad's reaction. My mom pulled away from me and walked over to him.

With a grin, my dad said, "Of course you have my permission! In fact, I've got two more, if you've got a couple of brothers or friends who are looking to get married."

My mom slapped him playfully on the arm, "Nathan, stop it! Don't talk about your daughters like they're pigs going to slaughter."

"Let me see the ring!" Tori grabbed my hand and inspected the ring I was wearing. "Wow! It's so beautiful!"

"Nick designed it," I said softly as my sister admired the diamond on my finger.

"Nice work, Nick. When I find the right guy, I'll be sure to send him your way when he starts his ring shopping." Tori flashed him a perfect smile then turned back to admire his handiwork.

"I can't really take credit for it. Cami described it and I just tried my best to remember what she said." Nick flashed me a smile and winked at me.

"Well, I can't take it anymore! I have to give you another hug," my mom said and wrapped her arms around Nick in a bear hug like the one she'd trapped me in. Nick laughed and squeezed her back.

"I'll get the wine!" Allison announced and left the room.

Instead of waiting for her in the living room, we all headed to the family dinner table and took our seats. My dad insisted that Nick sit next to him so that they could continue their conversation on sports. I sat on the other side of him. The food was already out and waiting for us.

Allison brought the wine and glasses while Tori brought out another place setting for Nick. We filled our plates and talked casually for a few minutes.

"I have to say, Cami, I'm impressed. You've definitely upgraded," Allison smirked at me as she sat and handed me a glass of wine.

"I'll say!" Tori added with a giggle as she took a glass of wine from Allison.

I blushed and avoided Nick's gaze, "I'm glad the two of you find him cuter than Jack, since you obviously couldn't stand him."

Both sisters laughed.

"Oh, honey, there's nothing cute about that man sitting next to you," my mom chimed in as she lifted her glass of wine to her mouth. "That man is sex in shoes! I can't blame you one bit for being smitten with him, or for wanting to get him naked and do bad things to him."

"Mom!" I shouted.

Both sisters laughed again.

"What? I can't appreciate what a fine looking man you've snagged for yourself?" my mom winked at Nick and took a big sip of her wine.

"You're not so bad yourself, Charlotte. I can see where your daughters get their looks," Nick said back with a grin and a wink.

"Do not encourage her!" I scolded Nick playfully. "Dad, are you hearing this?"

My dad laughed, "I'm just so happy there's finally going to be another man in this family, I could really care less how much your mother and sisters lust after him."

"Okay, that's enough! I'm not going to sit here and let you objectify him." I gave my sisters a stern warning look, but they kept giggling. I turned to my mom, "No more comments like that! They are inappropriate, and they weird me out! Also, you can't hug him anymore."

My mom giggled like my sisters but put her hands up in defeat.

I turned to my sisters, "As for you two," I pointed at them, "don't even start with the comments! I have dirt on both of you that could seriously jeopardize any future relationships with men. Don't make me use it!"

Both girls stopped laughing and put their hands up.

I didn't bother to look over at Nick to see what his reaction was. I could tell he was smiling. I picked up my fork and started eating my food. I was hoping that the conversation would turn to another topic, one that didn't revolve around Nick or me. Everyone started to eat and the table was silent as the meal continued.

Unfortunately, Allison wasn't quite ready to move on. After only a few minutes of blissful silence, she spoke up.

"So, I'm a little curious about something." She started in a fake concerned voice. "I talked to you two weeks ago, and you didn't mention a thing about Nick. Mom said she talked to you last week and you told her you weren't seeing anyone. Exactly how long have the two of you been together?"

I didn't look up, I just pushed the food around on my plate and answered dryly, "Well, since Nick was living in LA at the time, technically I wasn't *seeing* anyone."

"Smartass," Allison said under her breath.

"I'm curious about that too," Tori chimed in. "How long have the two of you been together?"

I glanced over at Nick then looked back down at my plate.

Nick cleared his throat and answered, "Until yesterday, we hadn't seen each other since the beach."

Once again, everyone at the table froze.

Allison was the first to break the silence, "Had you talked to each other since the beach? Was this a long distance thing?"

I shook my head.

She put her fork down, leaned on her elbows, and looked intently at me, "Let me get this straight, you two knew each other for a week this summer, haven't seen each other since, and now you're getting married?"

"I know it seems," I paused, looking for the right words to describe everything, but Nick jumped in and saved me.

"It seems crazy, we know. I've been trying for the past twenty-four hours to figure out how to put this into words, and the best I can come up with is that I just know she's the right one for me." Nick looked over at me and smiled. "I just know that we're meant to be together, it's just not something that I can describe to someone else. I never had all of this as a child," he pointed around the table at my family, "but, when I met Cami I felt like I had come home. I felt like she was what I'd been missing my whole life. I don't need to spend the next six months taking her on dates, when I know now what I want. I want to spend the rest of my life with her, and for some insane reason, she wants me too."

I looked up at him and he was smiling at me. Without caring who was around, he bent his head down and kissed me gently on the lips.

I heard my mom sigh loudly.

"Wow," Tori said softly from across the table. "That was amazing."

"I love you," Nick whispered in my ear before pulling away.

"That was pretty amazing," my dad added then cleared his throat.

"Do you think you could do that whole speech again," Tori asked with a dreamy look at Nick, "Only this time with your shirt off?"

Everyone, including me, laughed and the tension in the air released. Under the table, I grabbed Nick's hand and squeezed it. He leaned down and gave me another kiss, but this time on the cheek.

"Oh, shit!" my dad said suddenly, causing everyone to stop their laughing.

"What?" my mom asked, looking around for some cause to his outburst.

"I just realized that if Cami's getting married then you're going to make me watch even more episodes of that damn wedding dress show!" He said then threw himself back against his chair in defeat.

My mom's face lit up. "Yes! A wedding to plan! So, what are you two thinking? A summer wedding, I assume."

I grimaced and looked over at Nick, "We're thinking something a little sooner than that, mom."

"Oh," she said with a look of surprise. "Spring?"

"Sooner than that, too," I forced a smile to my face.

"It's going to be a tight fit, but I suppose we could pull off a winter wedding." My mom seemed to be lost in her head as she spoke.

"Actually, mom, we were thinking more like next week." I drew the words out hesitantly.

"Next week!" my mom shouted incredulously.

"What?" Tori dropped her fork onto her plate, causing a loud crash to echo through the house. "You're getting married next week?"

I blushed, "I don't really see the need for a big fancy wedding. Sorry," I added with a shrug.

"I don't think there's anything wrong with that, at all," my dad said matter-of-factly and put another bite of food into his mouth. With cheeks full of food, he flashed a grin at me.

"You're just happy that you won't have to pay for anything!" Allison said as she looked at our dad.

"Is that why you're planning to elope? Are you worried about the money?" my mom put a hand on my arm. "Nathan, this is just like Columbia. She got herself so worked up about the cost that she nearly gave herself an ulcer. Who knows what might have happened if she hadn't found that grant."

My dad sighed, "Cami, if this is about the cost then you know we would be happy to pay for whatever kind of wedding you want."

"I know that, dad." I smiled at him and turned to my mom. "This isn't about the money, I promise. I just don't see the need for a fancy ceremony when we can just go down to the courthouse one day next week and make it official."

"What about you Nick? Do you want a wedding?" Tori asked him from across the table.

"Yeah, you can't start off letting her bully you into everything. You'll never be able to think for yourself, if you do!" Allison added with a smirk.

"I don't really care either way. As long as it all ends with us married, I'll go with what she wants." He gave my hand a squeeze under table. "Also, for the record, I would be happy to foot the bill for a big fancy wedding if that's what she wanted."

My dad nodded appreciatively at him.

"Why so soon though?" my mom asked curiously.

My whole body tensed, but I played it off with a shrug. "Isn't the whole point of an engagement to give you time to plan the wedding? If there isn't going to be a wedding, why put it off?"

"Yeah, mom," Allison said with a snort, "It's not like she's knocked up or something. It's Saint Cami we're talking about!"

Reflexively, my hand went to my belly. Thankfully, the action was covered by the table. However, something must have shown on my face, or something on Nick's face gave it away, because Allison cocked an eyebrow at me. It only took her a second to figure it out. A small grin formed on her lips.

"You are, aren't you?" she said quietly.

"What?" I tried to play it off.

"I knew it!" she shouted. "I thought something was up when you walked in. Your boobs are bigger than usual and you always gain weight in your boobs first, you haven't touched your wine, and you're marrying some guy you barely know. What are you, five, six weeks along?"

I didn't answer her. Instead, I just stared at her.

"What is she saying?" my mom asked slowly.

"I'm saying that sweet innocent Cami hooked up with sexy pants here when she was at the beach. Had you done it yet when you called me, or was talking to me some kind of weird foreplay for you two?" Allison was smirking at me, obviously enjoying her recent epiphany.

"We didn't hook up. We had a short relationship that moved at a very fast pace." Nick said confidently. Next, he turned to my dad, "If it helps, sir, I did ask her to marry me before I knew."

"Hold on!" my mom shouted before my dad could say a word.

All heads turned to her.

"Are you saying that what Allison said is true? Are you getting married so soon because you're pregnant?" she held my gaze.

"No, we're getting married so soon because that's what we want." I took a deep breath then added, "But, I am pregnant."

"Ha!" Allison shouted triumphantly.

I didn't look away from my mom. I wasn't sure what her reaction was going to be, so I didn't want to miss it. She reached out her hand and cupped my face.

"Is this what you want? Are you happy?" she stared into my eyes with a look full of concern.

I smiled and nodded. By the time she'd gotten up out of her chair and wrapped her arms around me, I was sobbing. As soon as she heard me crying, she started crying.

"My baby is having a baby! I can't believe it!" she said as she buried her face in my hair.

My dad leaned closer to Nick and said, "Hormones, gets them every time."

"She's doing that because of the baby?" Nick asked.

"No, because she's a woman," my dad said with a smile. "Get used to it, son." He gave Nick a pat on the back and smiled. "How about if after dinner, us dads go out to the garage, drink beers, and tinker with the lawn mower or something?"

"Sounds good to me," Nick said with a laugh.

"Wait!" Allison slammed her glass down on the table. "How many times have we been lectured about safe sex, and how disappointing it would be if you had to tell all your friends that one of your daughters was having a baby out of wedlock? Are you serious?"

"She's not having a baby out of wedlock. They'll be married well before she even starts to show," my mom said proudly and smoothed my hair down.

"That doesn't negate the fact that she had sex with a guy she didn't know and got herself knocked up. What do you have to say about that? Where's the wrath of God you promised in all those lectures?" Allison was getting more upset the more she talked.

"They may not have known each other for very long, but they were clearly meant for each other. Their baby was made in love, and I don't want to hear another word about it. Do you hear me, Allison Marie?" my mom scolded my sister. She gave my face one last caress then sat back down in her chair.

"I can't believe this," Allison said with a shake of her head. "All that time you spent lecturing us, and when it finally happens, all you do is cry and defend her. Unbelievable!"

"What lectures are you talking about?" Tori asked.

"You know, the one mom gives about being smart when it comes to sex? I've heard it like a million times. Come on, you know the one?" Allison said with an eye roll.

Tori and I looked at each other from across the table. She looked to be as perplexed as I was. The only lecture mom had ever given me was the usual birds and the bees talk.

"Don't give me those innocent looks! You know what I'm talking about. She gave us the talk before big dances, and every summer before heading back to college." Allison looked expectantly between Tori and I.

I smiled and shook my head. "Sorry Al. I don't know what you're talking about. Mom never lectured me about safe sex."

"Me either," Tori said with a giggle.

"Now don't go thinking anything irrational, Allison. I wasn't trying to imply that I thought you were loose. I just happened to notice that you were a little less discriminating than your sisters seemed to be," our mom explained herself.

"Mom thinks you're a ho," I giggled loudly.

Allison glared at me, "Obviously she was worried about the wrong daughter."

"Girls! That's enough," mom stopped us with a firm warning. "It is my birthday and I would like to enjoy this occasion and the happy news that Cami has shared with us. Is it too much to ask you to not fight with each other for one day?"

"Sorry, mom," I said and lowered my eyes in shame.

Allison flashed an angry look, but apologized anyway.

My dad stood up and said, "Well, Nick, what do you say we head to the garage for some male bonding?"

Nick nodded and scooted his chair away from the table. Before he stood up though, he leaned over and whispered into my ear. "Your dad doesn't keep power tools and weapons in that garage does he?"

I giggled and turned to kiss him on the cheek. "Yes, but he doesn't actually know how to use any of them."

Nick flashed a worried grin and followed my dad outside.

"Even better from behind," my mom mumbled appreciatively when Nick disappeared from our view.

18.

"He's gorgeous!" Tori said with a dreamy look.

"I have to admit, Cami, you definitely picked an extremely attractive man to knock you up," Allison said as she dropped a handful of silverware in the sink.

"Allison, will you please stop saying that. You know how I hate that phrase!" my mom fussed and took the silverware out of the sink. "I really wish that you two girls would just put all that petty fighting aside and just be friends."

"Mom," I said dryly, "that's how she talks to her friends."

Allison smacked my arm.

"I can't believe you're going to be a mom," Tori gave me a sappy look. "Can I touch your belly?"

"There isn't much of a belly there to touch," I said and lifted my shirt a little.

Both of my sisters and my mom immediately put their hands on my bare stomach. It was a weird feeling.

"It's tiny, but there's definitely a bump there," my mom said with a grin.

"Tiny? I spotted it when she walked in, remember?" Allison flashed a smug smile. "I bet you'll be huge by Christmas."

My mouth flew open in surprise, "Shut up! I will not!"

"Oh!" my mom pulled her hand back and gave me a worried look. "Will you still be able to come with us to Grammy and Pop's, or will you have to go visit Nick's family?"

"We haven't really talked about it, but I guess we'll go to Grammy and Pop's." I shrugged nonchalantly and turned around to start loading the dishwasher.

"How do you know Nick won't want to have Christmas with his family?" Tori asked.

"Nick doesn't really talk to his family," I said quietly.

"What do you mean? Why doesn't he talk to his family?" my mom leaned against the counter next to me. "Are they upset about him moving here?"

I sighed, "It's not about anything recent."

"What is it about then?" Tori asked from where she sat on the opposite counter.

"It's about stuff from a long time ago," I answered. Trying to change the subject, I asked, "What do you all want for Christmas this year?"

"I don't think so, missy," my mom grabbed the sponge from my hand. "You aren't going to change the subject. If this man is going to be a part of our family, we need to know what he's bringing to the party. Spill it!"

I sighed and looked around, as if checking to see if Nick was listening. "Like he said at dinner, he didn't have a family like ours."

"What kind of family did he have?" Tori asked with a raised eyebrow. "Was he raised by wolves or something?"

Allison turned to Tori and gave her a look of disbelief. She shook her head and rolled her eyes.

"His dad was an alcoholic who was abusive, so he left home when he was fifteen," I practically whispered the information.

"He's been on his own since he was fifteen? How did he get where he is?" my mom's voice had a concerned tone to it.

"He stayed with friends for a little bit, and slept on beaches then met a surf shop owner who took him in. He worked hard to put himself through UCLA and ended up at Davis and Associates." I gave them a brief summary of what Nick had shared with me.

"When you say his dad was abusive, what does that mean?" Allison stared me down, "Was he a yeller?"

"Among other things," I answered and looked down at my feet.

My mom gasped, "Did he hit him?"

I nodded, "He burned him with cigarettes, too."

All three of them gasped.

My mom closed her eyes and shook her head. "How can people be so cruel?" she whispered sadly.

I turned back to the sink to let them deal with the information on their own. Part of me felt better for not having to carry the secret around any longer. However, another part of me felt as if I'd betrayed Nick by telling them. I had told him that he didn't need to share that information with my family, and then I told them everything.

"Cami," Allison said softly. "Are you sure about this?"

"I've seen the scars, Allison," I said without turning around.

"I meant are you sure about him?" she corrected the confusion. "I'm not trying to be mean. I just don't want you, or the baby, to get hurt."

I turned around and looked at her. "I trust him, Allison."

"I do too," my mom said confidently then smiled at me. "He loves your sister and I don't think he'd ever do anything to put her in danger."

"I agree," Tori added with a nod.

Allison exhaled loudly. "I don't understand why, but I trust him too."

"Do you think we should tell dad?" I asked hesitantly.

"I think you should let him tell your father." My mom picked up the dishtowel and wiped her hands. "Men have different ways of handling this stuff."

"Okay, enough about all this deep feelings crap! Tell me," Allison wiggled her eyes at me. "He's amazing in bed, isn't he?"

I felt the heat rise to my cheeks. "You can't honestly expect me to tell you that! Mom?" Stupidly, I turned to my mom for support.

With a grin, she said, "Well, maybe just a few details would be nice."

"So, what did you guys talk about in the garage?" I asked as I watched him working.

By the time we'd left my parents' house, I was both physically and emotionally exhausted. When I'd fallen asleep in the cab on the way to the train station, Nick just paid the driver to take us all the way back to the city. He said he didn't want to wake me from my adorably peaceful nap. Back at home, we'd changed into sweats and were lounging on the bed together.

"Just guy stuff," he shrugged, without looking up from his task.

"Like your hopes, dreams, and feelings?" I teased him.

"Don't forget about the rainbows and unicorns," he added with a laugh.

I laughed. "What did you really talk about?"

"Mostly sports, actually. Your dad seemed pretty amped that I like baseball. I think I might try to see if I can get us seats to a game this spring. I'm sure the company has a box or something."

I smiled. My dad would love that, and I suspected that Nick would too. "So, you think he liked you?"

"I think so," Nick nodded and looked up. "What do you think?"

"I think he liked you," I answered.

"No, what do you think of my work?" he asked and held my foot up so that I could see my toes. "Do you like?"

I looked down at my freshly polished toes. He'd painted my toenails a lovely shade of pink then skillfully spelled out on my toes "I LOVE NICK" with a shade of bright red.

I smiled and nodded my approval. "Wow, you are good at that! I should have let you do them that first day at the beach."

He put my feet down and tossed the bottle of red polish onto the side table. "You are a lot like your dad, you know?" He crawled up to where I was laying against the headboard.

"I know. My mom says it's amazing we actually get along, because we are so similar."

"He's really easy to talk to." Nick pulled me into his chest and wrapped an arm around me.

"So he didn't threaten you or anything?" I laughed, remembering the worried expression on Nick's face as he got up from the table.

He laughed, "Well, there was the awkward warning when we first got out to the garage."

"Tell me about that!" I said excitedly. Jack and my dad had never really hit it off. Usually when Jack would attend family functions, he'd just stay in the room with me and the other girls, while my dad would sneak off to hide somewhere.

"When he handed me the first beer, he looked sternly at me and said 'I'm only saying this because I think I'm supposed to. Judging by the things you said earlier, and the way you look at my daughter, I don't think I'm ever going to have to make good on this. However, just to be clear, if you hurt her or break her heart, I will kill you.'" Nick repeated my dad's words with a serious tone of his own.

"What did you say?" I asked with a grin on my face.

"Understood."

"Then you guys started talking about baseball?"

"Pretty much," Nick nodded.

"Men are so weird!" I laughed and snuggled into him.

"Why? What did you girls talk about?" he asked.

I blushed, remembering the conversation I'd had with my mom and sisters. "You don't want to know."

He laughed, "Was it about my body?" He wiggled and ran his other hand down his torso in a playful way.

"I am so sorry about that. They have never done that before. I do not know what got into them?"

"You mean they didn't sexually harass Jack? Why does that not surprise me?" Nick laughed, "I get the impression that they didn't exactly like him."

I shook my head, "I didn't realize how much they disliked him until you came along."

Nick laughed and pulled me tighter. "I don't mind being compared to him, as long as I always come out on top, of course!"

"I'll keep that in mind," I said with a smile.

He leaned down and pressed his lips to my cheek. He gave me a small kiss and whispered, "Don't get mad at me for noticing this, but did your bump get like two times bigger overnight?"

My hands went to my growing belly. "I was thinking the same thing!" I said excitedly. "Yesterday it was so small you couldn't even tell I had one, but today it's completely noticeable."

He pulled my shirt up over it and pulled the waistband of my sweats down. His hand rubbed against my skin, causing a shudder to run through me. I remembered how odd it had felt to have my sisters and mom touch me. Nothing about Nick's touch felt odd or uncomfortable. His skin against mine felt right.

"Your dad says it's perfectly normal to feel scared about our first one. He said to get used to the feeling, though." Nick watched his own hand rub against my skin as he talked.

"What does that mean?" I asked and studied his face.

He looked down at me with a smile, "Get used to it, because it will never go away. We will always be worried about our children, even when they're all grown up and move out."

"Children?" I repeated his word with a raised eyebrow. "How many are we planning on having?"

He laughed, "Just one the first time, I think."

"Yes, but how many altogether?"

He shrugged and smiled, "I don't know. How many do you want?"

I relaxed, "How about we get through this first one and see how that turns out before we start making plans for any more?"

He shifted and lay flat beside me, propping himself up on his arm so that he could look down at me. I fixed my shirt and pants so that my stomach was no longer exposed. When I looked up at him, he was staring down at my face.

"Sometimes, I'm afraid I'm going to wake up and realize that this has all been a dream. That you aren't really here, and that I'm going to have to go through this alone." I confessed quietly.

He brushed hair out of my face and spoke softly, "I'm not going anywhere, I promise."

I closed my eyes and nodded.

"Cami."

Nick said my name so softly that I almost couldn't hear him. I opened my eyes to see him studying my face.

His hand gently stroked my face as he whispered, "I meant everything that I said to your family today. You feel like home to me, and you have since the first day I met you. Because I'd never had it before, I didn't know how important that was. When you showed up, it changed everything. I've never felt like that with anyone."

I reached my hand up to his face and pulled him down to me for a kiss. When he pulled away, I smiled up at him.

"Why are you smiling?" he asked with a smile of his own.

"I was just thinking about that night at the beach when we made dinner. Do you remember what I said when you asked me why I wouldn't hook up with you?" I watched him intently as he tried to remember our conversation. "Remember, you asked if it was because I thought I wasn't pretty enough to be with you?"

He shook his head and gave me a smile. "I told you that I didn't mean it like that! I meant that if you thought that then you were wrong. I don't think that you aren't pretty enough to be with me."

I laughed, "Don't you remember what I said about it?"

He stopped and scanned his memory, "I think you gave me three reasons why I was wrong, right?"

"Yes, and one of them was because I'd seen enough chick flicks and read enough chick lit to know that I'd get you in the end. Remember that?" I asked with a smile.

"Yes," he nodded.

"I was right," I smiled and shrugged.

He shook his head, "Was there ever a doubt that you would get me? You had me that first day on the swing. Something in me knew I wanted to spend forever with you when I watched you scratching at your legs like you had fleas."

"And then you painted my legs for me," I smiled remembering the day.

"I would have done anything to get my hands on you," he said and shifted his body to be over top of me. "It worked, too. Of course, it took me a lot longer than I thought it would. I got you in the end, though."

I wiggled against him, "No, I got you. Don't forget that I'm the one who opened the door. If I hadn't come out of my room that night, you might have chickened out and stood outside my door forever."

"True," he kissed me on the lips. "Let us not forget, however, that I am the one who took that step across the hall for that first kiss."

"I'll give you that one," I said and planted a quick kiss on his lips, "but I let you kiss me. I could have stopped it, and I had stopped it twice before, but I didn't want to. I wanted you to kiss me." I ran my hands up and down his back as I spoke, causing his body to shudder this time.

"You wanted me to do a lot of things that night, if I remember," he said with a grin. He dipped his head back down to mine and kissed me passionately. I kissed him back, but as soon as his lips left mine, a yawn escaped.

"Are you bored with me already?" He laughed and tucked a piece of hair behind my ear.

"I'm sorry. I'm just really tired today," I smiled apologetically.

"How can you possibly be tired? You took an almost two hour nap earlier today."

I smiled, "We didn't exactly get a full night of sleep last night."

He ran a hand down my side, dipped his head, and nibbled on my ear. "I didn't get a full night's sleep either, and I'm not too tired." His breath against my skin sent another wave of uncontrollable shudders through my body.

"You're not creating a life on top of everything else." Just to punctuate my statement, I yawned again.

He rolled off me and sighed loudly.

I rolled over and pressed my body against his. "We have the rest of our lives to have sex. Can't we just snuggle tonight?"

He instinctively pulled me closer to him and moaned sadly. "I can't believe you just gave me the can't-we-just-cuddle line."

I laughed and kissed his chest. "I'm sorry."

"We're not even married yet and you've already cut me off."

I smiled and closed my eyes. "It's one night, Nick. You can survive one night without it."

He pulled the covers up over us and wrapped us up in them. "I know I can. I don't have to be happy about it, but I will survive it."

"If it makes you feel any better, there may come a time in this pregnancy when I won't be able to get enough of you," I yawned again and nuzzled my head against him.

"Those days cannot come soon enough," he said with a chuckle.

I wanted to say something else, but my mouth wouldn't move so the words just drifted off. I was too tired, and too content, to keep myself from drifting off to sleep.

Epilogue

"I'm home!" I heard Nick shout then heard the door slam behind him. "Are you done in the bathroom? I think I need to take a shower before dinner."

I stood in front of the closet, wearing nothing but my maternity bra and a pair of ridiculously huge underwear. I'd been standing that way for the past twenty minutes. The cute, and small, clothes that used to fit me taunted me from their hangers and shelves.

"Where are you?" Nick shouted to me.

"I'm gazing longingly at the clothes that will probably never fit me again," I said sadly in response.

He appeared in the door to our bedroom. "You look sexy like that. I think you should just wear that."

I gave him a disapproving look. "You're just being nice to me. I'm a cow and nothing fits."

He smiled and walked over to where I was standing. He leaned in and kissed me on the cheek, resting a hand on my huge protruding belly. "You are still the most beautiful woman in the world to me. I'm sure that you have plenty of clothes in that closet that will fit you." He stepped away and grabbed the black maternity dress I'd purchased a week ago. "What about this? You just bought this."

I frowned, "It fits, but it makes me look like I'm even more pregnant than I am."

"You're nine months pregnant, Cami. You can't get any more pregnant than that." He handed me the dress and kissed me on the cheek again. "Now put this on and finish getting ready."

I watched him pull his tie off and hang it on the rack. His shirt came off next. I turned away before he finished undressing. I loved him, and I loved his body, but seeing how fit and toned he was only made me feel more uncomfortable with my own bloated body.

"I talked to my dad today," I said as I closed the doors to the closet. "He said you had lunch together again."

"We did," he shouted from the bathroom door.

"That's like the third time this week that you've had lunch together, isn't it?"

"So?"

I smiled, "Nothing, I just think it's odd that you spend so much time with him."

He stuck his head out the door, "You don't want your husband to get along with your dad?"

I shook my head, "I do want you two to get along. I just don't know that I want you to be best friends."

"We're not best friends," Nick said and walked out of the bathroom. He had a towel wrapped around his waist. "I told you before that he's easy to talk to. He's really helped me with a lot of stuff these last few months."

I sighed and nodded. I knew that the two of them had been spending some time together, and I knew that Nick trusted my dad for advice.

"If it makes you upset, though, I can limit our lunches to once a week." He sat down on the bed and waited for my answer.

"You don't have to do that." I sighed softly, "I guess I'm just jealous because you get to spend so much time with him. I feel like all I do is work and go to the doctor's office."

He smiled at me, "After the baby comes, you can have lunch with me every day."

I exhaled loudly and plopped down on the bed. "I'm sorry I'm being such a grump. I'm just tired of being pregnant. I'm uncomfortable all the time. I can't sleep anymore, and I always have gas. Now my back is hurting." I couldn't hold it in anymore. Tears started streaming down my face. "I don't want to be pregnant anymore."

Nick stood up and wrapped me in his arms. "It's okay. You don't have much longer to go."

I sobbed against his bare skin. "I don't want to be pregnant, but I'm also scared about being a mom. What if I don't know what to do? What if I'm not good at it?"

Nick squeezed me tighter, "You are going to be a great mom." He rubbed my back as he comforted me.

"Thanks," I mumbled and pulled out of the hug. "I'm sorry for being so needy."

He smiled, "Stop apologizing. Why is your back hurting?" His face had a worried expression on it.

"I don't know. It's been bothering me all day." I put my hands on my hips and tried to stretch out the pain.

"Would you like me to give you a massage?" he asked and motioned for me to move so that he could massage my back. As soon as his hands started moving against my back, I relaxed.

"Lower," I moaned, encouraging him to get the trouble spot. His hands moved lower and I leaned against the bed to give him better access to the pain. He massaged my back for a minute and I felt much better.

"How's that?" he asked as his hands continued to knead my skin.

I moaned my answer and he kept working. Suddenly he started laughing.

"What's so funny?" I asked without looking at him.

"This is kind of hot," he said playfully.

"Hot? This is turning you on?" I asked in disbelief.

"Well, let's see. You have your butt up in the air, I'm standing behind you, and you're moaning. If memory serves me correctly, this is one of the positions that got us into this situation." Nick laughed and gave my butt a quick smack.

"Pervert," I said half-heartedly.

He laughed.

I turned my head and looked at him. "Is this really turning you on?"

He nodded and smiled at me.

"They say that sex can sometimes stimulate labor." I gave him a coy look.

He smiled, "Are you trying to seduce me, Mrs. Fletcher?" He held out his hand to help me up. "I've got to get in the shower. We're supposed to meet Darren at seven and we'll never make it if we get distracted with sex."

I made a face, "Do we have to go? Can't Darren just come over here and eat?"

"Cami," he said sternly, "Darren is only in town for a few days and he wants to take us to dinner to celebrate our wedding and this baby. Now stop trying to get out of it and put on that dress."

"Are you going to be one of those bossy dads?" I stuck my tongue out at him.

"Don't argue with me! Just do it!" he pointed at me and walked into the bathroom.

I laughed and picked up the dress. I pulled it on and adjusted it. The sound of water running, and of Nick singing along with it, floated out of the bathroom. I smiled at the sound. Singing in the shower was just one of the many things I'd come to learn about Nick since we moved in together and got married. He was also a neat freak, something that I was used to after sharing a room with Tori for so many years. We'd had a few arguments as we adjusted to our new life, but overall things had gone smoothly.

I left the room and headed to the nursery. We'd finished the room over a month ago, but I still added things when I found something I thought would make it even better. Since it was my last day at school, the school secretary had given me a blanket she'd knitted for me. It matched the colors of the beach-themed room perfectly. I folded it and set it on the shelf between the little beach figurines Nick and I had painted. As I did, I knocked a stuffed bear off the dresser. I let out a groan as I bent over to pick it up. When I stood up again, a pain shot through me. One hand went to my back and the other gripped the dresser, making me drop the bear again.

"Nick," I said through the pain. I knew I hadn't said it loud enough for him to hear me. When I thought I could move, I walked slowly back towards our bedroom. Nick was still in the shower and still singing. "Nick!" I called out again.

As I stepped into the bedroom, I felt something trickling down my leg. "Oh no!" I groaned, realizing what was happening. A puddle started to form underneath me. I stood there watching, as the puddle grew larger.

The shower shut off and I heard the shower door slide open.

"Nick!" I said and felt another sharp pain shoot through me.

"What?" he shouted back at me.

"I don't think we're going to make it to dinner."

He laughed and said, "Cami, we're not cancelling. Trust me when I say that you look amazing. You are the most beautiful pregnant woman ever to walk this earth. Please just put on that dress and smile."

"No, it's not that," I said through the pain.

"What then?" he said and appeared in the door completely naked.

"My water just broke and I think I'm having contractions."

"Nice try. We're not cancelling," he said dryly.

"Look down," I groaned and gripped the handle of the door tightly.

He looked down at the floor underneath me and gasped, "Oh, shit! You weren't kidding!"

I shook my head.

"What do we do? Who do we call? What do we need to get? Where's my cell? Where's the bag? Should we call your doctor?" he spit out a whole list of frantic questions. "I need to call your dad!" He threw his hands in the air and ran past me looking for his phone.

I grabbed his arm as he moved past me. "Focus," I said and looked into his eyes. I waited until he'd calmed down then continued. "The bag is packed and by the door. Your cell phone is on the table where it always is when you're home. I'll call for the car while you clean up the floor. We can call the doctor on the way to the hospital."

He nodded, "Right."

I let go of his arm and took a deep breath. "I'm going to put some dry clothes on then head to the living room."

"Okay," he said with a dazed expression. "What am I supposed to do again?"

He managed to pull himself together while I got dressed. I headed to the living room and called for a car. I stood by the door, waiting for him to join me. When he finally arrived in the living room, I smiled and watched him shake nervously as he reached for his keys.

"Ready?" he asked with a panicked voice.

Grinning, I said, "Did you forget something?"

He shook his head, "I cleaned up the floor. You called for the car, and I've got the bag," he lifted the bag up to prove his point. "I think we've got it all. We'll call the doctor while we're in the car."

I looked him up and down, letting my eyes roam over his naked body. "Do you think maybe you should put some clothes on?"

"Shit!" he said and ran down the hall back into our bedroom. Within a minute, he was back, wearing a pair of shorts, an old button-up shirt, and a pair of flip-flops. "Ready?"

"Is that really what you're going to wear?"

Five painfully long hours later, I leaned back against the bed and watched Nick as he held our son in his arms. As tired as I was, I couldn't take my eyes off the little blue bundle, or the man holding him in his arms.

"He's so little," Nick said quietly as he stared at our son.

"He's not that little, trust me. You haven't been carrying him around for the last nine months. You didn't have to push him out either." I laughed softly.

Nick looked up at me and smiled, "He's perfect. You did a great job."

I shrugged, “I had some help.”

Nick laughed. He looked back down at the baby sleeping in his arms and said, “I know we talked about if he was a boy that we’d name him Flynn, but he doesn’t look like a Flynn to me.”

We had stuck to our guns about not finding out the sex of the baby. It had led to some heated discussions about names. After two months of arguing, we’d finally settled on Flynn Michael for a boy and Cassie Faye for a girl.

“What do you mean?” I asked with a strange look.

Nick stood up and sat on the edge of the bed. He held our son so that I could get a good look at him. “He doesn’t look like a Flynn, see?”

I stared at the beautiful little face I’d been waiting to meet for the past nine months. He had very familiar features. “What does he look like to you?”

Nick sighed, “He looks like your dad.” He looked at me and smiled, “I think we should name him Nathan, but call him Nate.”

“You want to name him after my dad?” I could feel the tears stinging my eyes and the sob in my throat.

Nick nodded, “Nathan Flynn Fletcher.”

I smiled and nodded.

Nick leaned over and gave me a kiss. “I love you.”

“I love you, too,” I said with a smile. I leaned down and kissed the little blonde head wrapped in a blue blanket, “I love you too, little Nate.”

“I like it, Nate Fletcher,” Nick grinned down at our son.

“When did my parents say they would be here?” I asked as I watched him smiling at our baby.

“I texted them about an hour after he was born so they should be here any time.”

I fidgeted, worrying about the state of my hair. Three hours of labor was probably enough to mess up my hair. “How do I look?” I asked timidly.

“Beautiful,” Nick replied without even looking at me. He got up from the bed and put Nate back in his bed.

"Be serious, Nick! They're going to want to take pictures and I don't want to look like a mess."

He turned to me with a grin, "A brush wouldn't hurt."

"Oh! Get my bag, please!" I sat up straighter, frantic to fix myself before my parents walked in.

Nick chuckled and handed me my bag. "It doesn't matter to me that your hair is messed up you're still the most beautiful woman in the world." He leaned down and grabbed my face in both hands and covered my face in kisses.

I laughed and pushed him away, "Don't tease me. My mom is going to be showing everyone these pictures. I can't look awful in them."

"You're so vain!" he teased me and sat down on the bed. He pulled Nate's bed closer and gazed at him.

I brushed my hair, applied a little powder to my face, and put some lip gloss on. When I was done, I tossed the bag on the floor and turned to Nick, "Better?"

He smiled and winked at me, "How can you improve perfection?"

I rolled my eyes at him.

He stood up and leaned over me, "It seems pointless to do all that to your face and just let this stay open, don't you think?" He shifted my gown so that I wasn't flashing anyone.

"Why didn't you tell me my boob was showing?" Despite the fact that he'd seen them plenty in the last nine months, I was still red-faced by my exposure.

He laughed, "I didn't see anything wrong with it? I was enjoying the view, actually."

I punched him on the arm and he laughed. "What did you tell my parents?"

"I told them that the baby had arrived and then I told them what hospital and room number."

"Are you sure they're coming? It's after midnight." I asked, anxious to see my parents and have them meet Nate.

"Your dad wrote me back saying that they were on their way," he sat down on the bed next to me. He looked down at me then grabbed my hand, "You're shaking. Are you nervous?"

"A little," I admitted with a hesitant smile.

"Why? The hard work is over," he reached up and brushed a strand of hair behind my ear.

I sighed, "I know. I just want them to like him."

Nick smiled sweetly at me, "You know they'll love him. They've already made plans to spoil him rotten."

I looked at him with a smile, "You didn't tell them he was a boy, did you?"

Nick shook his head.

I turned my head to look at the blue bundle in the clear bed next to us, "My dad always wanted a boy, you know. He's going to be very excited."

"I know," he smiled. "He told me."

I turned back to him, "When?"

"When we were at a baseball game this spring," he smoothed the blanket around me. "He told me that he'd always hoped for a son so that he could take him to baseball games and teach him to throw a football."

I reached up and touched his face, "Was that before or after you told him about your dad?"

"Before," he smiled at me then took my hand in both of his. "Cami, I know I've said it at least a thousand times since you told me you were pregnant, but I promise you that I will never be anything like my dad. I was scared that I wouldn't know how to treat you and the baby, but your dad has really helped me. I will never hurt you like my dad hurt me and my mom."

My eyes started to water, "I know."

He held my gaze for what felt like a long time. Our breathing and the quiet sighing of our son were the only sounds in the room.

"I have something for you," he finally said in a soft voice. He smiled and pulled a long flat box out of his pocket.

I smiled and took the box, "You didn't have to get me anything."

He laughed, "Your dad told me to have a piece of jewelry ready for after you give birth. He said he gave your mom a necklace after you and your sisters were born, and she still wears them on your birthdays."

"She does?" I had never noticed the pattern of my mom's necklaces. He nodded and urged me to open the box he'd given me. With a smile, I lifted the lid of the box to find a silver pendant attached to a silver chain. I stared at it, trying to figure out what the pendant was supposed to be.

"It's a hammock," Nick said with the hint of a chuckle.

A huge grin broke across my face, "Oh, I was wondering what it was."

He took the necklace out of the box and unhooked it. He wrapped his arms around my neck and fastened the necklace for me. When it was hooked, he touched the pendant as it lay flat against my skin. "Do you know why I got you a hammock?"

"I'm guessing it has something to do that week at the beach?"

He nodded, "Actually, I got you a hammock because that's where I fell in love with you."

"It is?"

"Yes, in the hammock, under that house is where I fell in love with you. When I told you about my dad and you said that if we had been friends that your family would have taken me in, that was the moment everything changed for me. That hammock changed our lives, and I don't want to forget that." He leaned forward and kissed me on the lips.

"Knock, knock! Can we come in?" my mom's quiet voice broke through our little moment.

Nick gave me another quick kiss then leaned away from me.

"Come in, mom," I said cheerfully and grabbed Nick's hand.

"Oh, sweetheart, how are you? Did everything go well? Are you in any pain?" my mom rushed to my side.

I laughed at her, amazed that she was able to control the urge to immediately run over to the tiny bundle beside the bed. "I'm great, mom. Our son was very cooperative."

My mom's eyes welled up with tears, "A boy!" She put her hands on my face and leaned in to kiss my nose. When she pulled away she said, "Oh goodness! Let me meet this precious child!" She left my bed and walked quickly over to the small clear crib sitting next to my bed.

I watched and listened as she gasped loudly as she laid eyes on her grandson for the first time. "You can pick him up, if you want to."

She smiled and shook her head slowly before leaning down to pick up the blue swaddled bundle. "What's his name?"

I looked at Nick and nodded. I wanted him to tell them.

He smiled, "We'd picked out a name, Flynn Michael, but when we met him he just didn't look like a Flynn Michael."

"What does he look like?" my dad asked as he reached down and squeezed my hand.

"He looks like you, dad," I said with a laugh.

"He does," Nick added. "That's why we decided to name him Nathan Flynn Fletcher. We're going to call him Nate."

My dad closed his eyes and shook his head back and forth. He squeezed my hand, "Are you sure you want to give him my name? If the poor boy looks like me, isn't that punishment enough?"

I laughed, "It wasn't my idea, but I think it's perfect."

My dad stood up and wrapped his arms around Nick, "Thank you, son," he said quietly as he embraced him.

"Thank you," Nick said back before breaking their hug.

"Do you want to hold him?" my mom asked and walked over to where my dad was standing.

He nodded and took a seat in the recliner next to the bed. He smiled as my mom lowered the baby into his arms. "It's amazing how small they are at first. I remember when I held you when you were this small." My dad spoke absently as he stared at the baby in his arms. "God, I'd never been so happy and so scared in my whole life."

"I know the feeling," Nick said and sat down on the bed next to me.

My dad looked up at Nick, "You're going to do just fine, son. You just love these two, and any other little ones that come along after him, with everything you have in you."

My parents visited, and took a million pictures, for an hour before leaving. We'd given them the key to our apartment so that they wouldn't have to travel home and could come back and visit later in the day. Nate was starting to get fussy and the nurse came in to help me feed him for the first time. She left when he'd successfully latched on and was busy filling up.

"That was awkward," Nick said with a smile as he watched our son breastfeeding.

I laughed, "At least he caught on quickly. I read horror stories about babies who wouldn't latch on and all the things they had to do to teach them how to feed."

Nick grinned and grabbed our son's little hand, "Of course he's a natural. He's a Fletcher, we're breast men!"

I laughed again and Nate looked up at me. "Is this where it starts? Is he going to be obsessed with tits now because of me?"

Nick laughed, "Probably."

I sighed and turned to face him, "Thank you."

"For what?"

"For hooking up with me at the beach," I said with a grin.

He smiled, "We did not hook up. We had a very short relationship that moved at a very fast pace."

I smiled and put my free hand on his face, "I love you, baby, but let's not kid ourselves. We hooked up."

About the Author

Virginia Jewel lives a simple life with her dog and cat. When not working at her real job, or writing, she spends way too much time watching reruns and wasting time on the internet.

Follow her on her blog at http://virginiasbookshelf.blogspot.com or on Twitter @VaJewel

Made in the USA
Lexington, KY
06 July 2013